ACTION OFF THE SUNK

'Mains'l Mr Easton! And get the tops'l off her at once . . .' Men were already starting the tacks and sheets. Matchett's rattan rose and fell as he shoved the waisters towards the clew and buntlines, pouring out a rich and expressive stream of abuse. Even as the carronades opened fire *Virago* slowed and suddenly the leeward lugger was upon them.

Lining her rail a hedge of pikes and sword blades appeared.

'Boarders!' Drinkwater roared as the two vessels ground together. A grapnel struck the rail and Drinkwater drew his hanger and sliced the line attached to it.

He saw the men carrying Mason drop him half way down the poop ladder as they raced for cutlasses.

'God's bones!' Drinkwater screamed with sudden fury as the Frenchmen poured over the rail. His hanger slashed left and right and he seemed to have half a dozen enemies in his front. He pulled out a pistol and shot one through the forehead, then he was only aware of the swish of blades hacking perilously close to his face and the bite and jar in his mangled arm muscles as steel met steel.

The Bomb Vessel

RICHARD WOODMAN

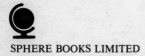

SPHERE BOOKS LIMITED

SPHERE BOOKS LTD

Penguin Books Ltd, 27 Wrights Lane, London W8 5TZ (Publishing and Editorial)
and Harmondsworth, Middlesex, England (Distribution and Warehouse)
Viking Penguin Inc., 40 West 23rd Street, New York, New York 10010, USA
Penguin Books Australia Ltd, Ringwood, Victoria, Australia
Penguin Books Canada Ltd, 2801 John Street, Markham, Ontario, Canada L3R 1B4
Penguin Books (NZ) Ltd, 182-190 Wairau Road, Auckland 10, New Zealand

First published in Great Britain by John Murray (Publishers) Ltd 1984
Published by Sphere Books Ltd 1985
Reprinted 1987

Printed and bound in Great Britain by Cox & Wyman Ltd, Reading
Set in 9/9pt Compugraphic Plantin

For
OSYTH LEESTON
with many thanks

Contents

Author's Note

The part played by Nathaniel Drinkwater in the Copenhagen campaign is not entirely fiction. Extensive surveying and buoy-laying were carried out prior to the battle, mainly by anonymous officers. It seems not unreasonable to assume that Drinkwater was among them.

Drinkwater's bomb vessel is not listed as being part of Parker's fleet but as she was nominally a tender this is to be expected. When ships of the line are engaged historians are apt to overlook the smaller fry, even, as occurred at Copenhagen, when it was the continuing presence of the bomb vessels left before the city after Nelson withdrew, that finally persuaded the Danes to abandon their intransigence. It has also been suggested that Nelson's success was not so much due to his battleships, which were in some difficulties at the time fighting an enemy who refused to capitulate, but to the effect of the bombs, throwing their shells into the capital itself.*

The presence of the Royal Artillery aboard bomb vessels is not generally known and it was 1847 before the three surviving artillerymen received recognition with the Naval General Service Medal and the clasp 'Copenhagen', confirmation of that famous regimental motto 'Ubique'.

Evidence suggests only four bombs got into station though contemporary illustrations show all seven. Quite possibly one of the four was *Virago*.

The hoisting of the contentious signal No 39 by Sir Hyde Parker has been the subject of controversy which has been clouded by myth. Given Parker's vacillating nature, his extreme caution and the subsequent apotheosis of Nelson, I have tried to put the matter in contemporary perspective.

As to the landing of Edward Drinkwater, the 'Berlingske Tidende' of 27th March 1802 stated that British seamen landed near Elsinore the day before 'for water' without committing any excesses. This landing does not appear to be corroborated elsewhere.

* See Journal of the Royal Artillery, Vol LXXVI Part 4, 1949, October, pages 285-294.

THE
COPENHAGEN
CAMPAIGN, 1801

PART ONE

Tsar Paul

'Whenever I see a man who knows how to govern, my heart goes out to him. I write to you of my feelings about England, the country that . . . is ruled by greed and selfishness. I wish to ally myself with you in order to end that Government's injustices.'

TSAR PAUL TO BONAPARTE, 1800

Chapter One   September 1800

A Fish Out of Water

Nathaniel Drinkwater did not see the carriage. He was standing disconsolate and preoccupied outside the bow windows of the dress-shop as the coach entered Petersfield from the direction of Portsmouth. The coachman was whipping up his horses as he approached the Red Lion.

Drinkwater was suddenly aware of the jingle and creak of harness, the stink of horse-sweat, then a spinning of wheels, a glimpse of armorial bearings and shower of filth as the hurrying carriage lurched through a puddle at his feet. For a second he stared outraged at his plum coloured coat and ruined breeches before giving vent to his feelings.

'Hey! Goddamn you, you whoreson knave! Can you not drive on the crown of the road?' The coachman looked back, his ruddy face cracking into a grin, though the bellow had surprised him, particularly in Petersfield High Street.

Drinkwater did not see the face that peered from the rear window of the coach.

'God's bones,' he muttered, feeling the damp upon his thighs. He shot an uneasy glance through the shop window. He had a vague feeling that the incident was retribution for abandoning his wife and Louise Quilhampton, and seeking the invigorating freshness of the street where the shower had passed, leaving the cobbles gleaming in the sudden sunshine. Water still ran in the gutters and tinkled down drainpipes. And dripped from the points of his new tail-coat, God damn it!

He brushed the stained breeches ineffectually, fervently wishing he could exchange the stiff high collar for the soft lapels of a sea-officer's undress uniform. He regarded his muddied hands with distaste.

'Nathaniel!' He looked up. Forty yards away the carriage had pulled up. The passenger had waved the coach on and was walking back towards him. Drinkwater frowned uncertainly. The man was older than himself, wore bottle-green velvet over silk breeches with a cream cravat at his throat and his elegance redoubled Drinkwater's annoyance at the spoiling of his own finery. He was about to open his mouth intemperately for the second time that morning when he recognised the engaging smile and penetrating hazel eyes of Lord Dungarth, former first lieutenant of the frigate *Cyclops* and a man

3

currently engaged in certain government operations of a clandestine nature. The earl approached, his hand extended.

'My dear fellow, I am most fearfully sorry . . .' he indicated Drinkwater's state.

Drinkwater flushed, then clasped the outstretched hand. 'It's of no account, my lord.'

Dungarth laughed. 'Ha! You lie most damnably. Come with me to the Red Lion and allow me to make amends over a glass while my horses are changed.'

Drinkwater cast a final look at the women in the shop. They seemed not to have noticed the events outside, or were ignoring his brutish outburst. He fell gratefully into step beside the earl.

'You are bound for London, my lord?'

Dungarth nodded. 'Aye, the Admiralty to wait upon Spencer. But what of you? I learned of the death of old Griffiths. Your report found its way onto my desk along with papers from Wrinch at Mocha. I was delighted to hear *Antigone* had been purchased into the Service, though more than sorry you lost Santhonax. You got your swab?'

Drinkwater shook his head. 'The epaulette went to our old friend Morris, my lord. He turned up like a bad penny in the Red Sea . . .' he paused, then added resignedly, 'I left Commander Morris in a hospital bed at the Cape, but it seems his letters poisoned their Lordships against further application for a ship by your humble servant.'

'Ahhh. Letters to his sister, no doubt, a venomous bitch who still wields influence through the ghost of Jemmy Twitcher.' They walked on in silence, turning into the yard of the Red Lion where the landlord, apprised of his lordship's imminent arrival by the emblazoned coach, ushered them into a private room.

'A jug of kill-devil, I think landlord, and look lively if you please. Well, Nathaniel, you are a shade darker from the Arabian sun, but otherwise unchanged. You will be interested to know that Santhonax has arrived back in Paris. A report reached me that he had been appointed lieutenant-colonel in a regiment of marines. Bonaparte is busy papering over the cracks of his oriental fiasco.'

Drinkwater gave a bitter laugh. 'He is fortunate to find employment . . .' He stopped and looked sharply at the earl, wondering if he might not have been unintentionally importunate. Colouring he hurried on: 'Truth to tell, my lord, I'm confounded irked to be without a ship. Living here astride the Portsmouth Road I see the johnnies daily posting down to their frigates. Damn it all, my lord,' he blundered on, too far advanced for retreat, 'it is against my nature to solicit interest, but surely there must be a cutter somewhere . . .'

Dungarth smiled. 'You wouldn't sail on a frigate or a line of battleship?'

Drinkwater grinned with relief. 'I'd sail in a bath-tub if it mounted a carronade, but I fear I lack the youth for a frigate or the polish for a battleship. An unrated vessel would at least give me an opportunity.'

Dungarth looked shrewdly at Drinkwater. It was a pity such a promising officer had not yet received a commander's commission. He recognised Drinkwater's desire for an unrated ship as a symptom of his dilemma. He wanted his own vessel, a lieutenant's command. It offered him his only real chance to distinguish himself. But passed-over lieutenants grew old in charge of transports, cutters and gun-brigs, involved in the tedious routines of convoy escort or murderous little skirmishes unknown to the public. Drinkwater seemed to have all the makings of such a man. There was a touch of grey at the temples of the mop of brown hair that was scraped back from the high forehead into a queue. His left eyelid bore powder burns like random ink-spots and the dead tissue of an old scar ran down his left cheek. It was the face of a man accustomed to hard duty and disappointment. Dungarth, occupied with the business of prosecuting an increasingly unpopular war, recognised its talents were wasted in Petersfield.

The rum arrived. 'You are a fish out of water, Nathaniel. What would you say to a gun-brig?' He watched for reaction in the grey eyes of the younger man. They kindled immediately, banishing the rigidity of the face and reminding Dungarth of the eager midshipman Drinkwater had once been.

'I'd say that I would be eternally in your debt, my lord.'

Dungarth swallowed his kill-devil and waved Drinkwater's gratitude aside.

'I make no promises, but you'll have heard of the *Freya* affair, eh? The Danes have had their ruffled feathers smoothed, but the Tsar has taken offence at the force of Lord Whitworth's embassy to Copenhagen to sort the matter out. He resented the entry of British men of war into the Baltic. I tell you this in confidence Nathaniel, recalling you to your assurances when you served aboard *Kestrel* . . .'

Drinkwater nodded, feeling his pulse quicken. 'I understand, my lord.'

'Vaubois had surrendered Malta to us. Pitt is of the opinion that Mahon is a sufficient base for the Mediterranean but many of us do not agree. We will hold Malta.' Dungarth raised a significant eyebrow. 'The Tsar covets the island, so too does Ferdinand of the Two Sicilies, but Tsar Paul is Grand Master of the Order of St John and his claim has a specious validity. At the present moment the Coalition against France threatens to burst like a rotten apple: Austria has not fired a shot since her defeat at Marengo in April. In short the Tsar has it in his power to break the whole alliance with ease. He is unstable enough to put his wounded pride before political sense.' He paused to toss off the rum. 'You will recollect at our last *contre-temps* with His Imperial Majesty, he offered to settle the differences between our two nations in single combat with the King!' Dungarth laughed. 'This time he has settled for merely confiscating all British property in Russia.'

Drinkwater's eyes widened in comprehension.

'I see you follow me,' went on Dungarth. 'For a change we are remarkably well informed of developments both at St Petersburg and at Copenhagen.' He smiled with an ironic touch of self-congratulation. 'Despite the massive subsidies being paid him the Tsar feigns solicitude for Denmark. A predatory concern, but that is the Danes' affair. To be specific, my dear fellow, the pertinent consequence of this lunatic's phobia is to revive the old Armed Neutrality of the Baltic States, moribund since the American War. The combination is already known to us and means the northern allies have an overwhelming force available for operations in concert with the French and Batavian fleets in the North Sea. I have no idea how to reconcile mad Paul with First Consul Bonaparte, but they are said to have a secret understanding. After your own experiences with the Dutch I have no need to conjure to your imagination the consequences of such a combined fleet upon our doorstep.'

Drinkwater shook his head. 'Indeed not.'

'So whatever the outcome . . .' A knock at the door was accompanied by an announcement that the fresh horses had been put-to. Dungarth picked up his hat. 'Whatever the outcome we must strike with pre-emptive swiftness.' He held out his hand. 'Good-bye, Nathaniel. You may rely on my finding something for you.'

'I am most grateful, my lord. And for the confidences.' He stood, lost in thought as the carriage clattered out of the yard. Less than half an hour had passed since the same coach had soiled his clothes. Already he felt a mounting excitement. The Baltic was comparatively shallow; a theatre for small ships; a war for lieutenants in gun-brigs. His mind raced. He thought of his wife with guilty disloyalty, then of Louise Quilhampton, abandoned in the dress-shop with Elizabeth, whose son he had brought home from the Red Sea with an iron hook in place of his left hand.

Drinkwater's mind skipped to thoughts of James Quilhampton, Mr Q as he had been known to the officers of the brig *Hellebore*. He too was unemployed and eager for a new appointment.

He picked up his hat and swore under his breath. There was also Charlotte Amelia, now nearly two years of age. Drinkwater would miss her sorely if he returned to duty. He thought of her bouncing upon Susan Tregembo's knee as they had left the house an hour earlier. And there was Tregembo, too, silently fretful on his own account at his master's idleness.

The old disease gnawed at him, tugging him two ways: Elizabeth and the trusting brown eyes of his daughter, the comforts and ease of domestic life. And against it the hard fulfilment of a sea-officer's duty. Always the tug of one when the other was to hand.

Elizabeth found him emerging from the Red Lion, noting both his dirtied clothes and the carriage drawing steadily up Sheet Hill.

'Nathaniel?'

'Eh? Ah. Yes, my dear?' Guilt drove him to over-played solicitude. 'Did you satisfy your requirements, eh? Where is Louise?'

'Taken offence, I shouldn't wonder. Nathaniel, you are cozening me. That coach . . .?'

'Coach, my dear?'

'Coach, Nathaniel, emblazoned three ravens sable upon a field azure, among other quarterings. Lord Dungarth's arms if I mistake not.' She slipped an arm through his while he smiled lopsidedly down at her. She was as lovely as when he had first seen her in a vicarage garden in Falmouth years earlier. Her wide mouth mocked him gently.

'I smell gunpowder, Nathaniel.'

'You have disarmed me, madam.'

'It is not very difficult,' she squeezed his arm, 'you are a poor dissembler.'

He sighed. 'That was Dungarth. It seems likely that we will shortly be at war with the Northern Powers.'

'Russia?'

'You are very perceptive.' He warmed to her and the conversation ran on like a single train of thought.

'Oh, I am not as scatter-brained as some of my sex.'

'And infinitely more beautiful.'

'La, kind sir, I was not fishing for compliments, merely facts. But you should not judge Louise too harshly though she runs on so. She is a good soul and true friend, though I know you prefer the company of her son,' Elizabeth concluded with dry emphasis.

'Mr Q's conversation is merely more to my liking, certainly . . .'

'Pah!' interrupted Elizabeth, 'he talks of nothing but your confounded profession. Come, sir, I still smell gunpowder, Nathaniel,' and added warningly, 'do not tack ship.'

He took a deep breath and explained the gist of Dungarth's news without betraying the details.

'So it is to be *Britannia contra mundum*,' she said at last.

'Yes.'

Elizabeth was silent for a moment. 'The country is weary of war, Nathaniel.'

'Do not exempt me from that, but . . .' he bit his lip, annoyed that the last word had slipped out.

'*But*, Nathaniel, *but*? But while there is fighting to be done it cannot be brought to a satisfactory conclusion without my husband's indispensable presence, is that it?'

He looked sharply at her, aware that she had great reason for bitterness. But she hid it, as only she could, and resorted to a gentle mockery that veiled her inner feelings. 'And Lord Dungarth promised you a ship?'

'As I said, my dear, you are very perceptive.'

He did not notice the tears in her eyes, though she saw the anticipation in his.

7

Chapter Two   October–November 1800

A Knight Errant

'Drinkwater!'

Drinkwater turned, caught urgently by the arm at the very moment of passing through the screen-wall of the Admiralty into the raucous bedlam of Whitehall. Recognition was hampered by the shoving that the two naval officers were subjected to, together with the haggard appearance of the newcomer.

'Sam? Samuel Rogers, by all that's holy! Where the deuce did you spring from?'

'I've spent the last two months haunting the bloody waiting room of their exalted Lordships, bribing those bastard clerks to put my name forward. It was as much as the scum could do to take their feet out of their chair-drawers in acknowledgement . . .' Rogers looked down. His clothes were rumpled and soiled, his stock grubby and it was clear that it was he, and not the notorious clerks, that were at fault.

'I must have missed you when I tarried there this morning.' Drinkwater fell silent, embarrassed at his former shipmate's penury. All around them the noise of the crowds, the peddlers, hucksters, the groans of a loaded dray and the leathery creak of a carriage combined with the ostentatious commands of a sergeant of foot-guards to his platoon seemed to emphasise the silence between the two men.

'You've a ship then,' Rogers blurted desperately. It was not a question. The man nodded towards the brown envelope tucked beneath Drinkwater's elbow.

Drinkwater feigned a laugh. 'Hardly, I was promised a gun-brig but I've something called a bomb-tender. Named *Virago*.'

'Your own command, eh?' Rogers snapped with a predatory eagerness, leaning forward so that Drinkwater smelt breath that betrayed an empty belly. Rogers seemed about to speak, then twisted his mouth in violent suppression. Drinkwater watched him master his temper, horrified at the sudden brightness in his eyes.

'My dear fellow . . . come . . .' Taking Rogers's elbow, Drinkwater steered him through the throng and turned him into the first coffee house in the Strand. When he had called for refreshment he watched Rogers fall on a meat pie and turned an idea over in his mind, weighing the likely consequences of what he was about to say.

'You cannot get a ship?'

Rogers shook his head, swallowing heavily and washing the last of the pie down with the small beer that Drinkwater had bought him. 'I have no interest and the story of *Hellebore's* loss is too well known to recommend me.'

Drinkwater frowned. The brig's loss had been sufficiently circumstantial to have Rogers exonerated in all but a mild admonishment from the Court of Enquiry held at Mocha the previous year. Only those who knew him well realised that his intemperate nature could have contributed to the grounding on Daedalus Reef. Drinkwater himself had failed to detect the abnormal refraction that had made the reckoning in their latitude erroneous. Rogers had not been wholly to blame.

'How was it so "well known", Sam?'

Rogers shrugged, eyeing Drinkwater suspiciously. He had been a cantankerous shipmate, at odds with most of the officers including Drinkwater himself. It was clear that he still nursed grievances, although Drinkwater had felt they had patched up their differences by bringing home the *Antigone*.

'You know well enough. Gossip, scuttlebutt, call it what you will. One man has the ear of another, he the ears of a dozen . . .'

'Wait a minute Sam. Appleby was a gossip but he's in Australia. Griffiths is dead. I'll lay a sovereign to a farthing that the poison comes from Morris!' Rogers continued to look suspiciously at Drinkwater, suspecting him still, of buying the pie and beer to ease his own conscience. Drinkwater shook his head.

'It was not me, Sam.' Drinkwater held the other's gaze till it finally fell. 'Come, what d'you say to serving as my first lieutenant?'

Rogers's jaw dropped. Suddenly he averted his face and leaned forward to grasp Drinkwater's hand across the table. His mouth groped speechlessly for words and Drinkwater sought relief from his embarrassment in questions.

'Brace up, brace up. You surely cannot be that desperate. Why your prize money . . . whatever happened to reduce you to this indigent state?'

Rogers mastered himself at last, shrugging with something of his old arrogance. 'The tables, a wench or two . . .' He trailed off, shamefaced and Drinkwater had no trouble in imagining the kind of debauch Samuel Rogers had indulged in with his prize money and two years celibacy to inflame his tempestuous nature. Drinkwater gave him a smile, recollecting Rogers's strenuous efforts in times of extreme difficulty, of his personal bravery and savage courage.

'Empty bellies make desperate fellows,' he said, watching Rogers, who nodded grimly. Drinkwater called for coffee and sat back. He considered that Rogers's chastening might not be such a bad thing, just as in battle his violent nature was such an asset.

'It is not exactly a plum command, Samuel, but of one thing I am certain . . .'

9

'And that is?'

'That we both need to make something of it, eh?'

Drinkwater lent Rogers ten pounds so that he might make himself more presentable. Their ship lay above Chatham and Rogers had been instructed to join Drinkwater at his lodgings the following morning. In the meantime Drinkwater had to visit the Navy Office and he left the latter place as the evening approached, his mind a whirl of instructions, admonitions and humiliation at being one of the lowest forms of naval life, a lieutenant in command, permitted into those portals of perfidy and corruption. It was then he had the second encounter of the day.

Returning west along the Strand he came upon a small but vicious mob who had pulled a coachman from his box. It was almost dark and the shouts of disorder were mixed with the high-pitched screams of a woman. Elbowing the indifferent onlookers aside Drinkwater pressed forward, aware of a pale face at the carriage window. He heard a woman in the crowd say, 'Serve 'im bleedin' right for takin' 'is whip to 'em!'

Drinkwater broke through the cordon round the coach to where a large grinning man in working clothes held the tossing heads of the lead-horses. The whites of their eyes were vivid with terror. Rolling almost beneath the stamping hooves, the triplecaped bundle of a bald-headed coachman rolled in the gutter while three men, one with a lacerated cheek, beat him with sticks.

The offending whip lay on the road and the coachman's huge tricorne was being rescued and appropriated by a ragged youth, to the whoops of amusement of his fellows. Several hags roared their approval in shrill voices, while a couple of drabs taunted the woman in the coach.

Drinkwater took in the situation at a glance. A momentary sympathy for the man who had been whipped faded in his angry reaction to disorder. The noise of riot was anathema to him. As a naval officer his senses were finely tuned to any hint of it. London had been wearing him down all day. This final scene only triggered a supressed reaction in him.

Still in full dress he threw back his cloak and drew his hanger. His teeth were set and he felt a sudden savage joy as he shoved his heel into the buttocks of the nearer assailant. A cry of mixed anger and encouragement went up from the mob. The man fell beneath the pawing hooves and rolled away, roaring abuse. The other two men paused panting, their staves ready to rebuff their attacker. Drinkwater stepped astride the coachman, who moaned distressingly, and brought his sword point up to the throat of the man with the whipped face. With his left hand he felt in his pocket.

'Come now,' Drinkwater snapped, 'you've had your sport. Let the lady proceed.'

The man raised his stave as though about to strike. Drinkwater

10

dropped the coin onto the back of the coachman. The glint of the half-crown caught the man's eye and he bent to pick it up, but Drinkwater's sword point caught the back of his neck.

'You will let the fellow go, eh? And set him upon his box if you please . . .' He could feel the man's indignation. 'I'm busy manning a King's ship, cully. Do you take the money and set the fellow up again.' Drinkwater sensed the man acquiesce, stepped back and put up his sword. Threat of the press worked better than the silver, but Drinkwater did not begrudge the money, disliking the arrogant use of corporal punishment for such trivialities.

The man rose and jerked his head at his accomplice. The coachman was hauled to his feet and bodily thrown onto the box. His hat had disappeared and he put his face into his hands as the crowd taunted him and cheered. Drinkwater turned to the window.

'Would you like me to accompany you, ma'am?' The face was pale and round in the gloom. He could not hear her whispered reply but the door swung open and he climbed in.

'Drive on!' he commanded as he closed the door. When he had pulled the blinds he sat opposite the occupant. She was little more than a child, still in her teens. The yellow carriage lights showed a plain face that seemed somehow familiar. He removed his hat.

'You are not hurt?' She shook her head and cleared her throat.

'I . . . I am most grateful, sir.'

'It was nothing. I think, ma'am, you should tell your coachman to be less eager to use his whip.'

She nodded.

'Are you travelling far?' he went on.

'To Lothian's hotel in Albemarle Street. Will that take you far out of your way? If so, I shall have poor Matthew drive you wherever you wish.' She began to recover her composure.

Drinkwater grinned. 'I think that inadvisable. My lodgings are off the Strand. I can return thither on foot. Please do not trouble yourself further.'

'You are very kind, sir. I see that you are a sea-officer. May I enquire your name?'

'Drinkwater, ma'am, Lieutenant Nathaniel Drinkwater. May I know whom I had the honour of assisting?'

'My name is Onslow, Lieutenant, Frances Onslow.'

'Your servant, Miss Onslow.' They smiled at each other and Drinkwater recognised the reason for her apparent familiarity. 'Forgive my curiosity but are you related to Admiral Sir Richard Onslow?'

'His daughter, Mr Drinkwater. You are acquainted with my father?'

'I had the honour to serve under him during the Camperdown campaign.' But Drinkwater was thinking he knew something else about Miss Onslow, something more keenly concerning herself, but he could not recollect it and a minute or two later the carriage turned off Piccadilly and drew to a halt in Albemarle Street.

After handing the young lady down he refused her invitation to reacquaint himself with the admiral.

'I regret I have pressing matters to attend to, Miss Onslow. It is enough that I have been of service to you.' He bent over her hand.

'I shall not forget it, Mr Drinkwater.'

Drinkwater forgot the encounter in the next few days. He became immersed in the countless details of preparing his ship for sea. He visited the Navy Board again, bribed clerks in the Victualling Office, wrote to the Regulating Captain in charge of the Impress Service at Chatham. He accrued a collection of books and ledgers; Muster books, Sick and Hurt books, Account books, Order books, orders directives. He had many masters; the Admiralty, the Navy Board, the Victualling Board, Greenwich hospital, even the Master-General of the Ordnance at Woolwich. Towards the end of November, he paid his reckoning, complaining about the exhorbitant charge for the candles he had burned in their Lordships' service. In company with a sprightlier Lieutenant Rogers he caught the Dover stage from the George at Southwark at four in the morning and set out for Chatham.

As the stage crossed the bridge at Rochester and he glimpsed the steel-grey Medway, cold beneath a lowering sky, he recalled the contents of a letter sent to his lodgings by Lord Dungarth. The earl had concluded, . . . *I realise, my dear Nathaniel, that she is not what you supposed would be in my power to obtain for you, nevertheless the particular nature of the service upon which you are to be employed would lend itself more readily to your purpose of advancement were you in a bomb.* Virago *is a bomb in fact, though not in name. I leave it to your ingenuity to alter the matter . . .*

Drinkwater frowned over the recollection. It might be a palliative, though it was unlike Dungarth to waste words or to have gone to any effort to further the career of a nobody. What interested Drinkwater was the hint underlying the encouragement. *Virago* had been built as a bomb vessel, though her present job was to act as a mere tender to the other bomb ships. That degrading of her made her a lieutenant's command, though she ought really to have a commander upon her quarterdeck. He could not resist a thrill of anticipation as the stage rolled to a halt outside the main, red-brick gateway of Chatham Dockyard. As they descended, catching the eye of the marine sentry, the wind brought them the scent of familiar things, of tar and hemp cordage, of stored canvas and coal-fired forges and the unmistakable, invigorating smell of saltings uncovered by the tide.

Despatching Rogers with their sea chests and a covey of urchins to lug them to an inn, Drinkwater was compelled to kick his heels for over an hour in the waiting room of the Commissioner's house, a circumstance that negated their early departure from the George and reminded Drinkwater that his belly was empty. In the end he was granted ten minutes by a supercilious secretary who clearly objected to rubbing shoulders with lieutenants, whether or not they were in command.

'She is one of several tenders preparing to serve the bombs,' he drawled in the languid and increasingly fashionable manner of the *ton*. 'As you may know your vessel was constructed as a bomb in '59 whereas the other tenders are requisitioned colliers. Your spars are allocated, your carpenter's and gunner's stores in hand. The Victualling Yard is acquainted with your needs. You have, lieutenant, merely to inform the Commissioner when your vessel is ready to proceed in order to receive your orders to load the combustibles, carcases, powder and so on and so forth from the Arsenal . . .' he waved a handkerchief negligently about, sitting back in his chair and crossing his legs. Drinkwater withdrew in search of Rogers, aware that if all had been prepared as the man said, then the dockyard was uncommonly efficient.

Fifteen minutes later, with Rogers beside him, he sat at the helm of a dockyard boat feeling the tiller kick gently under his elbow. The wind was keen on the water, kicking up sharp grey wavelets and whipping the droplets from the oar blades. The sun was already well down in the western sky.

'She's the inboard end of the western trot,' said the boatman curtly as he pulled upstream. Drinkwater and Rogers regarded the line of ships moored two and three abreast between the buoys. The flood tide gurgled round their bluff bows. Two huge ninety-eights rode high out of the water without their guns or stores, laid up in ordinary with only their lower masts stepped. Astern of them lay four frigates wanting men, partially rigged but with neglected paintwork, odd gun-ports opened for ventilation or the emergence of temporary chimneys. Upper decks were untidy with lines of washing which told of wives living on board with the 'standing officers', the warrant gunners, the masters, carpenters and boatswains. Drinkwater recognised two battered and decrepit Dutch prizes from Camperdown and remembered laying *Cyclops* up here in '83. There had been many more ships then, a whole fleet of them becoming idle at the end of the American War. The boatman interrupted his reverie.

'Put the helm over now, sir, if'ee please. She be beyond this'n.'

Drinkwater craned his neck. They began to turn under the stern of a shot-scarred sloop. The tide caught the boat and the two oarsmen pulled with increased vigour as they stemmed it. Drinkwater watched anxiously for the stern of *Virago*.

Chapter Three

The Bomb Tender

The richness of the carved decoration on her stern amazed him. It was cracked and bare of paint or gilt, but its presence gave him a pleasurable surprise. The glow of candles flickered through the stern windows. The boat bumped alongside and Drinkwater reached for the manropes and hauled himself on deck.

It was deserted. There were no masts, no guns. The paint on the mortar hatches was flaking; tatty canvas covers flapped over the two companionways. In the autumnal dusk it was a depressing sight. He heard Rogers cluck his tongue behind him as he came over the rail and for a moment the two officers stood staring about them, their boat cloaks flapping in the breeze.

'There's deal of work to be done, Mr Rogers.'

'Yes, sir.'

Drinkwater strode aft, mounted the low poop and flung back the companion cover. The smell of food and unwashed humanity rose, together with a babble of conversation. Drinkwater descended the steep ladder, turned aft in the stygian gloom of an unlit lobby and flung open the door of the after cabin. Rogers followed him into the room.

The effect of their entrance was instantaneous. The occupants of the cabin froze with surprise. If Drinkwater had felt a twinge of irritation at the sight of candles burning in his cabin, the scene that now presented itself was a cause for anger. He took in the table with its greasy cloth, the disorder of the plates and pots, the remnants of a meal, the knocked over and empty bottles. His glance rolled over the diners. In the centre lolled a small, rotund fellow in a well-cut coat and ruffled shirt. He had been interrupted in fondling a loosely-stayed woman who lay half across him, her red mouth opened in a grimace as the laughter died on her lips. Two other men also sprawled about the table, their dress in various states of disorder, each with a bare-shouldered woman giggling on his lap. There was a woman's shoe lodged in the cruet and several ankles were visible from yards of grubby petticoats.

The oldest of the women who sat on the round, well-dressed man's knee, was the first to recover. She hove herself upright, shrugged her shoulders in a clearly practised gesture and her bosom subsided from view.

'Who are you gentlemen then?' The other women followed her

example, there was a rustling of cotton and the shoe disappeared.

'Lieutenants Drinkwater and Rogers, madam. And you, pray?' Drinkwater's voice was icily polite.

'Mrs Jex,' she said, setting off giggles on either side of her, 'just married to 'Ector Jex, here . . . my 'usband,' she added to more giggles. 'My 'usband is purser of this ship.' There was a certain proprietory hauteur in her voice. Mr Jex remained silent behind the voluptuous bulk of his wife.

'And these others?'

'Mr Matchett, boatswain and Mr Mason, master's mate.'

'And the ladies?' Drinkwater asked with ironic emphasis, eyeing their professional status.

'Friends of mine,' replied Mrs Jex with the sharp certainty of possession.

'I see. Mr Matchett!'

Matchett pulled himself together. 'Sir?'

'Where are the remainder of the standing warrant officers?'

'H'hm. There is no gunner appointed, nor a master.'

'How many men have we?'

'Not including the warrant officer's mates, who number four men, we have eighteen seamen. All are over sixty years of age. That is all . . .'

'Well, gentlemen, I shall be in command of the *Virago*. Mr Rogers will be first lieutenant. I shall return aboard tomorrow morning to take command. I shall expect you to be at your duty.' He swept them with a long stare then turned on his heel and clattered up the ladder. He heard Rogers say something behind him as he regained the cold freshness of the darkened deck.

As they made for the ladder and the waiting dockyard boat a figure appeared wearing an apron, huge arms in shirtsleeves despite the chill wind. He touched his forehead.

'Beg pardon, sir. Willerton, carpenter. You've seen that pack of whores aft sir? Don't hold with it sir. 'Tis the wages of sin they have coming to 'em. There's nowt wrong with the ship, sir, she's as fine today as when they built her, she'll take two thirteen inch mortars and not crack a batten . . . nowt wrong with her at all . . .'

Slightly taken aback at this encounter Drinkwater thanked the man, reflecting, as he took his seat in the boat, that there were clearly factions at work on the *Virago* with which he would become better acquainted in the days ahead.

'You are required and directed without delay to take command of His Majesty's Bomb Tender *Virago*, which vessel you are to prepare for sea with all despatch . . .'

He read on in the biting wind, the commission flapping in his hands. When he had finished he looked at the small semi-circle of transformed warrant officers standing with their hats off. The sober blue of their coats seemed the only patches of colour against the flaked paintwork and bare timbers of the ship. They had clearly been at some pains to correct the impression their new commander had received the previous evening. They should be given some credit for that, Drinkwater thought.

'Good morning gentlemen. I am glad to see the adventures of the night have not prevented you attending to your duty.' He looked round. Matchett's eighteen seamen, barefoot and shivering in cotton shirts and loose trousers, were standing holding their holystones in one hand, their stockingette hats in the other. Drinkwater addressed them in an old formula. He tried to make it sound as though he meant it though there was a boiling anger welling up in him again.

'Do you duty men. You have nothing to fear.' He strode aft.

The cabin had been cleared. All that remained from the previous night were the table and chairs. Rogers followed him in. Drinkwater heard him sigh.

'There is a great deal to do, Sam.'

'Yes,' said Rogers flatly. From an adjacent cabin the sound of a cough was hurriedly muted and the air was still heavy with a mixture of sweat and lavender water.

Drinkwater returned to the lobby and threw open the door of the adjacent cabin. It was empty of people though a sea-chest, bedding and cocked hat case showed it was occupied. He tried the door on the opposite cabin. It gave. Mrs Jex was dressing. She feigned a decorous surprise then made a small, suggestive gesture to him. Her charms were very obvious and in the silence he heard Rogers behind him swallow. He closed the door and turned on the first lieutenant.

'Pass word for Mr Jex, Mr Rogers. Then make rounds of the ship. I want a detailed report on her condition, wants and supplied state. Come back in an hour.'

He went into the cabin and sat down. He looked round at the bare space, feeling the draughts whistling in through the unoccupied gunports. The thrill of first command was withering. The amount of work to be done was daunting. The brief hope of raising the status of *Virago* as Lord Dungarth suggested seemed, at that moment, to be utterly impossible. Then he remembered the odd encounter with Mr Willerton, that vestigial loyalty to his ship. Almost childlike in its pathetic way and yet as potent to the carpenter as the delights of the flesh had been to last night's revellers. Drinkwater took encouragement from the recollection and with the lifting of his spirits the draught around his feet seemed a little less noticeable, the cabin a little less inhospitable.

Mr Jex knocked on the cabin door and entered. 'Ah, Mr Jex, pray sit down.'

Jex's uniform coat was smartly cut and a gold ring flashed on his finger. His hands had a puffy quality and his cheeks were marred by the high colour of the bibulous. The Jexes, it seemed, were sybaritic in their way of life. Money, Nathaniel observed, was not in short supply.

'When I was at the Navy Board, Mr Jex, they did not tell me that you were appointed purser to this ship. Might I enquire as to how long you have held the post?'

'One month, sir.' Mr Jex spoke for the first time. His voice had the bland tone of the utterly confident.

'Your wife is still on board, Mr Jex . . .'

'It is customary . . .'

'It is customary to ask permission.'

'But I have, sir.' Jex stared levelly at Drinkwater.

'From whom, may I ask?'

'My kinsman, the Commissioner of the Dockyard offered me the appointment. I served as assistant purser on the *Conquistador*, Admiral Roddam's flagship, sir, the whole of the American War.' Drinkwater suppressed a smile. Mr Jex's transparent attempt to threaten him with his kindred was set at nought by the latter revelation.

'How interesting, Mr Jex. If I recollect aright, *Conquistador* remained guardship at the Nore for several years. Your experience in dealing with the shore must, therefore, be quite considerable.' Drinkwater marked the slightest tightening of the lips. 'I do not expect to see seamen on deck without proper clothing, Mr Jex. An officer of your experience should have attended to that.' Jex opened his mouth to protest. 'If you can see to the matter for me and, tomorrow morning, bring me a list of all the stores on board we may discuss your future aboard this ship.' Indignation now blazed clearly from Jex's eyes, but Drinkwater was not yet finished with him. In as pleasant a voice as he could muster he added:

'In the meantime I shall be delighted to allow you to retain your wife on board. Perhaps she will dine with all of the officers. It will give us the opportunity to discuss the progress of commissioning the ship, and the presence of a lady is always stimulating.' Jex's eyes narrowed abruptly to slits. Drinkwater had laid no special emphasis on the word 'lady' but there was about Mrs Jex's behaviour something suspicious.

'That will be all, Mr Jex. And be so kind as to pass word for Mr Willerton.'

Several days passed and Drinkwater kept Jex in a state of uncertainty over his future. The men appeared in guernseys and greygoes so that it was clear Jex had some influence over the dockyard suppliers. Drinkwater was pleased by his first victory.

He listened in silence as Rogers told of the usual dockyard delays, the unkept promises, the lack of energy, the bribery, the venality. He listened while Rogers hinted tactfully that he lacked the funds to expedite matters, that there were few seamen available for such an unimportant vessel and those drafted to them were the cast-offs from elsewhere. Drinkwater was dominated by the two problems of want of cash and men. He had already spent more of his precious capital than he intended and as yet obtained little more than a smartened first lieutenant, a few documents necessary to commission his ship, only obtained by bribing the issuing clerks, and victuals enough for the cabin for a week. Apart from the imposition of further bribing dockyard officials for the common necessities needed by a man of war, he had yet to purchase proper slops for his men, just a little paint that his command might not entirely disgrace him, a quantity of powder for practice, and a few comforts for his own consumption: a dozen live pullets, a laying hen, a case or two of blackstrap. He sighed, listening again to Rogers and his catalogue of a first lieutenant's woes. As he finished Drinkwater poured him a glass of the cheap port sold in Chatham as blackstrap.

'Press on Samuel, we do make progress.' He indicated the litter of papers on the table. Rogers nodded then, in a low voice and leaning forward confidentially he said, 'I, er, have found a little out about our friend Jex.'

'Oh?'

'More of his wife actually. It seems that after the last war Jex went off slaving. As purser he made a deal of money and accustomed himself to a fine time.' There was a touch of malice in Rogers as he sipped the wine, he was contemplating the fate of another brought low by excess. 'I gather he invested a good bit of it unwisely and lost heavily. Now, after some time in straightened circumstances, he is attempting to recoup his finances from the perquisites of a purser's berth and marriage to his lady wife.' Rogers managed a sneer. 'Though not precisely a trollop she did run a discreet little house off Dock Road. Quite a remunerative place, I am led to believe.'

'And a berth in a King's ship purchases *Madame* Jex a measure of respectability. Yes, I had noticed an assumption of airs by her ladyship,' concluded Drinkwater, grinning as an idea occurred to him. Making up his mind he slapped his hand on the table. 'Yes, I have it, it will do very nicely. Be so good as to ask Mr Jex to step this way.'

Jex arrived and was asked to sit. His air of confidence had sagged a little and was replaced by pugnacity. The purser's arms were crossed over his belly and he peered at his commander through narrowed eyes.

'I have come to a decision regarding you and your future.' Drinkwater spoke clearly, aware of the silence from the adjoining cabin. Mrs Jex would hear with ease through the thin bulkhead.

'Your influence with the dockyard does you credit, Mr Jex. I would be foolish not to take advantage of your skill and interest in that direction . . .' Drinkwater noted with satisfaction that Jex was relaxing. 'I require that you do not sleep out of the ship until you have completed victualling for eighty souls for three months. Your wife may live on board with you. You will be allowed the customary eighth on your stores, but a personal profit exceeding twelve and one half per cent will not be tolerated. You will put up the usual bond with the Navy Board and receive seven pounds per month whilst on the ship's books. Until the ship is fully manned you may claim a man's pay for your wife but she shall keep the cabin clean until my servant arrives. You will ensure that the stores from the Victualling Yard are good, not old, nor in split casks. You may at your own expense purchase tobacco and slops for the men. You will, as part of this charge, purchase one hundred new greygoes, one hundred pairs of mittens, a quantity of woollen stockings and woollen caps, together with some cured sheepskins from any source known to you. You will in short, supply the ship with warm clothes for her entire company. Do you understand?'

Jex's jaw hung. In the preceeding minutes his expression had undergone several dramatic changes but the post of purser in even the meanest of His Britannic Majesty's ships was sought after as a source of steady wealth and steadier·opportunity. Drinkwater had not yet finished with the unfortunate man.

'We have not, of course, mentioned the fee customarily paid to the captain of a warship for your post. Shall we say one hundred? Come now, what do you say to my terms?'

'Ninety.'

'Guineas, my last offer, Mr Jex.'

Drinkwater watched the purser's face twist slowly as he calculated. He knew he could never stop the corruption in the dockyards, nor in the matter of the purser's eighth, but he might put the system to some advantage. There was a kind of rough justice in Drinkwater's plan. Mrs Jex's wealth came from the brief sexual excesses of a multitude of unfortunate seamen. It was time a little was returned in kind.

Virago presented something of a more ordered state a day or two later. Both Matchett and Mason, despite their unprepossessing introduction a few days earlier, turned out to be diligent workers. With a third of Jex's ninety guineas Drinkwater was able to 'acquire' a supply of paint, tar, turpentine, oakum, rosin and pitch to put the hull in good shape. He also acquired some gilt paint and had Rogers rig staging over the stern to revive the cracked-acanthus leaves that roved over the transom.

While Drinkwater sat in his cloak in the cabin, the table littered with lists, orders, requisitions and indents, driving his pen and dispatching Mason daily to the dockyard or post-office on ship's business, Rogers stormed about the upper deck or terrorised the dockyard foremen with torrents of foul-mouthed invective that forced reaction from even their stone-walling tactics. Storemen and clerks who complained about his bullying abuse usually obliged Drinkwater to make apologies for him. So he developed an ingratiating politeness that disguised his contempt for these jobbers. With a little greasing of palms he could often reverse the offended clerk's mind and thus obtain whatever the ship required.

Drinkwater made daily rounds of the ship. Forward of the officers' accommodation under the low poop stretched one huge space. It was at once hold and berthing place for the hammocks of her crew.

Gratings decked over the lower section into which the casks of pork, peas, flour, oatmeal, fish and water were stowed. Here too, like huge black snakes, lay the vessel's four cables. Extending down from deck to keelson in the spaces between the two masts were two massive mortar beds. These vast structures were of heavy crossed timbers, bolted and squeezed together with shock-absorbant hemp poked between each beam. Drinkwater suspected he was supposed to dismantle them, but no one had given him a specific order to do so and he knew that the empty shells, or carcases, stowed in the gaps between the timbers. He would retain those shell rooms, and therefore the mortar beds, for without them, opportunity or not, *Virago* would be useless as anything but a cargo vessel. Store rooms, a carpenter's workshop and cabin each for Matchett and Willerton were fitted under the fo'c's'le whilst beneath the officers' accommodation aft were the shot rooms, spirit room, fuse room and bread room. Beneath Drinkwater's own cabin lay the magazine space, reached through a hatchway for which he had the only key.

It was not long before Drinkwater had made arrangements to warp *Virago* alongside the Gun Wharf, but he was desperate for want of men to undertake the labour of hoisting and mounting the eight 24-pounder carronades and two 6-pounder long guns that would be *Virago*'s armament. They received a small draft from the Guardship at the Nore and another from the Impress service but still remained thirty men short of their complement. By dint of great effort, by the second week in December, the carronades were all on their slides, the light swivels in their mountings and the two long guns at their stern ports in Drinkwater's cabin. The appearance of the two cold black barrels upon which condensation never ceased to form, brought reality to both Mrs Jex and to Drinkwater himself. To Mrs Jex they disturbed the domestic symmetry of the place, to Drinkwater they reminded him that a bomb vessel was likely to be chased, not do the chasing.

Virago had been built as one of a number of bomb ships constructed at the beginning of the Seven Years War. She was immensely strong, with futtocks the size of a battleship. Though only 110 feet long she displaced 380 tons. She would sit deep in the water when loaded and, Drinkwater realised, would be a marked contrast to the nimble cutter *Kestrel* or the handy brig *Hellebore*. She was reduced to a tender by the building of a newer class of bomb vessel completed during the American War. Normally employed on the routine duties of sloops, the bomb vessels only carried their two mortars when intended for a bombardment. For this purpose they loaded the mortars, powder, carcases and shells from the Royal Artillery Arsenal at Woolwich, together with a subaltern and a detachment of artillerymen. The mortars threw their shells, or bombs (from which the ships took their colloquial name) from the massive wooden beds Drinkwater had left in place on *Virago*. The beds were capable of traversing, a development which had revolu-

20

tionised the rig of bomb vessels. As of 1759 the ketch rig had been dispensed with. It was no longer necessary not to have a foremast, nor to throw the shells over the bow, training their aim with a spring to the anchor cable. Now greater accuracy could be obtained from the traversing bed and greater sailing qualities from the three-masted ship-rig.

Even so, Drinkwater thought as he made one of his daily inspections, he knew them to be unpopular commands. *Virago* had fired her last mortar at Le Havre in the year of her building. And convoy protection in a heavily built and sluggish craft designed to protect herself when running away was as popular as picket duty on a wet night. So although the intrusion of the stern chasers into the cabin marked a step towards commissioning, they also indicated the severe limitations of Drinkwater's command.

However he cheered himself up with the reflection that *Virago* would be sailing in company with a fleet, the fleet destined for the 'secret expedition' mentioned in every newspaper, and for the 'unknown destination' that was equally certain to be the Baltic.

Even as Mr Matchett belayed the breechings of the intrusive six-pounders, muttering about the necessity of a warrant gunner, Drinkwater learned of the collapse of the Coalition. The Franco-Austrian armistice had ended, hostilities had resumed and the Austrians had been smashed at Hohenlinden. Suddenly the Baltic had become a powder keg.

Although Bonaparte, now first consul and calling himself Napoleon, was triumphant throughout Europe, it was to the other despot that all looked. Sadistic, perverted and unbalanced, Tsar Paul was the cynosure for all eyes. The thwarting of his ambitions towards Malta had led to mistrust of Britain, despite the quarter of a million pounds paid him to which a monthly addition of £75,000 was paid to keep 45,000 Russian soldiers in the field. When Napoleon generously repatriated, at French expense, 5,000 Russian prisoners of war after Britain had refused to ransom them, Tsar Paul abandoned his allies.

The Tsar's influence in the Baltic was immense. Russia had smashed the Swedish empire at Poltava a century earlier, and Denmark was too vulnerable not to bend to a wind from the east. Her own king was insane, her Crown Prince, Frederick, a young man dominated by his ministers.

When the Tsar revived the Armed Neutrality he insisted that the Royal Navy should no longer be able to search neutral ships, particularly for naval stores, those exports from the Baltic shores that both Britain and France needed. The Baltic states wanted to trade with whomsoever they wished and under the double-headed eagle of the Romanovs they would be able to do so; the British naval blockade would be rendered impotent and France, controlling all the markets of Europe, triumphant. With one head of the Russian eagle ready tensed to stretch out a talon to cripple impotent Turkey, the effect of the other's influence in the Baltic would finish Britain at a stroke.

So, inferred Drinkwater, argued Count Bernstorff, Minister to Crown Prince Frederick. And though Russia was the real enemy it was clear that the Royal Navy could not go into the Baltic leaving a hostile Denmark in its rear.

Drinkwater coughed as clouds of smoke erupted into the cabin from the bogey stove.

'I beg you, Mrs Jex, to desist. I would rather sit in my cloak than be suffocated by that thing.' He leant helplessly on the table, covered, as was usual, with papers.

' 'Twill not draw, Mr Drinkwater, 'tis the wind. For shame I will perish with the marsh ague if I do not freeze first.' She sniffed and snuffled with a streaming cold.

'Perhaps madam, if you wore more clothes . . .' offered Drinkwater drily.

She gave him a cold look. Her early attempt to flirt with him had ceased when she learned of the bargain he had driven with her husband. He bent once more to the tedious task of the inventory, almost welcoming the interruption of a knock at the door, though the blast of icy air made him swear quietly as it blew papers from his desk.

'Beg pardon, sir . . .'

'Mr Willerton, come in, come in, and shut that door. What can I do for you?'

'We needs a leddy, sir.'

'A leddy? Ah, a *lady*, a figurehead, d'you mean?'

'Aye sir.'

Drinkwater frowned. It was an irrelevance, an expensive irrelevance too, one that he would have to pay for himself since he had spent the rest of Mr Jex's contribution on barrels of sauerkraut. He shook his head. 'I'm afraid that ain't possible, Mr Willerton. We have a handsome scroll and, in accordance with regulations, as I have no doubt you well know, ships below the third rate are not permitted individual figureheads. Most make do with a lion, we have a handsome scroll . . .' He tailed off, aware that Mr Willerton was not merely stubborn, but felt strongly enough to oppose his commander. Mr Willerton's almost bald head was shaking.

'Won't do sir. Bad luck to have a ship without a figurehead, sir. I was in the *Brunswick* at the First of June, sir. Damned Frogs shot the duke's hat off. We lashed a laced one on and sent the *Vengeur* to the bottom, sir. Ships without figureheads are like dukes without hats.'

Drinkwater met the old man's level gaze. There was not a trace of humour in his eyes. Mr Willerton spoke with the authority of holy writ.

'Well, Mr Willerton, if you feel that strongly . . .'

'I do, sir, and so does the men. We've raised a subscription of fifteen shillings.'

'Upon my soul!' Drinkwater's astonishment was unfeigned. Together with the realisation that his financial preoccupations were making him mean, came the reflection that the carpenter's request and the response of his motley little crew somehow reflected credit on the ship. He suddenly felt a pang of self-reproach for his tight-fistedness. If that shivering huddle of men he had seen on deck the morning he had read his commission at the gangway had enough esprit-de-corps to raise a subscription for a figurehead, the least he could do was encourage it. He tried to supress any too obvious emotion, but the brief silence had not gone unnoticed. Mr Willerton pressed his advantage. 'I have ascertained, sir, that a virago is a bad tempered, shrewish woman what spits fire.' Drinkwater watched a slight movement of his eyes to Mrs Jex, who sat huddled in sooty disarray over the smoking stove. As the former madame of a brothel she would have had a choice phrase or two to exchange with the men in one of her less ladylike moods.

'I believe that is correct, Mr Willerton,' replied Drinkwater gravely, mastering sudden laughter.

'I have my eye on a piece of pine, sir, but it cost eight shilling. Then there is paint, sir.'

'Very well, Mr Willerton.' Drinkwater reached into his pocket and laid a guinea on the table. 'The balance against your craftsmanship, but be careful how you pick your model.'

For a second their eyes met. Willerton's were a candid and disarming blue, as innocent as a child's.

Chapter Four   December 1800–January 1801

A Matter of Family

Lieutenant Drinkwater was in an ill humour. It was occasioned by exasperation at the delays and prevarications of the dockyard and aggravated by petty frustrations, financial worries and domestic disappointment.

The latter he felt keenly for, as Christmas approached, he had promised himself a day or two ashore in lodgings in the company of his wife. Elizabeth was to have travelled to Chatham with Tregembo and his own sea-kit, but now she wrote to say she was unwell and that her new pregnancy troubled her. She had miscarried before and Drinkwater wrote back urging her not to risk losing the child, to stay with Charlotte Amelia and Susan Tregembo in the security of their home.

Tregembo was expected daily. The topman who had, years ago, attached himself to young Midshipman Drinkwater, was now both servant and confidant. Also expected was Mr Midshipman Quilhampton. Out of consideration for Louise, Drinkwater had left her son at home when he himself went to London. Later he had written off instructions to the young man to recruit hands for *Virago*. Now Drinkwater waited impatiently for those extra men.

But it was not merely men that Drinkwater needed. As Christmas approached, the dockyard became increasingly supine. He wanted masts and spars, for without them *Virago* was as immobile as a log, condemned to await the dockyard's pleasure. And Drinkwater was by no means sure that Mr Jex was not having his revenge through the influence of his kinsman, the Commissioner. As the days passed in idleness Drinkwater became more splenetic, less tolerant of Mrs Jex, less affable to Rogers. He worried over the possibilities of desertion by his men and fretted over their absence every time a wooding party went to search the tideline for driftwood. Unable to leave his ship by Admiralty order he sat morosely in his cloak, staring gloomily out over the dull, frosty marshes.

His misgivings over his first lieutenant increased. Rogers's irascibility was irritating the warrant officers and Drinkwater's own doubts about selecting Rogers grew. They had already argued over the matter of a flogging, Drinkwater ruling the laxer discipline that customarily prevailed on warships in port mitigated the man's offence to mere impudence. The knock at the door brought him out of himself.

24

'Come in!'

'Reporting aboard, sir.'

'James! By God, I'm damned glad to see you. You've men? And news of my wife?'

James Quilhampton warmed himself over the smoking stove. He was a tall, spare youth, growing out of his uniform coat, with spindle-shanked legs and a slight stoop. Any who thought him a slightly ridiculous adolescent were swiftly silenced when they saw the heavy iron hook he wore in place of a left hand.

'Aye sir, I have fifteen men, a letter from your wife and a surgeon.' He stood aside, pulling a letter from his breast. Taking the letter Drinkwater looked up to see a second figure enter his cabin.

'Lettsom, sir, surgeon; my warrant and appointment.' Drinkwater glanced at the proferred papers. Mr Lettsom was elderly, small and fastidious looking, with a large nose and a pair of tolerant eyes. His uniform coat was clean, though shiny and with overlarge, bulging pockets.

'Ah, I see you served under Richard White, Mr Lettsom, he speaks highly of you.'

'You are acquainted with Captain White, Lieutenant Drinkwater?'

'I am indeed, we were midshipmen together in the *Cyclops*, I saw him last at the Cape when he commanded the *Telemachus*.'

'I served with him in the *Roisterer*, brig. He was soon after posted to *Telemachus*.'

'I have no doubt we shall get along, Mr Lettsom.' Drinkwater riffled through the papers on his table. 'I have some standing orders here for you. You will find the men in reasonable shape. I have had their clothes replaced and we may thus contain the ship-fever. As to diet I have obliged the purser to buy in a quantity of sauerkraut. Its stink is unpopular, but I am persuaded it is effective against the scurvy.' Lettsom nodded and glanced at the documents.

'You are a disciple of Lind, Mr Drinkwater, I congratulate you.'

'I am of the opinion that much of the suffering of seamen in general is unnecessary.'

Lettsom smiled wryly at the earnest Drinkwater. 'I'll do my best, sir, but mostly it depends upon the condition of the men:

When people's ill, they come to I,
I physics, bleeds and sweat's 'em;
Sometimes they live, sometimes they die,
What's that to I? I let's 'em.'

For a second Drinkwater was taken aback, then he perceived the pun and began to laugh.

'A verse my cousin uses as his own, sir,' Lettsom explained, 'he is a physician of some note among the fashionable, but of insufficient integrity not to claim the verse as his own. I regret that he plagiarised it from your humble servant.' Lettsom made a mock bow.

'Very well, Mr Lettsom, I think we shall get along . . . Now gentlemen, if you will excuse me . . .'

He slit open Elizabeth's letter impatiently and began to read, lost for a while to the cares of the ship.

> *My Dearest Husband,*
> *It is with great sadness that I write to say I shall not see you at Christmastide. I am much troubled by sickness and anxious for the child whom, from the trouble he causes, I know to be a boy. Charlotte chatters incessantly . . .*

There was a page of his daughter's exploits and a curl of her hair. He learned that the lateness of Tregembo's departure was caused by a delay in the preparation of his Christmas gift and that Louise Quilhampton was having her portrait painted by Gaston Bruilhac, a paroled French *sous-officier*, captured by Drinkwater in the Red Sea who had executed a much admired likeness of his captor during the homeward voyage. There was town gossip and Elizabeth's disapproval of Mr Quilhampton's recruiting methods. Then, saved in Elizabeth's reserved manner for a position of importance in the penultimate paragraph, an oddly disquieting sentence:

> *On Tuesday last I received an odd visitor, your brother Edward whom I have not seen these five or six years. He was in company with a lively and pretty French woman, some fugitive from the sans culottes. He spoke excellent French to her and was most anxious to see you on some private business. I explained your whereabouts but he would vouchsafe me no further confidences. I confess his manner made me uneasy . . .*

Drinkwater looked up frowning only to find Quilhampton still in the cabin.

'You wish to see me, Mr Q?'

'Beg pardon, sir, but I am rather out of pocket. The expense of bringing the men, sir . . .'

Drinkwater sighed. 'Yes, yes, of course. How much?'

'Four pounds, seventeen shillings and four pence ha'penny, sir. I kept a strict account . . .'

The problem of the ship closed round him again, driving all thoughts of his brother from his mind.

Mr Easton, the sailing master, with a brand new certificate from the Trinity House and an equally new warrant from the Navy Board joined them on the last day of the old century. Six days later Drinkwater welcomed his final warrant officer aboard. They had served together before. Mr Trussel was wizened, stoop-shouldered and yellow-skinned. Lank hair fell to his shoulders from the sides and back of his head, though his crown was bald.

'Reporting for duty, Mr Drinkwater.' A smile split his face from ear to ear.

'God bless my soul, Mr Trussel, I had despaired of your arrival, but you are just in time. Pray help yourself to a glass of blackstrap.' He indicated the decanter that sat on its tray at the end of the table, remembering Trussel's legendary thirst which he attributed to a lifelong proximity to gunpowder.

'The roads were dreadful, sir,' said Trussel, helping himself to the cheap, dark wine. 'I gather we are a tender, sir, servicing bombs.'

'Exactly so, Mr Trussel, and as such most desperately in want of a gunner. I shall rely most heavily upon you. As soon as we are rigged we are ordered to Blackstakes to load ammunition and ordnance stores. You will of course have finished your preparations of the magazines by then. Willerton, the carpenter, has a quantity of tongued deals on board and has made a start on them. I've no need to impress upon your mind that not a nail's to be driven once we've a grain of powder on board.'

'I understand, sir.' He paused. 'I saw Mr Rogers on deck.' The statement of fact held just the faintest hint of surprise. Trussel had been gunner of the brig *Hellebore* when Rogers wrecked her in the Red Sea.

'Mr Rogers is proving a most efficient first lieutenant Mr Trussel.' Drinkwater paused, watching Trussel's face remain studiously wooden. 'Well, I'd be obliged if you would be about your business without delay; time is of the very essence.'

Trussel rose. 'One other thing, sir.'

'Yes, what is that?'

'Are we to embark a detachment of artillerymen?'

Drinkwater nodded. 'I have received notice to that effect. It is customary to do so when ordnance stores are loaded.'

'Then we are for the Baltic, sir?'

Drinkwater smiled. 'You may conjecture as you see fit. I have no orders beyond those to load powder at Blackstakes.' Trussel grinned comprehendingly back.

'I hear Lord Nelson is to be employed upon a secret expedition. The papers had it as I came through London.' He smiled again, aware that the news had come as a surprise to the lieutenant.

'Lord Nelson . . .' mused Drinkwater, and it was some moments before he bent again to his work.

'I congratulate you, Mr Willerton.' Drinkwater regarded the brilliantly painted figurehead that perched on *Virago*'s tiny fo'c's'le. The product of Willerton's skill with mallet and gouge was the usual mixture of crude suggestion and mild obscenity. The half bust showed a ferociously staring woman with her head thrown back. A far too beautiful mouth gaped violently revealing a protruding scarlet tongue, like the tongue of flame that must once have issued from *Virago*'s mortars.

To the face of this harpy Mr Willerton's artistry had added the pert, up-tilted breasts of a virgin, too large for nature but erotic

27

enough to satisfy the prurience of his shipmates. But it was the right arm that attested to Mr Willerton's true genius. While the left trailed astern the right crooked under an exaggerated breast, its nagging forefinger erect in the universally recognisable position of the scold. The 'leddy' was both termagant wanton and nagging wife, a spitfire virago eminently suitable to a bomb vessel. It was a pity, thought Drinkwater as he nodded his approval, that they were not so commissioned.

The handful of men detailed by Lieutenant Rogers to assist Willerton in fitting the figurehead grinned appreciatively, while Willerton sucked his teeth with a peculiar whistling noise.

'Worthy of a first rate, Mr Willerton. A true virago. I am glad you heeded my advice,' he added in a lower voice.

Willerton grinned, showing a blackened row of caried teeth. 'The right hand, sir, mind the right hand.' His blue eyes twinkled wickedly.

Drinkwater regarded the nagging finger. Perhaps there was some suggestion of Mrs Jex there, but it was not readily recognisable to him. He gave Willerton formal permission to fit the figurehead and turned aft.

A keen easterly wind canted *Virago*'s tub-like hull across the river as she lay to her anchor clear of the sheer hulk. The three lower masts had been stepped and their rigging, already made up ashore and 'lumped' for hoisting aboard, had been fitted over the caps and hove tight to the channels by deadeyes and lanyards. The double hemp lines of fore, main and mizzen stays had been swigged forward and tightened. Rogers and Matchett were at that moment hoisting up the maintopmast, its heel-rope leading down to the barrel windlass at the break of the fo'c's'le, the pawls clicking satisfactorily as the topmast inched aloft.

Drinkwater began to walk aft, past the sweating gangs of sea and landsmen being bullied and sworn at by the bosun's mates, round the heaps and casks being counted by Mr Jex, and ascended the three steps to the low poop. He cast a glance across the river where Mr Quilhampton brought the cutter out from the dockyard, towing the mainyard from the mast pond. Over the poop with its huge tiller, a mark of *Virago*'s age, fluttered the ensign. In its upper hoist canton it bore the new Union flag with St Patrick's saltire added after the recent Act of Union with Ireland. For a second he regarded it curiously, seeing a fundamental change in something he had come to regard as almost holy, something to fight and perhaps to die under. Of the Act and its implication he thought little, though it seemed to make sense to his ordered mind as did Pitt's attempt to emancipate the Roman Catholics of that unfortunate island.

He descended the companionway into his cabin. Mrs Jex had been evicted. On 27th January the Admiralty had ordered a squadron of bombs and their tenders to assemble at Sheerness. The dockyard had woken to its responsibilities. All was now of the utmost urgency before their Lordships started asking questions of the Commissioner.

Tregembo was hanging Elizabeth's gift, the cause of his delay in joining. Drinkwater watched, oddly moved. Bruilhac's skill as a portraitist showed Elizabeth cool and smiling with Charlotte Amelia chubby and serious. He was suddenly filled with an immense pride and tenderness. From his position at the table his two loved ones looked down at him, illuminated by the light that entered the cabin from the stern windows behind him, the moving light that, even on a dull day, did not enter his cabin without reflecting from the sea.

Mr Quilhampton interrupted his reverie. 'Mainyard's alongside, sir, and I've a letter left for you at the main gate.' He handed the paper over and Drinkwater slit the wafer.

> *My Dear Nathaniel,*
>   *I'd be obliged if you would meet me at the sign of the Blue Fox this evening.*
>   *Your brother, Edward*

He looked up. 'Mr Q. Be so good as to ask the first lieutenant to have a boat for me at four bells.'

The Blue Fox was in a back street, well off the Dock Road and in an alley probably better known for its brothels than its reputable inns. But the place seemed clean enough and the landlord civil, evincing no surprise when Drinkwater asked for his brother. The man ushered Drinkwater to a private room on the upper floor.

Edward Drinkwater rose to meet him. He was of similar height to Nathaniel, with a heavier build and higher colour. His clothes were fashionably cut, and though not foppish, tended to the extremes of colour and decoration then *de rigeur*.

'Nathaniel! My dear fellow, my dear fellow, you are most kind to come.'

'Edward. It has been a very long time.' They shook hands.

'Too long, too long . . . here I have some claret mulling, by heaven damned if it ain't colder here than in London . . . there, a glass will warm you. Your ship is nearly ready then?'

Nathaniel nodded as he sipped the hot wine.

'Then it seems I am just in time, just in time.'

'Forgive me, Edward, but why all the mysterious urgency?'

Edward ran a finger round his stock with evident embarrassment. He avoided his brother's eyes and appeared to be choosing his words with difficulty. Several times he raised his head to speak, then thought better of it.

'Damn it Ned,' broke in Drinkwater impatiently, ' 'tis a woman or 'tis money, confound it, no man could haver like this for ought else.'

'Both Nat, both.' Edward seized on the opportunity and the words began to tumble from him. 'It is a long story, Nat, one that goes back ten or more years. You recollect after mother died and you married, I

29

went off to Enfield to work for an India merchant, with his horses. I learned a deal about horses, father was good with 'em too. After a while I left the nabob's employ and was offered work at Newmarket, still with horses. I was too big to race 'em but I backed 'em and over a long period made enough money to put by. I was lucky. Very lucky. I had a sizeable wager on one occasion and made enough in a single bet to live like a gentleman for a year, maybe two if I was careful.' He sighed and passed a hand over his sweating face.

'After the revolution in France, when the aristos started coming over there were pickings of all sorts. I ran with a set of blades. We took fencing lessons from an impoverished marquis, advanced an old dowager some money on her jewels, claimed the debt . . . well, in short, my luck held.

'Then I met Pascale, she was of the minor nobility, but penniless. She became my mistress.' He paused to drink and Drinkwater watching him thought what a different life from his own. There were common threads, perceptible if you knew how to identify them. Their boyhood had been dominated by their mother's impecunious gentility, widowed after their drunken father had been flung from a horse. Nathaniel was careful of money, neither unwilling to loot a few gold coins from an American prize when a half-starved midshipman, nor to lean a little on the well-heeled Mr Jex. But where he had inherited his mother's shrewdness Edward had been bequeathed his father's improvidence as he now went on to relate.

'Things went well for a while. I continued to gamble and, with modest lodgings and Pascale to keep me company, managed to cut a dash. Then my luck changed. For no apparent reason. I began to lose. It was uncanny. I lost confidence, friends, everything.

'Nathaniel, I have twenty pounds between me and penury. Pascale threatens to leave me since she has received an offer to better herself . . .' He fell silent.

'As another man's mistress?'

Edward's silence was eloquent.

'I see.' Drinkwater felt a low anger building up in him. It was not enough that he should have spent a great deal of money in fitting out His Britannic bloody Majesty's bomb tender *Virago*. It was not enough that the exigencies of the service demanded his constant presence on board until sailing, but that this good-for-nothing killbuck of a brother must turn up to prey on his better nature.

'How much do you want?'

'Five hundred would . . .'

'Five hundred! God's bones, Edward, where in the name of Almighty God d'you think I can lay my hands on five hundred pounds?'

'I heard you did well from prize money . . .'

'Prize money? God, Ned, but you've a damned nerve. D'you know how many scars I've got for that damned prize money, how many sleepless nights, hours of worry . . .? No, of course you don't.

30

You've been cutting a dash, gaming and whoring like the rest of this country's so-called gentry while your sea-officers and seamen are rotting in their wooden coffins. God damn it, Ned, but I've a wife and family to be looked to first.' His temper began to ebb. Without looking up Edward muttered:

'I heard too, that you received a bequest.'

'Where the hell d'you learn that?' A low fury came into his voice.

'Oh, I learned it in Petersfield.' That would not be difficult. There were enough gossips in any town to know the business of others. It was true that he had received a sizeable bequest from the estate of his former captain, Madoc Griffiths. 'They say it was three thousand pounds.'

'They may say what the hell they like. It is no longer mine. Most is in trust for my children, the remainder made over to my wife.' He paused again and Edward looked up, disappointed yet irritatingly unrepentant.

It suddenly occurred to Drinkwater that the expenses incurred in the fitting out of a ship, even a minor one like *Virago*, were inconceivable to Edward. He began to repent of his unbrotherly temper; to hold himself mean, still reproved in his conscience for the trick he had played on Jex, no matter how many barrels of sauerkraut it had bought.

'Listen, Ned, I am more than two hundred pounds out of pocket in fitting out my ship. That is why we receive prize money, that and for the wounds we endure in an uncaring country's service. You talk of fencing lessons but you've never known what it is to cut a man down before he kills you. You regard my uniform as some talisman opening the salons of the *ton* to me when I am nothing but a dog of a sailor, lieutenant or not. Why, Ned, I am not fit to crawl beneath the bootsoles of a twelve-year-old ensign of horse whose commission costs him two thousand pounds.' All the bitterness of his profession rose to the surface, replacing his anger with the gall of experience.

Edward remained silent, pouring them both another drink. After several moments Nathaniel rose and went to a small table. From the tail pocket of his coat he drew a small tablet and a pencil. He began to write, calling for wax and a candle.

After sealing the letter he handed it to his brother. 'That is all I can, in all conscience, manage.'

Then he left, picking up his hat without another word, leaving Edward to wonder over the amount and without waiting for thanks.

He was too preoccupied to notice Mr Jex drinking in the taproom as he made his way through to the street.

The Pyroballogist

Drinkwater raised the speaking trumpet. 'A trifle more in on that foretack, if you please Mr Matchett.' He transferred his attention to the waist where the master attended the main braces. 'You may belay the main braces Mr Easton.'

'Aye, aye, sir.'

Virago slid downstream leaving the dockyard to starboard and the ships laid up in ordinary to larboard. 'Full and bye.'

'Full an' bye, zur.' Tregembo answered from the tiller. Drinkwater, short of men still, had rated the Cornishman quartermaster.

They cleared the end of the trot, slipping beneath the wooded hill at Upnor.

'Up helm!' *Virago* swung, turning slowly before the wind. Drinkwater nodded to Rogers. 'Square the yards.' Rogers bawled at the men at the braces as *Virago* brought the wind astern, speeding downstream with the ebb tide under her, her forecourse, three topsails and foretopmast staysail set. The latter flapped now, masked by the forecourse.

They swung south east out of Cockham Reach, the river widening, its north bank falling astern, displaced by the low line of Hoo Island. They passed the line of prison hulks, disfigured old ships, broken, black and sinister. The hands swung the yards as the ship made each turn in the channel, the officers attentive during this first passage of the elderly vessel. They rounded the fort on Darnetness.

'Give her the main course, Mr Rogers.'

'Aye, aye, sir. Main yard there! Let fall! Let fall! Let fall! Mind tacks and sheets there, you blasted lubbers! Look lively there! Watch, God damn it, there's a kink in the starboard clew garnet! It'll snag in the lead block, Mr Quil-bloody-hampton!'

Virago gathered speed, the tide giving Drinkwater a brief illusion of commanding something other than a tub of a ship. He smiled to himself. Though slow, *Virago* was heavy enough to carry her way and would probably handle well enough in a seaway. She had a ponderous certainty about her that might become an endearing quality, Drinkwater thought. He swung her down Kethole Reach and Rogers braced the yards up again as the wind veered a point towards the north. To the west the sky was clearing and almost horizontal beams of sunlight began to slant through the overcast, shining ahead of them to where the fort at Garrison Point and the Sheerness Dockyard gleamed dully against the monotones of marsh and islands.

'Clew up the courses as we square away in Saltpan Reach, Mr Rogers.' He levelled his glass ahead. Half a dozen squat hulled shapes were riding at anchor off Deadman's Island, a mile up stream from Sheerness. They were bomb vessels anchored close to the powder hulks at Blackstakes.

A chattering had broken out amidships. 'Silence there!' snapped Rogers. Drinkwater watched the line of bombs grow larger. 'Up courses if you please.'

Rogers bawled, Quilhampton piped and Matchett shouted. The heavy flog of resisting canvas rose above Drinkwater's head as he studied the bombs through his glass, selecting a place to bring *Virago* to her anchor.

They were abeam the upstream vessel, a knot of curious officers visible on her deck. There was a gap between the fourth and fifth bomb vessel, sufficient for *Virago* to swing. Drinkwater felt a thrill of pure excitement. He could go downstream and anchor in perfect safety at the seaward end of the line; but that gap beckoned.

'Stand by the braces, Mr Rogers! Down helm!'

'Down helm, zur!' *Virago* turned to starboard, her yards creaking round in their parrels, the forestaysail filling with a crack.

'Brace sharp up there, damn it!' he snapped, then to the helm, 'Full and bye!'

'Full an' bye, zur,' replied the impassive Tregembo.

Drinkwater sailed *Virago* as close to the wind as possible as the ebb pushed her remorselessly downstream. If he made a misjudgement he would crash on board the bomb vessel next astern. He could see a group of people forward on her, no doubt equally alerted to the possibility. He watched the relative bearing of the other vessel's foremast. It drew slowly astern: he could do it.

'Anchor's ready, sir,' muttered Rogers.

'Very well.' They were suddenly level with the bow of the other ship.

'Down helm!' *Virago* turned to starboard again, her sails about to shiver, then to flog. She carried her way, the water chuckling under her bow as she crept over the tide, leaving the anxious watchers astern and edging up on the ship next ahead.

Drinkwater watched the shore, saw its motion cease. 'All aback now! Let go!'

He felt the hull buck as the anchor fell from the cathead and watched the cable rumble along the deck, saw it catch an inexperienced landsman on the ankle and fling him down while the seamen laughed.

'Give her sixty fathoms, Mr Matchett, and bring her up to it.'

He nodded to Rogers. 'Clew up and stow.'

Mr Easton went below to plot their anchorage on the chart and when the vessel was reported brought to her cable Drinkwater joined him. Looking at the chart Drinkwater felt satisfied that neither ship nor crew had let him down.

His satisfaction was short-lived. An hour later he stood before Captain Martin, Master and Commander of His Majesty's bomb vessel *Explosion*, senior officer of the bomb ships assembled at Sheerness. Captain Martin was clearly intolerant of any of his subordinates who showed the least inclination to further their careers by acts of conspicuousness.

'Not only, lieutenant, was your manoeuvre one that endangered your own ship but it also endangered mine. It was, sir, an act of wanton irresponsibility. Such behaviour is not to be tolerated and speaks volumes on your character. I am surprised you have been entrusted with such a command, Mr Drinkwater. A man responsible for carrying quantities of powder upon a special service must needs be steady, constantly thoughtful, and never, ever hazard his ship.'

Drinkwater felt the blood mounting to his cheeks as Martin went on. 'Furthermore you have been most dilatory in the matter of commissioning your ship. I had reason to expect you to join the bombs under my command some days ago.'

Martin looked up at Drinkwater from a pair of watery blue eyes that stared out of a thin, parchment coloured face. Drinkwater fought down his sense of injustice and wounded pride. Feeling like a whipped midshipman he applied the resilience of the orlop, learned years ago.

'If my conduct displeased you I apologise, sir. I had no intention of causing you any concern. As to the manner of my commissioning I can only say that I exerted every effort to hasten the matter. I was prevented from so doing by the officials of the dockyard.'

'The dockyard officers have their own job to attend to, Mr Drinkwater, you cannot expect them to give priority to a bomb tender . . .'

Aware that he had offended (Martin was probably related to some jobber in the dockyard), Drinkwater could not resist the opening.

'Precisely my point, sir,' he said drily. Martin's upper lip curled slightly, a mark of obvious displeasure, and Drinkwater added hastily, 'I mean no offence, sir.'

He stared down the commander who eventually said, 'Now, to your orders for the next week . . .'

'Your sport was most profitable, Mr Q,' said Drinkwater laying down his knife and fork upon an empty plate.

'Thank you sir. Did you favour the widgeon or the teal?'

'I fancy the teal had the edge. Mr Jex, would you convey my appreciation to the cook.'

Jex nodded, his mouth still full. Drinkwater looked round the table. It was a cramped gathering, sharing his small cabin with the officers were the two stern chasers and two 24-pound carronades in the aftermost side ports.

34

The cloth was drawn and the decanter of blackstrap placed in front of Drinkwater. They drank the loyal toast at their seats then scraped their chairs back. A cigar or two appeared, Trussel brought out a long churchwarden pipe and Willerton slipped a surreptitious quid of tobacco into his mouth. Lettsom took snuff and Drinkwater reflected that apart from himself and Rogers and Mr Quilhampton all those present, which excepted Mr Mason on deck, were well over forty-five, possibly over fifty. The preponderance of warrant officers carried by *Virago* ensured this, but it sometimes made Drinkwater feel old before his time, condemned to spend his life in the society of elderly men. He sighed, remembering the attitude of Captain Martin. Then he remembered something else, something he had been saving for this moment. 'By the way gentlemen, when I was aboard *Explosion* this morning I learned some news from London that will affect us all. Has anyone else learned of it?'

'We know that Admiral Ganteaume got out of Brest with seven of the line,' said Rogers.

'Aye, these damned easterlies, but I heard that Collingwood's gone in pursuit,' added Matchett. Drinkwater shook his head.

'You mean, sir, that it is intended to defend the Thames by dropping stone blocks into it?' asked Quilhampton ingenuously.

'No, young shaver, I do not.' He looked round. No one seemed to have any idea. 'I mean that Billy Pitt's resigned and that Mr Speaker Addington is to form a new government . . .' Exclamations of surprise and dismay met the news.

'Well, 'twill be of no account, Addington's Pitt's mouthpiece . . .'

'No wonder there are no orders for us . . .'

'So the King would not stomach emancipating the papists.'

'Damned good thing too . . .'

'Come Mr Rogers, you surely cannot truly think that?'

'Aye, Mr Lettsom, I most certainly do, God damn them . . .'

'Gentlemen please!' Drinkwater banged his hand on the table. The meal was intended to unite them. 'Perhaps you would like to know who is to head the Admiralty?' Their faces turned towards him. 'St Vincent, with Markham and Troubridge.'

'Who is to replace St Vincent in the Channel, sir?'

'Lord Cornwallis.'

'Ah, Billy Blue, well I think that is good news,' offered Lettsom, 'and I hear St Vincent will be at Sir Bloody Andrew Snape Hammond's throat. He has sworn reform and Hammond is an infernal jobber. Pray heaven they start at Chatham, eh?'

'I'll drink to that, Mr Lettsom,' said Drinkwater smiling.

'What d'you say Jex?' said the surgeon turning to the purser, 'got your dirty work done just in time, eh?' There was a rumble of laughter round the table. Jex flushed.

'I protest . . . sir . . .'

'I rule that unfair, Mr Lettsom,' said Drinkwater still smiling. 'Consider that Mr Jex paid for the sauerkraut.'

'The hands'll not thank you for that sir, however good an anti-scorbutic it is.'

Drinkwater ignored Jex's look of startled horror. He did not see it subside into an expression of resentment. 'What about the other members of the cabinet?' asked Lettsom.

'I forget, Mr Lettsom. Only that that blade Vansittart is to be Joint Secretary to the Treasury or something. That is all I recollect . . .'

'Well the damned politicians forget us; why the hell should we remember them?' Rogers's flushed face expressed approval at his own jest.

'I have it!' said Lettsom suddenly, snapping his fingers as the laughter died away.

'Have what sir?' asked Quilhampton in precocious mock horror, 'The lues? The yaws?'

'An epigram, gentlemen, an epigram!' He cleared his throat while several banged the table for silence. Lettsom struck a pose:

'If blocks can from danger deliver,
Two places are safe from the French,
The first is the mouth of the river,
The second the Treasury Bench.'

'Bravo! Bravo!' They cheered, banged the table and were unaware of the strange face that appeared round the doorway. Drinkwater saw it first, together with that of Mason behind. He called for silence. 'What is it Mr Mason?'

The assembled officers turned to stare at the newcomer. He wore a royal blue tail coat turned back to reveal scarlet facings. His breeches were white and a cocked hat was tucked underneath his arm. His face was round and red, covered by peppery hair that grew out along his cheekbones, though his chin was shaved yet it had the appearance of being constantly rasped raw as if to keep down its beard. The man's head sat low upon his shoulders, like a 12-pound shot in the garlands.

'God damn my eyes, it's a bloody lobster,' said Rogers offensively and even though the man wore the blue uniform of the Royal Artillery his apoplectic countenance lent the welcome an amusing aptness.

'Lieutenant Tumilty of the artillery, sir,' said Mason filling the silence while the artillery officer stared aggressively round his new surroundings.

Drinkwater rose. 'Good day, lieutenant, pray sit down. Mr Q, make way there. You are to join us then?' He passed the decanter down the table and the messman produced a glass. The other occupants of the cabin eyed the stranger with ill-disguised curiosity.

Tumilty filled his glass, downed it and refilled it. Then he fixed Drinkwater with a tiny, fiery eye.

'I'm after asking if you're in command of the ship?' The accent was pugnaciously Irish.

36

'That is correct, Mr Tumilty.'

'It's true then! God save me but 'tis true, so it is.' He swallowed again, heavily.

'What exactly is true, Mr Tumilty?' asked Drinkwater, beginning to feel exasperated by the artilleryman's circumlocution.

'Despite appearances to the contrary, and begging your pardon, but you being but a lieutenant, then this ain't a bomb vessel, sir. Is that, or is that not the truth of the matter?'

Drinkwater flushed. Tumilty had touched a raw nerve. '*Virago* was built as a bomb vessel, but at present she is commissioned only as a tender . . .'

'Though there's nothing wrong with her structure,' growled the hitherto silent Willerton.

'Does that answer your question?' added Drinkwater, ignoring the interruption.

Tumilty nodded. 'Aye, God save me, so it does. And I'll not pretend I like it lieutenant, not at all.' He suddenly struck his hat violently upon the table.

'Devil take 'em, do they not know the waste; that I'm the finest artilleryman to be employed upon the service?' He seemed about to burst into tears, looking round the astonished faces for agreement. Drinkwater was inclined to forgive him his behaviour; clearly Mr Tumilty was acting as a consequence of some incident at Woolwich and cursing his superiors at the Royal Arsenal.

'Gentlemen, pity me, I beg you. I'm condemned to hand powder like any of your barefoot powder-monkeys. A fetcher and carrier, me!'

'It seems, Mr Tumilty, that, to coin a phrase, we are all here present in the same boat.' A rumble of agreement followed Drinkwater's soothing words.

'But me, sir. For sure I'm the finest pyroballogist in the whole damned artillery!'

Chapter Six

Powder and Shot

'Pyroballogy, Lieutenant Drinkwater, is the art of throwing fire. 'Tis both scientific and alchemical, and that is why officers in my profession cannot purchase their commissions like the rest of the army, so it is.'

Drinkwater and Tumilty stood at the break of the poop watching the labours of the hands as they manned the yardarm tackles, hoisting barrel after barrel of powder out of the hoy alongside. They had loaded their ordinary powder and shot, naval gunner's stores for their carronades and long guns, from the powder hulk at Blackstakes. Now they loaded the ordnance stores, sent round from Woolwich on the Thames. From time to time Tumilty broke off his monologue to shout instructions at his sergeant and bombadier who, with *Virago's* men, were toiling to get the stores aboard before the wind freshened further.

'No sir, our commissions are all issued by the Master-General himself and a captain of artillery may have more experience than a field officer, to be sure. I'm not after asking if that's a fair system, Mr Drinkwater, but I'm telling you that a man can be an expert at his work and still be no more than a lieutenant.'

Drinkwater smiled. 'And I'd not be wanting to argue with you Mr Tumilty,' he said drily.

' 'Tis an ancient art, this pyroballogy. Archimedes himself founded it at the seige of Syracuse and the Greeks had their own ballistic fireballs. Now tell me, Mr Drinkwater, would I be right in thinking you'd like to be doing a bit of the fire-throwing yourself?'

Drinkwater looked at the short Irishman alongside him. He was growing accustomed to his almost orientally roundabout way of saying something.

'I think perhaps we both suffer from a sense of frustration, Mr Tumilty.'

'And the carpenter assures me the ship's timbers are sound enough.' Drinkwater nodded and Tumilty added, ' 'Tis not to be underestimated, sir, a thirteen-inch mortar has a chamber with a capacity of thirty-two pounds. Yet a charge in excess of twenty will shake the timbers of a mortar bed to pieces in a very short time and may cause the mortar to explode.'

'But we do not have a mortar, Mr Tumilty.'

'True, true, but you've not dismantled the beds Mr Drinkwater. Now why, I'm asking myself, would that be?'

Drinkwater shrugged. 'I was aware that they contained the shell rooms, I assumed they were to remain in place . . .'

'And nobody told you to take them to pieces, eh?'

'That is correct.'

'Well now that's very fortunate, Mr Drinkwater, very fortunate indeed, for the both of us. What would you say if I was to ship a couple of mortars on those beds?'

Drinkwater frowned at Tumilty who peered at him with a sly look.

'I don't think I quite understand.'

'Well look,' Tumilty pointed at the hoy. The last sling of fine grain cylinder powder with its scarlet barrel markings rose out of the hoy's hold, following the restoved and mealed powder into the magazine of *Virago*. The hoy's crew were folding another section of the tarpaulin back and lifting off the hatchboards to reveal two huge black shapes. 'Mortars, Mr Drinkwater, one thirteen-inch weighing eight-two hundredweights, one ten-inch weighing forty-one hundredweights. Why don't we ship them on the beds, eh?'

'I take it they're spares.' Tumilty nodded. Drinkwater knew the other bomb vessels already had their own mortars fitted for he had examined those on the *Explosion*. There seemed no very good argument against fitting them in the beds even if they were supposed to be struck down into the hold. After all *Virago* had been fitted to carry them. He wondered what Martin would say if he knew, as doubtless he would in due course.

'By damn, Mr Tumilty, it is getting dark. Let us have those beauties swung aboard as you suggest. We may carry 'em in their beds safer than rolling about in the hold.'

'That's the spirit, Mr Drinkwater, that's the spirit to be sure.'

'Mr Rogers! A word with you if you please.' Rogers ascended the ladder.

'Sir?'

'We have two mortars to load, spares for the squadron. I intend to lower them on the beds. D'you understand Sam? If we've two mortars fitted we may yet get a chance to do more than fetch and carry . . .'

The gleam of enthusiasm kindled in Roger's eye. 'I like the idea, damned if I don't.' He shot a glance at Tumilty, still suspicious of the artilleryman who seemed to occupy a position of a questionable nature aboard a King's ship. The Irishman was gazing abstractedly to windward.

'Now, 'twill be ticklish with this wind increasing but it will likely drop after sunset. Brace the three lower yards and rig preventers on 'em, then rig three-fold purchases as yard and stay tackles over both beds. Get Willerton to open the hatches and oil the capsquares. Top all three yards well up and put two burtons on each and frap the whole lot together. That should serve.'

'What weights, sir?'

'Eighty-two hundred weights to come in on the after bed and . . .'

'Forty-one on the forward . . .'

'*Forrard*, Mr Tumilty.'

'I'm sure I'm begging your pardon, Mr Rogers.' Rogers hurried away shouting for Matchett and Willerton. 'Why he's a touchy one, Mr Drinkwater.'

'We're agreed on a number of things, Mr Tumilty, not least that we'd both like to add 'Captain' to our name, but I believe there was much bad blood between the artillery and the navy the last time an operation like this took place.'

'Sure, I'd not be knowing about that sir,' replied Tumilty, all injured innocence again.

Virago creaked and leaned to starboard as the weight came on the tackles. The sun had already set and in the long twilight the hands laboured on. The black mass of the ten-inch mortar, a little under five feet in length, hung above the lightened hoy.

At the windlass Mr Matchett supervised the men on the bars. Yard and stay tackles had been rigged with their hauling parts wound on in contrary directions so that as the weight was eased on the yard arms it was taken up on the stay tackles. The doubled-up mainstay sagged under the weight and Rogers lowered the mortar as quickly as possible. Mr Willerton's party with handspikes eased the huge iron gun into its housing and snapped over the capsquares. *Virago* was upright again, though trimming several inches by the head.

'Throw off all turns, clear away the foretackles, rig the after tackles!'

It was as Drinkwater had said. The wind had died and the first mortar had come aboard without fuss. Mr Tumilty had left the pure seamanship to the navy and gone to closet himself with his sergeant and Mr Trussel, while they inspected the powder stowage and locked all the shell rooms, powder rooms, fuse rooms and filling rooms that Willerton had lined with the deal boards supplied by Chatham Dockyard.

The tackles suspended from the main and crossjack yards were overhauled and hooked onto the carefully fitted slings round the thirteen-inch mortar. Next the two centreline tackles were hooked on. To cope with the additional weight of the larger mortar Drinkwater had ordered these be rigged from the main and mizzen tops, arguing the mizzen forestay was insufficient for the task.

Again the hauling parts were led forward and the slack taken up. There were some ominous creakings but after half an hour the trunnions settled on the bed and Mr Willerton secured the second set of capsquares. The sliding section of the mortar hatches were pulled over and the tarpaulins battened down. The last of the daylight disappeared from the riot of cloud to the west and the hands, grumbling or chattering according to their inclination, were piped below.

For the first time since the days of disillusion that followed his joining the ship, Nathaniel Drinkwater felt he was again, at least in part, master of his own destiny.

'Well, Mr Tumilty, perhaps you would itemise the ordnance stores on board.'

'Sure, and I will. We have two hundred of the thirteen-inch shell carcases, two hundred ten-inch, one hundred and forty round, five-vented carcases for the thirteens, forty oblong carcases for the tens. Five thousand one pound round shot, the same as you have for your swivels . . .'

'What do you want them for?' asked Rogers.

'Well now, Mr Rogers,' said Tumilty, tolerantly lowering his list, 'if you choke up the chamber of a thirteen inch mortar with a couple of hundred of they little devils, they fall like iron rain on trenches, or open works without casemates, or beaches, or anywhere else you want to clear of an enemy. Now to continue, we have loaded two hundred barrels of powder, an assortment as you know of fine cylinder, restoved and mealed powder. I have three cases of flints, five of fuses, six rolls of worsted quick-match, a quantity of rosin, turpentine, sulphur, antimony, saltpetre, spirits of wine, isinglass and red orpiment for Bengal lights, blue fires and fire balls. To be sure, Mr Rogers, you're sitting on a mortal large bang.'

'And you've everything you want?' Tumilty nodded. 'Are you happy with things, Mr Trussel?'

'Aye, sir, though I'd like Mr Willerton to make a new powder box. Ours is leaky and if you're thinking that . . . well, maybe we might fire a mortar or two ourselves, then you'll need one to carry powder up to the guns.'

'Mr Trussel's right, Mr Drinkwater. The slightest leak in a powder box lays a trail from the guns to the filling room in no time at all. If the train fires the explosion'll be even quicker!' They laughed at Tumilty's diabolical humour; the siting of those ugly mortars had intoxicated them all a little.

'Very well, gentlemen. We'll look at her for trim in the morning and hope that Martin does not say anything.'

'Let us hope Captain Martin'll be looking after his own mortars and not overcharging them so that we haven't to give up ours,' said Tumilty, blowing his red nose. He went on:

'And who had you in mind to be throwing the shells at, Mr Drinkwater?'

'Well it's no secret that the Baltic is the likely destination, gentlemen,' he looked round at their faces, expectant in the gently swinging light from the lamp. From the notebooks he had inherited from old Blackmore, sailing master of the frigate *Cyclops*, he had learned a great deal about the Baltic. Blackmore had commanded a snow engaged in the timber trade. 'If the Tsar leagues the navies of the north, we'll have the Danes and Swedes to deal with, as well as the Russians. If he doesn't, we've still the Russians left. They're based at

41

Revel and Cronstadt; iced up now, but Revel unfreezes in April. As to the Swedes at Carlscrona, I confess I know little of them. Of the Danes at Copenhagen,' he shrugged, 'I do not think we want to leave 'em in our rear.'

'It's nearly the end of February now,' said Trussel, 'if we are to fight the Danes before the Russkies get out of the ice, we shall have to move soon.'

'Aye, and with that dilatory old bastard Hyde Parker to command us, we may yet be too late,' added Rogers.

'Yes, I'm after thinking it's the Russkies.' Tumilty nodded, tugging at the hairs on his cheeks.

'Well, they say Hyde Parker's marrying some young doxy, so I still say we'll be too late.' Rogers scratched the side of his nose gloomily.

'They say she's young enough to be his daughter,' grinned Trussel.

'Dirty old devil.'

'Lucky old sod.'

' 'Tis what comes of commanding in the West Indies and taking your admiral's eighth from the richest station in the service,' added the hitherto silent Easton.

'Well well, gentlemen, 'tis of no importance to us whom Admiral Parker marries,' said Drinkwater, 'I understand it is likely that Nelson will second him and *he* will brook no delay.'

'Perhaps, perhaps, sir, but I'd be willing to lay money on it,' concluded Rogers standing up, taking his cue from Drinkwater and terminating the meeting.

'Let us hope we have orders to proceed to the rendezvous at Yarmouth very soon, gentlemen. And now I wish you all a good night.'

Chapter Seven

February 1801

Action off the Sunk

Lieutenant Drinkwater hunched himself lower into his boat cloak, shivering from the effects of the low fever that made his head and eyes ache intolerably. The westerly wind had thrown a lowering overcast across the sky and then whipped itself into a gale, driving rain squalls across the track of the squadron as it struggled out of the Thames Estuary into the North Sea.

Their visible horizon was circumscribed by one such squall which hissed across the wave-caps and made *Virago* lean further to leeward as she leapt forward under its impetus. A roil of water foamed along the lee scuppers, squirting inboard through the closed gunports and Drinkwater could hear the grunts of the helmsmen as they leaned against the cant of the deck and the kicking resistance of the big tiller. A clicking of blocks told where the quartermaster took up the slack on the relieving tackles. Drinkwater shivered again, marvelling at the chill in his spine which was at odds with the burning of his head.

He knew it could be typhus, the ship-fever, brought aboard by the lousy draft of pressed men, but he was fastidious in the matter of bodily cleanliness and had not recently discovered lice or fleas upon his person. He had already endured the symptoms for five days without the appearance of the dreaded 'eruption'. Lettsom had fussed over him, forcing him to drink infusions of bark without committing himself to a diagnosis. The non-appearance of a sore had led Drinkwater to conclude he might have contracted the marsh-ague from the mists of the Medway. God knew he had exposed himself to chills and exhaustion as he had striven to prepare his ship, and his cabin stove had been removed with Mrs Jex, prior to the loading of powder.

He thought of the admonition he had received from Martin and the recollection made him search ahead, under the curved foot of the forecourse to where *Explosion* led the bomb vessels and three tenders to the north eastward. What he saw only served to unsettle him further.

'Mr Easton!' he shouted with sudden asperity, 'do you not see the commodore's signalling?' Martin, the epitome of prudence tending to timidity, was reducing sail, brailing up his courses and snugging down to double reefed topsails and a staysail forward. Drinkwater left Easton to similarly reduce *Virago*'s canvas and repeat the signal to the vessels astern. He fulminated silently to himself, having already decided that Martin was a cross they were all going to have to bear. As senior officer he had been most insistent upon being addressed as

43

'commodore' for the short passage from Sheerness to Yarmouth. Drinkwater found that sort of pedantry a cause for contempt and irritation. He was aware, too, that Martin was not simply a fussy senior officer. It was clear that whatever advancement Drinkwater expected to wring out of his present appointment was going to have to be despite Captain Martin, who seemed to wish to thwart the lieutenant. Drinkwater threw off his gloomy thoughts, the professional melancholy known as 'the blue devils', and watched a herring gull glide alongside *Virago*, riding the turbulent air disturbed by the passage of the ship. With an almost imperceptible closing of its wings it suddenly side-slipped and curved away into the low trough of a wave lifting on *Virago*'s larboard quarter.

'Sail reduced sir.'

'Very well, Mr Easton. Be so good as to keep a sharp watch on the commodore, particularly in this visibility.'

Easton bit his lip. 'Aye, aye, sir.'

'When will we be abeam the Gunfleet beacon?'

' 'Bout an hour, sir.'

'Thank you.'

Easton turned away and Drinkwater looked over the ship. His earlier premonition had been correct. She had an immensely solid feel about her, despite her lack of overall size. Her massive scantlings gave her this, but she was also positive to handle and gave him a feeling of confident satisfaction as his first true command.

He looked astern at the remainder of the squadron. *Terror*, *Sulphur*, *Zebra* and *Hecla* could just be made out. *Discovery* and the other two tenders, both Geordie colliers, were lost in the rain to the south westward. The remaining bomb, *Volcano*, was somewhere ahead of *Explosion*.

He saw one of the tenders emerge from the rain astern of *Hecla*. She was a barque rigged collier called the *Anne Reed*, requisitioned by the Ordnance Board and fitted up as an accommodation vessel for the Royal Artillery detachment, some eight officers and eighty men who, in addition to half a dozen ordnance carpenters from the Tower of London, would work the mortars when the time came. Lieutenant Tumilty was somewhere aboard her, no doubt engaged in furious and bucolic debate with his fellow 'pyroballogists' over the more abstruse aspects of fire-throwing.

Drinkwater smiled to himself, missing the man's company. Doubtless there would be time for that later, when they reached Yarmouth and again when they entered the Baltic.

A stronger gust of wind dashed the spray of a breaking wave and whipped it over *Virago*'s quarter. A cold trickle wormed its way down Drinkwater's neck, reminding him that he need not stand on deck all day. Already the Swin had opened to become the King's Channel, now that too merged with the Barrow Deep. Easton lifted his glass and stared to the north. The rain would prevent them seeing the Naze and its tower. Drinkwater fumbled in his tail pocket and brought out his

44

own glass. He scanned the same arc of the horizon, seeing it become indistinct, grey and blurred as yet another rain squall obscured it. He waited patiently for it to pass, then looked again. This time Easton beat him to it.

'A point forrard of the beam, sir.'

Drinkwater hesitated. Then he saw it, a pole surmounted by a wooden cage over which he could just make out a faint, horizontal blur. The blur was, he knew, a huge wooden fish.

'Very well, Mr Easton, a bearing if you please and note in your log.'

A quarter of an hour later the Gunfleet beacon was obliterated astern by more rain and as night came on the wind increased.

By midnight the gale was at its height and the squadron scattered. Drinkwater had brought *Virago* to an anchor, veering away two full cables secured end to end. For although they were clear of the long shoals that run into the mouth of the Thames they had yet to negotiate the Gabbards and the Galloper and the Shipwash banks, out in the howling blackness to leeward.

The fatigue and anxiety of the night seemed heightened by his fever and he seemed possessed of a remarkable energy that he knew he would pay dearly for later, but he hounded his officers and took frequent casts of the lead to see whether his anchor was dragging. At six bells in the middle watch the atmosphere cleared and they were rewarded by a glimpse of the lights of the floating alarm vessel* at the Sunk. With relief he went below, collapsing across his cot in his wet boat cloak, his feet stuck out behind him still in their shoes. Only his hat rolled off his head and into a damp corner beneath a carronade slide.

Lieutenant Rogers relieved Mr Trussel at four in the morning.

'Wind's abating, sir,' added Trussel after handing the deck over to the lieutenant.

'Yes.'

'And veering a touch. Captain said to call him if it veered, sir.'

'Very well.' Rogers wiped his mouth with the back of his hand and slipped the pewter mug that was now empty of coffee into the bottom shelf of the binnacle. He looked up at the dark streamer of the masthead pendant, then down at the oscillating compass. The wind was indeed veering.

'Mr Q!'

'Sir?'

'Pass word to the Captain that the wind's veering, north west a half west and easing a touch, I fancy.'

'Aye, aye, sir.'

The cloud was clearing to windward and a few stars were visible. Rogers crossed the deck to look at the traverse board then hailed the masthead to see if anything was visible from there.

Drinkwater arrived on deck five minutes later. It had taken him a

---

* Early lightvessel with fixed lights; that at the Sunk was established in 1799.

great effort to urge his aching and stiffened limbs to obey him.

'Morning sir.'

'Mornin',' Drinkwater grunted, 'any sign of the commodore or the Sunk alarm vessel?'

'No sign of the commodore but the Sunk's still in sight. She's held to her anchor.'

'Very well. Wind's easing ain't it?'

'Aye, 'tis dropping all the time.'

'Turn the hands up then, we'll prepare to weigh.'

Drinkwater walked aft and placed his hands on the carved taffrail, drawing gulps of fresh air into his lungs and seeking in vain some invigoration from the dawn. Around him the ship came to life. The flog of topsails being cast loose and sheeted home, the dull thud of windlass bars being shipped. There was no fiddler aboard *Virago* and the men set up a low chant as they began to heave the barrels round to a clunking of pawls. The cable came in very slowly.

They had anchored north east of the Sunk, under the partial shelter of the Shipwash Sand and *Virago* rolled as her head was pulled round to her anchor. Already a faint lightening of the sky was perceptible to the east. Drinkwater shook the last of the sleep from him and turned forward.

'Forrard there, how does she lead?'

'Two points to larboard, sir, and coming to it.' Matchett's voice came back to him from the fo'c's'le. Drinkwater drummed his fingers on the poop rail.

'Up and down, sir.'

'Anchor's aweigh!'

'Topsail halliards, away lively there . . . haul away larboard braces, lively now! Ease away that starboard mainbrace damn you . . .!' The backed topsails filled with wind even before their yards had reached their proper elevation. *Virago* began to make a stern board.

'Foretopmast staysail, aback to larboard Mr Matchett.' The ship began to swing. 'Helm a-lee!'

'Hellum's a-leek, zur.'

'Larboard tack, Mr Rogers, course nor' nor' east.'

He left Rogers to haul the yards again and steady *Virago* on her new course. They would be safely anchored in Yarmouth Roads before another midnight had passed. Around him the noises of the ship, the clatter of blocks, the grind of the rudder, the flog of canvas and creak of parrels, told him Rogers was steadying *Virago* on her northward course. He wondered how the other members of the squadron had fared during the night and considered that 'commodore' Martin might be an anxious and exasperated man this morning. The thought amused him, although it was immediately countered by the image of Martin and the other ships sitting in Yarmouth Roads awaiting the arrival of *Virago*.

The ship heeled and beneath him the wake began to bubble out from under her stern as she gathered headway. Instinctively he threw

46

his weight on one hip, then turned and began pacing the windward side of the poop. The afterguard padded aft and slackened the spanker brails, four men swigging the clew out to the end of the long boom by the double outhauls.

'Course, nor' nor' east, sir.'

'Very well, Sam. You have the deck, carry on.'

Rogers called Matchett to pipe up hammocks. The routine of *Virago*'s day had begun in earnest. Drinkwater walked forward again and halted by the larboard mizzen rigging at the break of the poop. He searched for a glimpse of Orfordness lighthouse but his attention was suddenly attracted by something else, an irregularity in the almost indistinguishable meeting of sea and sky to the north of them. He fished in his tail pocket for the Dolland glass.

'Mr Rogers!'

'Sir?'

'What d'you make of those sails,' said Drinkwater without lowering his glass, 'there, half a point on the larboard bow?'

Rogers lifted his own glass and was silent for a moment. 'High peaks,' he muttered, 'could be bawleys out of Harwich, but not one of the squadron, if that's what you're thinking.'

'That ain't what I'm thinking Sam. Take another look, a good long look.'

Rogers whistled. One of the approaching sails had altered course, slightly more to the east and they were both growing larger by the second.

'Luggers, by God!'

'And if I'm not mistaken they're in chase, Sam. French *chassemarées* taking us for a fat wallowing merchantman. I'll wager they've been lying under the Ness all night.'

'They'll eat the logline off this tub, God damn it, and be chock full of men.'

'And as handy as yachts', added Drinkwater, remembering the two stern chasers in his cabin and his untried crew. He would be compelled to fight for he could not outrun such swift enemies.

'Wear ship, Sam, upon the instant. Don't be silly man, we're no match for two Dunkirkers, we'll make the tail of the bank and beat up for Harwich.'

Rogers shut his gaping mouth and turned to bawl abusively at the hands milling in the waist as they carried the hammocks up and stowed them in the nettings. The first lieutenant scattered them like a fox among chickens.

Drinkwater considered his situation. To stand on would invite being out-manoeuvred, while by running he would not only have his longest range guns bearing on the enemy, but might entice the luggers close enough to pound them with his carronades. If he could outrun them long enough to make up for the Sunk and Harwich they might abandon the chase, privateers were unwilling to fight if the odds were too great and there was a guardship in Harwich harbour.

The spanker was brailed up again as *Virago*'s stern passed through the wind. Drinkwater tried to conceal the trembling of his hand, which was as much due to his fever as his apprehension, while he tried to hold the images of the approaching luggers in the circle of the glass. Thanks to the twilight they had been close enough when first spotted. They were scarcely a mile distant as Rogers shrieked at topmen too tardily loosing the topgallants for his liking.

'Look lively you damned scabs, you've a French hulk awaiting you if you don't stop frigging about . . .'

'Beg pardon, sir.'

Drinkwater bumped into a crouching seaman scattering sand on the deck. He abandoned a further study of the enemy and looked to the trim of the sails. Easton was at the con now, still rubbing the sleep out of his eyes.

'We'll make up for Harwich as soon as we're clear of the Shipwash Sand, Mr Easton. Do you attend to the bearing of the alarm vessel.'

'Aye, aye, sir.'

Daylight was increasing by the minute and Drinkwater looked astern again. He could see the long, low hulls, the oddly raked masts and the huge spread of canvas set by the luggers. He was by no means confident of the outcome, and both of the pursuing sea-wolves were coming up fast.

Drinkwater walked forward again. Rogers reported the ship cleared for action.

'Very well. Mr Rogers, you are to command the two chasers in the cabin. We will do what damage we can before they close on us. They will likely take a quarter each and try to board.' Rogers and Easton nodded.

'Mr Easton, you have the con. From time to time I may desire you to ease away a little or to luff half a point to enable Mr Rogers to point better.'

'Aye, sir, I understand.'

'Mr Mason the larboard battery, Mr Q the starboard. Rapid fire as soon as you've loosed your first broadside. For that await the command. Mr Rogers you may fire at will.'

'And the sooner the better.'

Drinkwater ignored Rogers's interruption. 'Is that clear gentlemen?'

There was a succession of 'ayes' and nods and nervous grins.

Drinkwater stood at the break of the low poop. The waisters were grouped amidships, the gun crews kneeling at their carronades. They all looked expectantly aft. They had had little practice at gunnery since leaving Chatham and Drinkwater was acutely conscious of their unpreparedness. He looked now at the experienced men to do their best.

'My lads, there are two French privateers coming up astern hand over fist. They've the heels of us. Give 'em as much iron as they can stomach before they close us. A Frog with a bellyful of iron can't jump a ditch . . .' He paused and was gratified by a dutiful ripple of nervous laughter at the poor jest. 'But if they do board I want to see you busy with those pikes and cutlasses . . .' He broke off and gave them what he thought was a confident, bloodthirsty grin. He was again relieved to see a few leers and hear the beginnings of a feeble cheer.

He nodded. 'Do your duty, lads.' He turned to the officers, 'Take post gentlemen.'

It suddenly occurred to him that he was unarmed. 'Tregembo, my sword and pistols from the cabin if you please.'

He looked aft and with a sudden shock saw the two luggers were very much closer. The nearer was making for *Virago*'s lee quarter, the larboard.

'God's bones,' muttered Drinkwater to himself, trying to fend off a violent spasm of shivering that he did not want to be taken for fear.

'Here zur,' Tregembo held out the battered French hanger and Drinkwater unhooked the boat cloak from his throat and draped it over Tregembo's outstretched arm. He buckled on the sword then took the pistols.

'I've looked to the priming, zur, and put a new flint in that 'un, zur.'

'Thank you, Tregembo. And good luck.'

'Aye, zur.' The man hurried away with the cloak and reappeared on deck almost at once.

A fountain of water sprung up alongside them, another rose ahead.

'In range, sir,' said Easton beside him, 'they'll be good long nines, then.'

'Yes,' said Drinkwater shortly, aware that his tenure of command might be very short indeed, his investment in *Virago* a wasted one. An uncomfortable vision of the fortresses of Verdun and Bitche rose unbidden into his mind's eye. He swore again softly, cursing his luck, his fever and the waiting.

Beneath his feet he felt a faint rumble as Rogers had the chaser crews run the 6-pounders through the stern ports. He thought briefly of the two portraits hanging on the forward bulkhead and then forgot all about them as the roar of *Virago*'s cannon rang in his ears.

He missed the fall of shot, and that of the second gun. At least Samuel Rogers would do his utmost, of that Drinkwater was certain.

At the fourth shot a hole appeared in the nearer lugger's mizen. Beside Drinkwater Easton ground his right fist into the palm of his left hand with satisfaction.

'Mind you attend to the con, Mr Easton,' Drinkwater said and caught the crest-fallen look as Easton turned to swear at the helmsmen.

The nearer lugger was overhauling them rapidly, her relative bearing opening out broader on the quarter with perceptible speed. 'Luff her a point Mr Easton!'

'Aye, aye, sir.'

Virago's heel eased a little and Rogers's two guns fired in quick succession.

Drinkwater watched intently. He fancied he saw a shower of splinters somewhere amidships on the Frenchman then Mason was alongside him.

'Beg pardon sir, but I can get the aftermost larboard guns to bear on that fellow, sir.' The enemy opened fire at that very moment and a buzz filled the air together with a whooshing noise as double shotted ball and canister scoured *Virago*'s deck. Drinkwater heard cries of agony and the bright gout of blood appeared as his eye sought out the damage to his ship.

'Very well, Mr Mason . . .' But Mason was gone, he lay on the deck silently kicking, his face contorted with pain.

'You there! Get Mr Mason below. Pass word to Mr Q to open fire with both batteries. Independent fire . . .'

His last words were lost in a crack from aloft and the roar of gunfire from the enemy. The mainyard had been shot through and was sprung, whipping like a broomstick.

'Mains'l Mr Easton! And get the tops'l off her at once . . .' Men were already starting the tacks and sheets. Matchett's rattan rose and fell as he shoved the waisters towards the clew and buntlines, pouring out a rich and expressive stream of abuse. Even as the carronades opened fire *Virago* slowed and suddenly the leeward lugger was upon them.

Lining her rail a hedge of pikes and sword blades appeared.

'Boarders!' Drinkwater roared as the two vessels ground together. A grapnel struck the rail and Drinkwater drew his hanger and sliced the line attached to it.

He saw the men carrying Mason drop him half way down the poop ladder as they raced for cutlasses.

'God's bones!' Drinkwater screamed with sudden fury as the Frenchmen poured over the rail. His hanger slashed left and right and he seemed to have half a dozen enemies in his front. He pulled out a pistol and shot one through the forehead, then he was only aware of the swish of blades hacking perilously close to his face and the bite and jar in his mangled arm muscles as steel met steel.

The breath rasped in his throat and the fever fogged him with the first red madness of bloodlust longer than was usual. The cool fighting clarity that came out of some chilling primeval past revived him at last. The long fearful wait for action was over and the realisation that he was unscathed in those first dreadful seconds left him with a detachment that seemed divorced from the grim realities of hand to hand fighting. He was filled with an extraordinary nervous energy that could only have owed its origins to his fevered state. He seemed wonderfully possessed of demonic powers, the sword blade sang in his hand and he felt an overwhelming and savagely furious joy in his butchery.

He was not aware of Tregembo and Easton rallying on him. He was oblivious to James Quilhampton a deck below still pouring shot after shot into the French lugger's hull at point blank range with two

24-pounder carronades. Neither did he see Rogers emerge on deck with the starboard gun crews who had succeeded in dismasting the other lugger at a sufficient distance, nor that Quilhampton had so persistently hulled their closer adversary that her commander realised he had caught a Tartar and decided to withdraw.

He did not know that the Viragos were inspired by the sight of their hatless captain, one foot on the rail, hacking murderously at the privateersmen like a devil incarnate.

Drinkwater was only aware that it was over when there were no more Frenchmen to be killed and beneath him a widening gulf between the two hulls. He looked, panting, at his reeking hands; his right arm was blood-soaked to the elbow. He was sodden from the perspiration of fever and exertion. He watched their adversary drop astern, her sails flogging. She was low in the water, sinking fast. Several men swam round her, the last to leave *Virago* he presumed. Staggering as though drunk, he looked for the second lugger. Her foremast was gone and her crew were sweeping her up to the assistance of her foundering consort.

Drinkwater was aware of a cheer around him. Men were shouting and grinning, all bloody among the wounded and the dead. Rogers was coming towards him, his face cracked into a grin of pure delight. Then there was another cheer out to starboard and *Virago* surged past the anchored red bulk of the Sunk alarm vessel, her crew waving from the rail, her big Trinity House ensign at the dip.

'They bastards've bin 'anging round three days 'n' more,' he heard her master shout in the Essex dialect as they passed.

'I fancy we fooled the sods then, God damn 'em,' said Rogers as the cheers died away. Drinkwater's head cleared to the realisation that he was shivering violently. He managed a thin smile. Ship and company had passed their first test; they were blooded together but now there was a half-clewed main course to furl, a topsail to secure and a mainyard to fish.

'Do you wish to put about and secure a prize, sir?' asked the ever hopeful Rogers.

'No Sam, Captain Martin would never approve of such a foolhardy act. Do you put about for Yarmouth, we must take the Shipway now. Those luggers'll not harm the alarm vessel and have problems enough of their own. Mr Easton, a course to clear Orfordness if you please. See word is passed to Willerton to fish that bloody yard before it springs further, and for Christ's sake somebody get that poor fellow Mason below to the surgeon.'

Drinkwater was holding the poop rail to prevent himself keeling over. He was filled with an overwhelming desire to go below but there was one last thing to do.

'Mr Q!'

'Sir?'

'Do you bring me the butcher's bill in my cabin directly.'

PART TWO

Sir Hyde Parker

'If you were here just to look at us! I had heard of manoeuvres off
Ushant, but ours beat all ever seen. Would it were over, I am really
sick of it!'

NELSON, March 1801

Chapter Eight   February–March 1801

An Unlawful Obligation

'Hold him!' Lettsom snapped at his two mates as they struggled to hold Mason down on the cabin table. A cluster of lanterns illuminated the scene as Lettsom, stripped to the shirt-sleeves, his apron stained dark with blood, bent again over his task.

Despite a dose of laudanum Mason still twitched as the surgeon probed the wound in his lower belly. The bruised flesh gaped bloodily, the jagged opening in the groin where the splinter had penetrated welled with blood.

Drinkwater stood back, against the bulkhead. Since the action with the luggers that morning he had slept for five hours and fortified himself against his fever with half a bottle of blackstrap. *Virago* was now safely anchored in Yarmouth Roads in company with a growing assembly of ships, partly the preparing Baltic fleet, partly elements of Admiral Dickson's Texel squadron. Drinkwater was feeling better and the absence of *Explosion* had further encouraged him.

Mason was the last of the three serious casualties to receive Lettsom's attention. One seaman had lost an arm. Another, like Mason, had received severe splinter wounds. An additional eight men had received superficial wounds and there were four of their own people dead. The seven French corpses left on board had been thrown overboard off Lowestoft without ceremony.

Lettsom had left Mason until *Virago* reached the relative tranquility of the anchorage. He knew that the long oak sliver that had run into Mason's body could only be extracted successfully under such conditions.

Drinkwater watched anxiously. He knew Lettsom was having difficulties. The nature of the splinter was to throw out tiny fibres of wood that acted like barbs. As these carried fragments of clothing into the wound the likelihood of a clean excision was remote. The set of Lettsom's jaw and the perspiration on his forehead were evidence of his concern.

Lettsom withdrew the probe, inserted thin forceps and drew out a sliver of wood with a sigh. He held it up to the light and studied it intently. Drinkwater saw him swallow and his eyes closed for a moment. He had been unsuccessful. He rubbed his hand over his mouth in a gesture of near despair, leaving a smear of blood across his face. Then his shoulders sagged in defeat.

'Put him in my cot,' said Drinkwater, realising that to move Mason further than was absolutely necessary would kill him. Lettsom caught his eye and the surgeon shook his head. The two men remained motionless while the surgeon's mates bound absorbent pledgets over the wound and eased Mason into the box-like swinging bed. Lettsom rinsed his hands and dropped his reeking apron on the tablecloth while his mates cleaned the table and cleared Drinkwater's cabin of the gruesome instrument chest. Drinkwater poured two glasses of rum and handed one to the surgeon who slumped in a chair and drained it at a swallow.

'The splinter broke,' Lettsom said at last. 'It had run in between the external iliac vein and artery. They were both intact. That gave me a chance to save him . . .' He paused, looked at Drinkwater, then lowered his eyes again. 'That was a small miracle, Mr Drinkwater, and I should have succeeded, but I bungled it. No don't contradict me, I beg you. I bungled it. The splinter broke with its end lodged in the obturator vein, the haemorrage was dark and veinous. When he turns in his sleep he will move it and puncture his bladder. Part of his breeches and under garments will have been carried into the body.'

'You did your utmost, Mr Lettsom. None of us can do more.'

Lettsom looked up. His eyes blazed with sudden anger. 'It was not enough, Mr Drinkwater. God damn it, it simply was not enough.'

Drinkwater thought of the flippant quatrain with which Lettsom had introduced himself. The poor man was drinking a cup of bitterness now. He leaned across and refilled Lettsom's glass. Drinkwater was a little drunk himself and felt the need of company.

'You did your duty . . .'

'Bah, duty! Poppycock, sir! We may all conceal our pathetic inadequacies behind our "duty". The fact of the matter is I bungled it. Perhaps I should still be probing in the poor fellow's guts until he dies under my hands.'

'You cannot achieve the impossible, Mr Lettsom.'

'No, perhaps not. But I wished that I might have done more. He will die anyway and might at least have the opportunity to regain his senses long enough to make his peace with the world.'

Drinkwater nodded, looking at the hump lying inert in his own bed. He felt a faint ringing in his ears. The fever did not trouble him tonight but he seemed to float an inch above his chair.

'I don't believe a man must shrive his soul with a canting priest, Mr Drinkwater,' Lettsom went on, helping himself to the bottle. 'I barely know whether there is an Omnipotent Being. A man is only guts sewn up in a hide bag. No anatomist has discovered the soul and the divine spark is barely perceptible in most.' He nodded at the gently swinging cot. 'See how easily it is extinguished. How much of the Almighty d'you think he contains to be snuffed like this?' he added with sudden vehemence.

'You were not responsible for Mason's wound, Mr Lettsom,' Drinkwater said with an effort, 'those luggers . . .'

'Those luggers, sir, were simply a symptom of the malignity of mankind. What the hell is this bloody war about, eh? The king of Denmark's mad, Gustav of Sweden's mad, Tsar Paul is a dangerous and criminal lunatic and each of these maniacs is setting his people against us. And what in God's name are we doing going off to punish Danes and Swedes and Russians for the crazy ambitions of their kings? Why, Mr Drinkwater, it is even rumoured that our very own beloved George is not all that he should be in the matter of knowing what's what.' Lettsom tapped his head significantly.

'We are swept up like chaff in the wind. Mason is hit by the flail and I bungle his excision like a student. That's all there is to it, Mr Drinkwater. One may philosophise over providence, or what you will, as long as you have a belly empty of splinters, but that *is* all there is to it . . .'

He fell silent and Drinkwater said nothing. His own belief in fate was a faith that drew its own strength from such misgivings as Lettsom expressed. But he could not himself accept the cold calculations of the scientific mind, could not agree with Lettsom's assumption of ultimate purposelessness.

They were both drunk, but at that brief and peculiarly lucid state of drunkenness that it is impossible to maintain and is gone as soon as attained. In this moment of clarity Drinkwater thought himself the greater coward.

'Perhaps,' said Lettsom at last, 'the French did themselves a service by executing King Louis, much as we did the first Charles. Pity of the matter is we replaced a republic by a monarchy and subjected ourselves voluntarily to the humbug of parliamentary politics . . .'

'You are an admirer of the American rebels, Mr Lettsom?'

The surgeon focussed a shrewd eye on his younger commander. 'Would you not welcome a world where ability elevated a man quicker than birth or influence, Mr Drinkwater?'

'Now you sound like a leveller. You know, you quacks stand in a unique position in relationship to the rest of us. Wielding the knife confers a huge moral advantage upon you. Like priests you are apt to resort to pontification . . .'

'Moral superiority is conferred on *any* man with a glass in his hand . . .'

'Aye, Mr Lettsom, and when we rise tomorrow morning the world will be as it is tonight. Imperfect in all its aspects, yet oddly beautiful and full of hidden wonders, cruel and harsh with battles to be fought and gales endured. There is more honesty at a cannon's mouth than may be found elsewhere. Kings and their ambition are but a manifestation of the world's turbulence. As a scientist I would have expected you to acknowledge Newton's third law. It governs the entire travail of humanity Mr Lettsom, and is not indicative of tranquil existence.'

Lettsom looked at Drinkwater with surprise. 'I had no idea I was commanded by such a philosopher, Mr Drinkwater.'

'I learnt the art from a surgeon, Mr Lettsom,' replied Drinkwater drily.

'Your journals, Mr Q.' Drinkwater held out his hand for the bound notebooks. He opened the first and turned over the pages. The handwriting was large and blotchy, the pages wrinkled from damp.

'They were rescued from the wreck of the *Hellebore*, sir,' offered the midshipman.

Drinkwater nodded without looking up, stifling the images that rose in his mind. He took up a later book. The calligraphy had matured, the entries were briefer, less lyrical and more professional. A drawing appeared here and there: *The arrangement of yards upon a vessel going into mourning.* Drinkwater smiled approvingly, discovering a half-finished note about mortars.

'You did not complete this, Mr Q?'

'No sir. Mr Tumilty left us before I had finished catechising him.'

'I see. How would you stow barrels, Mr Q?'

'Bung up and bilge free, sir.'

'A ship is north of the equator. To find the latitude, given the sun's declination is south and the altitude on the meridian is reduced to give a correct zenith distance, how do you apply that zenith distance to the declination?'

'The declination is subtracted from the zenith distance, sir, to give the latitude.'

'A vessel is close hauled on the larboard tack, wind south-westerly and weather thick. You have the deck and notice the air clearing with blue sky to windward. Of what would you beware and what steps would you take?'

'That the ship might be thrown aback, the wind veering into the north west. I would order the quartermaster to keep the vessel's head off the wind a point more than was necessary by the wind.'

'Under what circumstances would you not do this?'

Quilhampton's face puckered into a frown and he caught his lip in his teeth.

'Well, Mr Q? You are almost aback, sir.'

'I . . . er.'

'Come now. Under what circumstances might you not be able to let the vessel's head pay off? Come, summon your imagination.'

'If you had a danger under the lee bow, sir,' said Quilhampton with sudden relief.

'Then what would you do?'

'Tack ship, sir.'

'You have left it too late, sir, the ship's head is in irons . . .' Drinkwater looked at the sheen of sweat on the midshipman's brow. There was enough evidence in the books beneath Drinkwater's hands of Quilhampton's imagination and he was even now beset by anxiety on his imaginary quarterdeck.

'Pass word for the captain, sir?' Quilhampton suggested hopefully.

'The captain is incapacitated and you are first lieutenant, Mr Q, you cannot expect to be extricated from this mess.'

'Make a stern board and hope to throw the ship upon the starboard tack, sir.'

'Anything else?' Drinkwater looked fixedly at the midshipman. 'What if you fail in the sternboard?

'Anchor, sir.'

'At last! Never neglect the properties of anchors, Mr Q. You may lose an anchor and not submit your actions to a court-martial, but it is quite otherwise if you lose the ship. A prudent man, knowing he might be embayed, would have prepared to club-haul his ship with the larboard anchor. Do you know how to club-haul a ship?'

Quilhampton swallowed, his prominent Adam's apple bobbing round his grubby stock.

'Only in general principle, sir.'

'Make it your business to discover the matter in detail. Now, how is a topmast stuns'l set?'

'The boom is rigged out and the gear bent. Pull up the halliards and tack, keeping fast the end of the deck sheet. The stops are cut by a man on the lower yard. The tack is hauled out and the halliards hove. The short sheet is rove round the boom heel and secured in the top.'

Drinkwater smiled, recognising the words. 'Very well, Mr Q. Consequent upon the death of Mr Mason I am rating you acting master's mate. You will take over Mason's duties. Please take your journals with you.'

He waved aside Quilhampton's thanks. 'You will not thank me when the duty becomes arduous or I am dissatisfied with your conduct. Go and look up how to club-haul in that excellent primer of yours.'

Drinkwater picked up his pen and returned to the task he had deliberately interrupted by summoning Quilhampton.

Dear Sir, he began to write, *It is with great regret that my painful duty compels me to inform you of the death of your son* . . .

Explosion and the rest of the squadron came into Yarmouth Roads during the next two days to join the growing number of British men of war anchored there. Most of the other bomb vessels had been blown to leeward and Martin merely nodded when Drinkwater presented his report. The fleet was reduced to waiting while the officers eagerly seized on the newspapers to learn anything about the intentions of the government in respect of the Baltic crisis.

A number of British officers serving with the Russian navy returned to Britain. One in particular arrived in Yarmouth: a Captain Nicholas Tomlinson, who had been reduced to half-pay after the American War and served with the Russians at the same period as the American John Paul Jones. He volunteered his services to the commander-in-chief. Admiral Parker, comfortably ensconced at the

Wrestler's Inn with his young bride, refused to see Tomlinson.

No orders emanated from either Parker or London. It was a matter that preoccupied the officers of *Virago* as they dined in their captain's absence.

'Lieutenant Drinkwater is endeavouring to discover some news of our intentions either from Martin or anyone else who knows,' explained Rogers as he took his place at the head of the cabin table and nodded to the messman.

'I hear the King caught a severe chill at the National Fast and Humiliation,' said Mr Jex in his fussy way, 'upon the thirteenth of last month.'

'National Farce,' corrected Rogers, sarcastically.

'*I* heard he caught a cold *in the head*,' put in the surgeon with heavy emphasis.

'At all events we must wait until either Addington's kissed hands or Parker has got out of his bed,' offered Easton.

'At Parker's age he'll be a deuced long time getting up with a young bride in his bed,' added Lettsom with a grin, sniping at the more accessible admiral in the absence of a king.

'At Parker's age he'll be a deuced long time getting *it* up, you mean Mr Lettsom,' grunted Rogers coarsely.

'Yes, I wonder who exhausts whom, for it is fearful unequal combat to pit eighteen years against sixty-four.'

'Experience against enthusiasm, eh?'

'More like impotence against ignorance, but wait, I have the muse upon me,' Lettsom paused. 'I am uncertain on whom to lay the greater blame for our woes.

'Why here is a thing to raise liberal hopes;
Government can't do as it pleases,
While the entire fleet 'waits the order to strike
Addington awaits the King's sneezes.'

A cheer greeted this doggerel but Lettsom shook his head with dissatisfaction.

'It don't scan to my liking. I think the admiral the better inspiration:

' 'Tis not for his slowness in firing his shot
That our admiral is known every night,
But his laxness in heaving his anchor aweigh
Must dub him a most tardy knight.'

There were more cheers for the surgeon and it was generally accepted that the second verse was much better than the first.

'But the lady's no fool, Mr Lettsom, and I'll not subscribe to her ignorance,' Rogers said as the laughter died away. 'Parker flew his flag in the West Indies. He's the richest admiral on the list. His fortune is supposed to be worth a hundred thousand and all she has to put up with is a few years of the old pig grunting about the sheets before the lot'll fall into her lap. Why 'tis a capital match and I'll drink to Lady Parker. There's many a man as would marry for the same reason, eh Mr Jex?' Rogers leered towards the purser.

Jex shot a venomous look at the first lieutenant. His conduct during the fight with the luggers had not been exactly valorous and he had dreaded this exposure as the butt of the officers' jests.

'Ah, Mr Jex has seen victory betwixt the sheets and is accustomed to seek it between the sails, eh?' There was another roar of laughter. At the end of the action off the Sunk Jex had been discovered hiding in the spare sails below decks.

'You are being uncharitable towards Mr Jex, Mr Rogers. I have it on good authority he was looking for his honour,' Lettsom said as Jex stormed from the cabin the colour of a beetroot.

'Come in. Yes Mr Q, what is it?' Drinkwater's voice was weary.

'Beg pardon, sir, but the vice-admiral's entering the anchorage.' Drinkwater looked up. There was a light in the young man's eyes. 'Lord Nelson, sir,' he added excitedly. Drinkwater could not resist Quilhampton's infectious enthusiasm.

'Thank you, Mr Q,' he said smiling. The hero of the Nile had a strange way of affecting the demeanour of his juniors. Drinkwater remembered their brief meeting at Syracuse and that same infectious enthusiasm that had seemed to imbue Nelson's entire fleet, despite their vain manoeuvrings in chase of Bonaparte. What a shame the same spirit was absent from the present assembly of ships. Drinkwater sighed. The subsequent scandal with Hamilton's wife and the vainglorious progress through Europe that followed the victory at Aboukir Bay, had curled the lip of many of Nelson's equals, but Drinkwater had no more appetite for his paper-work and he found himself pulling a muffler round his neck under his boat cloak to join the men at *Virago*'s rail cheering the little admiral as the *St George* stood through the gatway into Yarmouth Roads.

The battleship with her three yellow strakes flew a blue flag at her foremasthead and came in with two other warships. Hardly had her sheet anchor dropped from her bow than her cannon boomed out in salute to Parker's flag, flying nominally at the mainmasthead of the 64-gun *Ardent* until the arrival of Parker's proper flagship. The flag's owner was still accommodated at the Wrestler's Inn and this fact must have been early acquainted to Nelson for his barge was shortly afterwards seen making for the landing jetty. It was later rumoured that, although he received a cordial enough welcome from the commander-in-chief, Parker refused to discuss arrangements for the fleet on their first meeting.

Although a man who appeared to have lost both head and heart to Emma Hamilton, Nelson had never let love interfere with duty. It was soon common knowledge in the fleet that his criticisms of Parker were frank, scatological and scathing. Nelson's dissatisfaction spread like wildfire, and ribald jests were everywhere heard, particularly among the hands on the ships that waited in the chill winds and shivered in their draughty gun decks while Sir Hyde banked the bedroom fire in the Wrestler's Inn. In addition to Lettsom's doggerel there were other ribaldries, mostly puns upon the name of the hostelry where Parker lodged and all of them enjoyed with relish in gunrooms as on gun decks, in cockpits and in state-rooms. Nelson had given a dinner the evening of his arrival and expressed his fears on the consequences of a delay. His impatience did not improve as day succeeded day.

The final preparations for the departure of the expedition were completed. Nearly eight hundred men of the 49th Foot with a company of rifles had been embarked under Colonel Stewart. Eleven masters of Baltic trading ships and all members of the Trinity House of Kingston-upon-Hull had joined for the purpose of piloting the fleet through the dangers of the Baltic Sea. On Monday 9th March Parker's flagship the *London* arrived and his flag was ceremoniously shifted aboard her at eight o'clock the next morning. The admiral remained ashore.

Later that day an Admiralty messenger arrived in Yarmouth with an order for Parker to sail, but still he prevaricated. His wife had arranged a ball for the coming Friday and, to indulge his Fanny, Parker postponed the fleet's departure until after the event.

That evening Lieutenant Drinkwater also received a message, scribbled on a piece of grubby paper:

> *Nathaniel*
> *I beg you come ashore at eight of the clock tonight.*
> *I must see you on a matter of the utmost urgency.*
> *I beg you not to ignore this plea and I will*
> *await you on the west side of the Yare ferry.*
>
> *Ned*

The word *must* was underlined heavily. Drinkwater looked up at the longshoreman who had brought the note and had refused to relinquish it to Mr Quilhampton who now stood protectively suspicious behind the ragged boatman.

'The man was insistent I give it to you personal, sir,' he said in the lilting Norfolk accent.

'What manner of man was it gave you this note?'

'Why, I'd say he were a serving man, sir. Not a gentleman like you sir, though he was gen'rous with his master's money . . .' The implication was plain enough without looking at the man's face. Drinkwater drew a coin from his pocket.

'Here,' he passed it to the boatman, frowning down at the note. He dismissed the man. 'Mr Q.'

'Sir?'

'A boat, please, in an hour's time.'

'Aye, aye, sir.'

'And Mr Q, not a word of this to anyone if you please.' He fixed

Quilhampton with a baleful glance. If Edward was reduced to penury in a matter of weeks he did not want the world to know of it.

A bitter easterly wind blew across the low land south of the town. The village of Gorleston exhibited a few lights on the opposite bank as he descended into the ferry. Darkness had come early and the fresh wind had led him to order his boat off until the following morning. To the half guinea the note had cost him it now looked as though he would have to add the charge of a night's lodging ashore. Brotherly love was becoming an expensive luxury which he could ill afford. And now, he mused as the ferryman held out a fist, there was an added penny for the damned ferry.

Clambering up the far bank he allowed the other passengers to pass ahead of him. He could see no one waiting, then a shadow detached itself from a large bush growing on the river bank.

'God damn it, Ned. Is that you?'

'Ssh, for the love of Christ . . .'

'What the devil are you playing at?'

'I must talk to you . . .' Edward loomed out of the shadows, standing up suddenly in front of Drinkwater. Beneath a dark cloak Drinkwater could see the pale gleam of a shirt. Edward's hair was undressed and loosely blowing round his face. Even in the gloom Drinkwater could see he was in a dishevelled state. He was the longshoreman's 'serving man'.

'What in God's name . . .?'

'Walk slowly, Nat, and for heaven's sake spare me further comment. I'm deep in trouble. Terrible trouble . . .' Edward shivered, though whether from cold or terror his brother could not be sure,

'Well come on, man, what's amiss? I have not got all night . . .' But of course he had. 'Is it about the money, Edward?'

He heard the faint chink of gold in a purse. 'No, I have the remains of that here. It is not a great deal . . . Nat, I am ruined . . .'

Drinkwater was appalled: 'D'you mean you have lost that two hundred and fifty . . .? My God, you'll have no more!'

'God, Nat, it isn't money that I want.'

'Well what the devil is it?'

'Can you take me on your ship? Hide me? Land me wherever you are going. I speak French. Like a German they say. For God's sake, Nat you are my only hope, I beg you.'

Drinkwater stopped and turned to his brother. 'What the hell is this all about, Ned?'

'I am a fugitive from the law. From the extremity of the law, Nat. If I am taken I . . .' he broke off. 'Nat, when I heard your ships were assembling at Yarmouth and arrived to find *Virago* anchored off the shore I . . . I hoped . . .'

'What are you guilty of?' asked Drinkwater, a cold certainty settling round his heart.

'Murder.'

There was a long silence between the brothers. At last Drinkwater said, 'Tell me what happened.'

'I told you of the girl? Pascale?'

'Aye, you did.'

'I found her abed with her God damned marquis.'

'And whom did you murder?'

'Both of them.'

'God's bones!' Drinkwater took a few paces away from his brother, his brain a turmoil. Like at that moment in the Strand, his instinct for order reeled at the prospect of consigning his brother to the gallows. He remembered his mother, then his wife and child in a bewildering succession of images that drove from his mind the necessity of making a decision and only further confused him. Edward was guilty of Edward's crimes and should suffer the penalty of the law; yet Edward was his brother. But protecting Edward would make him an accessory, while Edward's execution would ensure his own professional oblivion.

He swore beneath his breath. In his passion Edward had murdered a worthless French aristocrat and his whore. How many Frenchmen had Nathaniel murdered as part of his duty? Lettsom's words about duty came back to him and he swore again.

But those were moral judgements of an unrecognised morality, a morality that might appeal to Lettsom and his Paine-like religion of humanity. In the harsher light of English justice he had no choice: Edward was a criminal.

The vain pontifications of the other night, as he and Lettsom had exchanged sallies over the dying body of Mason, came back to confront him now like some monstrous ironic joke. He felt like a drowning man. What would Elizabeth think of him if he assisted his brother up the steps of the scaffold? Would she understand his quixoticism if he helped Edward escape? Was his duty to Edward of greater significance than that he owed his wife?

'Nat, I beg you . . .'

'I do not condone what you have done. You confront me with an unlawful obligation.'

A thought occurred to him. At first it was no more than a half-considered plan and owed its inception to a sudden vicious consideration that it might cost this wastrel brother his life. Edward would have to submit to the harsh judgement of fate.

'How much money have you left?'

'Forty-four pounds.'

'You must return it to me. You have no need of money.' He heard the sigh of relief. 'You will accompany me back to the ship and will be entered on the books as Edward Waters, a landsman volunteer. Tell your messmates you are a bigamist, that you have seduced a young girl while being married yourself, any such story will suffice and guarantee they understand your morose silences. You will make no approach to me, nor speak to me unless I speak to you. If you

64

transgress the regulations that obtain on board you will not be immune from the cat. As far as I am concerned you importuned me whilst ashore and asked to volunteer. Being short of men I accepted your offer. Do you understand?'

'Yes, Nat. And thank you, thank you . . .'

'I think you will have little to thank me for, Ned. God knows I do not do this entirely for you.'

Batter Pudding

Drinkwater woke in the pre-dawn chill. By an inexplicable reflex of the human brain he had fallen instantly asleep the night before, but now he awoke, his mind restlessly active, his body in a lather of sweat, not of fever, but of fear.

His first reaction was that something was terribly wrong. It took him a minute to separate fact from fancied dreaming, but when he realised the extent of reality he was appalled at his own conduct. He got out of his cot, dragged his blankets across the deck and slumped in the battered carver he had inherited as cabin furniture in the *Virago*.

Staring unseeing into the darkness it was some time before he had stopped cursing himself for a fool and accepted the events of the previous evening as accomplished facts. The residual effects of his fever sharpened his imagination so that, for a while, his isolation threatened to prevent him thinking logically. After a little he steadied himself and began to examine his actions in returning to the ship.

The first point in his favour was that he and Edward had returned in a hired beach boat picked up in the River Yare. The boatmen had got a good price for the passage out through the breakwaters and Edward a soaking by way of an introduction to the sea-service. Drinkwater had insisted on his brother leaving the cloak on the bank of the Yare, thinking the more indigent he looked the better. The fugitive had been frozen, wet and dishevelled enough not to excite any comment as to there being any connection between the two men. Indeed the silence between them had been taken for disdain on Drinkwater's part to the extent of one of the longshoremen offering a scrap of tarpaulin to the shuddering Edward. And, now that he recollected it, he had heard a muttered comment about 'fucking officers' from the older of the two boatmen as he had agilely scrambled up *Virago*'s welcome tumblehome.

He wondered if he had over-played his hand in arriving upon the deck, for in the darkness the officer on watch, already expecting the captain to remain ashore until the morning, had not manned the side properly. Trussel's embarrassment was obvious and Drinkwater pitied the quartermaster who had not spotted the boat in time.

Trussel's apologies had been profuse and Drinkwater had excused them abruptly.

''Tis no matter, Mr Trussel, I went upon a fool's errand and am glad to be back.' Drinkwater turned aft and had one foot on the poop ladder when he appeared to recollect something. 'Oh, Mr Trussel,' he looked back at the rail over which the sopping figure of Edward was clambering. He had clearly been sluiced by the sea as he jumped from the boat and even in the gloom the dark stain of water was visible around his feet. He stood shivering, pathetically uncertain.

'This fellow importuned me ashore. Damned if he didn't volunteer; on the run from some jade's jealous husband I don't wonder. See he's wrapped up for the night and brought before Lettsom and the first lieutenant in the morning.'

He heard Trussel acknowledge the order and knew Edward's reception would be cruel. Trussel would not welcome the necessity of turning out blankets and hammock at that late hour and Jex, the issuing officer, would be abusive at being turned from his cot to oblige the gunner. Trussel's own irritation at being found wanting in his duty on deck only added to the likelihood of Edward becoming a scapegoat. Now, in the cold morning air, Drinkwater hoped that his play-acted unconcern had sounded more genuine to Trussel and the other members of the anchor watch than to his own ears.

He made to find his flint to light a lantern, then realised that it would not do to let the morning anchor watch know he was awake by the glow in the skylight. He continued to sit until the wintry dawn threw its cold pale light through the cabin windows, gleaming almost imperceptibly on the black breeches of the two stern chasers. Then he roused himself and passed word for hot water. Already the hands were turning up to scrub decks. After he had shaved and dressed his mind was more composed. He had formulated a plan to save Edward's neck and his own honour. By the time he was ready to put it into practice there was enough light in the cabin by which to write.

The easterly wind had died in the night and the morning proved to be one of light airs and sunshine, picking out the details of the fleet with great clarity, lending to the bright colours of the ensigns, jacks, command flags and signals the quality of a country fair; quite the reverse of their stern military purpose. Had Drinkwater been less preoccupied by his dilemma he might have remarked on the irony of the situation, for the Baltic enterprise seemed to be in abeyance while preparations were made for Lady Parker's ball. Around *St George* there congregated an early assortment of captain's gigs; water beetles collecting round the core of disapproval at the frivolous attitude of the fleet's commander-in-chief.

Pacing his tiny poop Drinkwater resisted the frequent impulse to touch the sealed letter in his breast pocket. He should have called his own boat away half an hour ago but morbid curiosity kept him on deck to see what his brother would make of his first forenoon in the Royal Navy. Edward had one powerful incentive to keep his mouth shut and Drinkwater had advised him of it just before he hailed the boatman on the beach the previous night.

'If the people ever learn they've their captain's brother among them they will make your life so hellish you'd wish you'd not asked for my protection.'

If Edward had doubted his brother then, he had little cause to this morning. Graham, bosun's mate of the larboard watch, was giving him a taste of the starter as he hustled the new recruit aft to where Mr Lettsom sat on the breech of a gun waiting to give the newcomer his medical examination.

Drinkwater stopped his pacing at the poop rail. 'Is that our new man, Mr Lettsom?'

'Aye sir.' Lettsom looked up at his commander. Drinkwater studiously ignored his brother although he felt Edward's eyes upon him.

'I don't want that fellow bringing the ship-fever aboard. God knows what hole he's out of, but if he wants a berth aboard *Virago* he must formerly have been quartered in a kennel.'

Lettsom grinned with such complicity that Drinkwater thought his own performance must be credible. With an assumed lofty indifference he resumed his pacing as Lettsom commanded 'Strip!'

As Drinkwater paced up and down he caught glimpses of his unfortunate brother. First shivering naked, then being doused by a washdeck hose pumped enthusiastically by grinning seamen, and finally bent double while Lettsom examined him for lice.

'Well, Mr Lettsom?'

'No clap, pox or crabs, sir. Teeth fair, no hernias, though a little choleric about the gills. Good pulse, no fever. Sound in wind and limb. Washed from truck to keel in the German Ocean and fit for service in His Britannic Majesty's Navy.'

'Very well. Ah, Mr Rogers . . .' Drinkwater touched his hat in acknowledgement of Rogers's salute.

'Good morning sir.'

'I have a new hand for you. Volunteered last night and I knew you were still short of men. God knows what induces voluntary service but a mad husband or a nagging wife may drive a man to extremes.'

'Not a damned felon are you, cully?' Rogers asked in a loud voice that started the sweat prickling along Drinkwater's spine.

Already ashamed of his nakedness Edward did not raise his eyes. 'N . . . No . . .'

Graham's starter sliced his buttocks and the bosun's mate growled 'No *sir*.'

'No sir.'

Drinkwater had had enough. 'Take him forward, Graham, the fellow's cold. Volunteers are rare enough without neglecting 'em. See he washes the traps he wore aboard and is issued with slops from the purser, including a greygoe. Oh, and Graham, get that hair cut.'

'Aye, aye, sir.'

Graham hustled Edward forward. Drinkwater had one last thought. Afterwards he thought the timing capped the whole performance. 'By the way, what's your name?'

'Waters, sir . . . Edward Waters.'

'Very well Waters, do your duty and you have nothing to fear.' The old formula had a new meaning and the two brothers looked at each other for a moment then Drinkwater nodded his dismissal and Graham led 'Waters' away.

Drinkwater resumed his pacing, aware that he was shaking with relief. When he had calmed himself he called for his gig.

Great Yarmouth is a town built on the grid pattern, squeezed into the narrow isthmus between the North Sea and the River Yare that flows southwards, parallel to the sea from the tidal Broadlands, then turns abruptly, as if suddenly giving up its independence and surrendering to the ocean. More than once in its history the mouth had moved and the population turned out to dig a cut to preserve the river mouth that ensured their prosperity.

The walled section of the old town had streets running from north to south between the quays lining the Yare and a sea road contiguous with the beach. At right angles to the streets, alleys cut east to west, from sea to river, and Drinkwater was hopelessly lost in these before he eventually discovered the Wrestler's Arms in the market place.

He walked past it three or four times before making up his mind to carry out his plan. The metaphor to be hung for a sheep as a lamb crossed his mind with disquieting persistence, but he entered the coffee room and called for a pot of coffee. It was brought by a pleasant looking girl with soft brown hair and a smile that was pretty enough to distract him. He relaxed.

'Be that all, sir?' she asked, her lilting accent rising on the last syllable.

'No, my dear. Have you pen, paper and ink, and would you oblige me by finding out if Lady Parker is at present in her rooms?'

The girl nodded. 'Oh, yes sir. Her ladyship's in sir, her dressmaker's expected in half an hour sir and she's making preparations for a gala ball on Friday, sir . . .'

'Thank you,' Drinkwater cut in abruptly, 'but the paper, if you please . . .'

The girl flushed and bobbed a curtsey, hurrying away while Drinkwater sipped the coffee and found it surprisingly delicious.

When the girl returned he asked her to wait while he scribbled a note requesting permission for Lieutenant Drinkwater to wait upon her ladyship at her convenience, somewhat annoyed at having to use such a tone to an eighteen-year-old girl, but equally anxious that the gala would not turn her ladyship's mind from remembering her deliverer in the Strand.

Giving the girl the note and a shilling he watched her bob away, her head full of God knew what misconceptions. She returned after a few minutes with the welcome invitation that Lady Parker would be pleased to see Lieutenant Drinkwater at once.

He found her ladyship in an extravagant silk morning dress that would not have disgraced Elizabeth at the Portsmouth Assembly Rooms. The girl's plain face was not enhanced by the lace cap that she wore. Drinkwater much preferred the French fashion of uncovered hair, and he could not but agree with Lord St Vincent's nickname for her: *Batter Pudding*. But somehow her very plainness made his present task easier. Her new social rank had made her expect deference and her inexperience could not yet distinguish sincerity from flattery.

Drinkwater bent over her hand. 'It is most kind of your ladyship to receive me.' He paused and looked significantly at a door which communicated with an adjacent room and from which the low tone of male voices could be heard. 'I do hope I am not disturbing you . . .'

'Not at all. Thank you Annie, you may go.' The girl withdrew and Lady Parker seated herself at a table. There was a stiffness about her, as though she were very conscious of her deportment. He felt suddenly sorry for her and wondered if she had yet learned to regret being unable to behave like any eighteen-year-old.

'Would you join me in a cup of chocolate, Lieutenant?'

He felt it would be churlish to refuse despite his recent coffee. 'That would be most kind of you.'

'Please sit down.' She motioned to the chair opposite and turned to the tray with its elegant silver pot and delicate china cups.

'May I congratulate you, Lady Parker. At our last meeting I had not connected your name with Admiral Parker's. You must forgive me.'

She smiled and Drinkwater noticed that her eyes lit up rather prettily.

'I had hoped, sir, that you had come to see me as a friend and were not calling upon me as your admiral's wife . . .'

The blow was quite sweetly delivered and Drinkwater recognised a certain worldly shrewdness in her that he had not thought her capable of. It further reassured him in his purpose.

'Nothing was further from my mind, ma'am. I came indeed to see you and the matter has no direct connection with your husband. I come not so much as a friend but as a supplicant.'

'No direct *connection*, Mr Drinkwater? And a *supplicant*? I will willingly do anything in my power for you but I am not sure I understand.'

'Lady Parker forgive me. I should not have importuned you like this and I do indeed rely heavily upon having been able to render you assistance. The truth of the matter is that I have a message I wish delivered in London. It is both private and public in that the matter must remain private, but it is in the public interest.'

She lowered her cup and Drinkwater knew from the light in her eyes that her natural curiosity was aroused. He went on: 'I know I can rely upon your discretion, ma'am, but I have been employed upon special services. That is a fact your own father could verify, though I

70

doubt your husband knows of it. In any event please confirm the matter with the recipient of this letter before you deliver it, if you so wish.' He drew out the heavily sealed letter from his coat and held it out. She hesitated.

'It is addressed to Lord Dungarth at his private address . . .'

'And the matter *is* in the public interest?'

'I believe it to be.' His armpits were sodden but she took the letter and Drinkwater was about to relax when the sound of raised voices came from the other room. He saw her eyes flicker anxiously to the door then return to his face. She frowned.

'Lieutenant Drinkwater, I hope this is not a matter of spoiling my ball.'

'I am sorry ma'am, I do not understand.'

'Certain gentlemen are of the opinion that it would be in the public interest if I were not to hold a ball on Friday, they are urging Sir Hyde to sail at once, even threatening to write to London about it.'

'Good heavens, ma'am, my letter has no connection with the fleet. I would not be so presumptuous . . .' He had appeased her, it seemed. 'The matter is related to affairs abroad,' he added with mysterious significance, 'I am sorry I cannot elaborate further.'

'No, no, of course not. And you simply wish me to deliver this to his lordship?'

'Aye, ma'am, I should consider myself under a great obligation if you would.'

She smiled and again her eyes lit attractively. 'You will be under no obligation Mr Drinkwater, provided you will promise to come to my ball.'

'It will give me the greatest pleasure, ma'am, and may I hope for a dance?'

'Of course, Lieutenant.' He stood. The noises from the other room sounded hostile and he wished to leave before the door opened. 'It would be better if no one knew of the letter, your ladyship,' he indicated the sealed paper on the table.

'My dressmaker comes soon . . .' She reached for her reticule and hid the letter just as the door burst open. As Drinkwater picked up his hat he came face to face with a short florid man in a grey coat. He was shaking his head at someone behind him.

'No, damn it, no . . . Ah, Fanny, my dear,' he saw Drinkwater, 'who the deuce is this?'

'May I present Lieutenant Drinkwater, Hyde dear.' Drinkwater bowed.

'Of which ship, sir?' Parker's eyes were hostile.

'*Virago*, bomb-tender, sir. I took the liberty . . .'

'Lieutenant Drinkwater took no liberties, my dear, it was he who rescued me from the mob in the Strand last October. The least I could do was present him to you.'

Parker seemed to deflate slightly. He half faced towards the man

71

in the other room, whose identity was still unknown to Drinkwater, then turned again to the lieutenant.

'Obliged, I'm sure, Lieutenant, and now, if you'll excuse me . . .'

'Of course sir. I was just leaving . . .' But Lady Parker had a twinkle in her eye and Drinkwater, grateful and surprised at the skill of her intervention, suspected her of enjoying herself.

'Lieutenant Drinkwater served under father at Camperdown, Hyde, I am sure he is worthy of your notice.'

Parker shot him another unfriendly glance and Drinkwater wondered if the admiral thought he had put his wife up to this currying of favour. Clearly the other man was forming some such notion for he appeared disapprovingly in the doorway. The shock of recognition hit Drinkwater like a blow. If he thought Parker saw him in a poor light it was clear Lord Nelson saw him in a worse.

'If you want your dance, Sir Hyde, and your wife wants her *amusements*, then the fleet and I'll go hang. But I tell you time, time is everything; five minutes makes the difference between a victory and a defeat.'

Chapter Ten

Truth in Masquerade

Drinkwater began Tuesday afternoon pacing his poop as the sky clouded over and the wind worked round to the west. The encounter with Lord Nelson had made him resentful and angry. He paced off his fury at being taken by his lordship for one of Lady Parker's *amusements*. The sight of the little admiral, his sleeve pinned across his gold-laced coat, his oddly mobile mouth in its pale, prematurely worn face, with the light of contempt in his one good eye had had an effect on Lieutenant Drinkwater that he was still trying to analyse. It had, he concluded, been like receiving raking fire, so devastating was Nelson's disapproval. The second and more powerful emotion which succeeded in driving from his mind all thoughts of his brother, was the despair he felt at having earned Nelson's poor opinion.

He found Sir Hyde Parker's assurance of 'taking notice of the Lieutenant's conduct to please my wife', which ordinarily ought to have been a matter for self-congratulation, brought him no comfort at all. Nelson had cut him as they both left the Wrestler's Inn and Drinkwater felt the slight almost as intensely as a physical wound.

Drinkwater began to realise the nature of Nelson's magic. He had glimpsed it two years earlier at Syracuse animating a weary fleet that had been beaten by bad luck, bad weather and compounded the break-out of the French through their blockade of Toulon by an over-zealous pursuit that had made them overtake the enemy without knowing it. Yet Nelson had led them back east to smash Brueys in Aboukir Bay in the victory that was now known as The Nile. Now Drinkwater stood condemned as the epitome of all that Nelson despised in Parker and Parker's type.

And because it was unjust he burned with a fury to correct Nelson's misconception.

As he paced up and down he realised the hopelessness of his case. He began to regret asking Dungarth for his own command. What hope had he of distinguishing himself in the old tub that *Virago* really was? Those two mortars that Tumilly had so slyly placed in their beds were no more than a charade. There would be no 'opportunity' in this expedition, only drudgery, probable mismanagement and a glorious débâcle to amuse Europe. No fleet orders had been issued to the ships, no order of sailing. All was confusion with a few of Nelson's intimates forming a cabal within the hierarchy of the fleet which threatened to overset the whole enterprise.

Added to the demoralisation of the officers were the chills, fevers, agues and rheumatism being experienced by many of the seamen. The much publicised Baltic Fleet had the constitution of an organism in an advanced state of rot. Drinkwater's own condition was merely a symptom of that decay.

Only that morning on his return from the shore Rogers had brought a man aft for spitting on the deck. Although Drinkwater suspected the fellow had fallen into an uncontrollable fit of violent coughing he had ordered the grating rigged and the man given a dozen lashes. It was only hours later that he felt ashamed, unconsoled by the reflection that many captains would have ordered three dozen, and only recognising the unpleasant fact that events of the last few days had brutalised him. He had watched Edward's face as Cottrell had been flogged. Only once had his brother looked up. Nathaniel realised now that he had flogged Cottrell as an example to Edward, and he cursed the rottenness of a world that penned men in such traps.

But Lieutenant Drinkwater's wallow in the mire of self-pity did not last long. It was an unavoidable concomitant of the isolation of command and the antidote, when it came in the person of a midshipman from *Explosion*, was most welcome. He was invited to dine on the bomb vessel within the hour. The thought of company among equals, even equals as bilious-eyed as Martin, was preferable to his own morbid society.

It proved to be a surprisingly jolly affair. After a sherry or two he relaxed enough to cast off the 'blue-devils'. If they were going to war he might as well enjoy himself. In a month he might be dead. If they ever did sail of course, and it was this subject that formed the conversation as the officers of the bomb vessels gossiped. The fleet was buzzing with a rumour that delighted both the naval and the artillery officers crowded into Martin's after cabin. Lord Nelson, it was said, had written direct to Earl St Vincent, the First Lord. Lady Parker's ball and the delay it was causing was believed to be the subject of his lordship's letter. Among the assembly an atmosphere of almost school-boy glee prevailed. They waited eagerly for the outcome, arguing on whether it would be the supercession of Parker by Nelson or an order to sail.

Drinkwater exchanged remarks with two white-haired lieutenants who were in command of the other tenders and normally employed by the Transport Board. They were both over sixty and he soon gravitated towards Tumilty and the other artillery officers who were more his own age. The merry-eyed Lieutenant English, attached to *Explosion*, sympathised with him over Martin's apparent animosity and cursed his own ill-luck in being appointed to the ship. Fitzmayer of the *Terror* and Jones of the *Volcano* seemed intent on insulting Admiral Parker and had embarked on a witty exchange of military *double entendres* designed to throw doubts on the admiral's ability to be a proper husband to his bride. The joke was becoming rather stale. From Captain-Lieutenant Peter Fyers of *Sulphur* he learned something of the defences of Copenhagen where Fyers had served the previous year in a bomb vessel sent as part of Lord Whitworth's embassy. Captain-Lieutenant Lawson, attached to *Zebra*, was expatiating on the more scandalous excesses and perverted pastimes of the late Empress Catherine and the even less attractive sadism of her son Tsar Paul, 'the author', as he put it, 'of our present misfortune, God-rot his Most Imperial Majesty.'

'There seems a deal of hostility to kings among these king's officers,' remarked Drinkwater to Tumilty, thinking of the regicide tendencies of his own surgeon.

'Ah,' explained Tumilty with inescapable Irish logic, 'but we're not exactly *king's* officers, my dear Nat'aniel, no we're not. As I told you our commissions are from the Master General of the Ordnance, d'you see. Professional men like yourself, so we are.' He paused to drink off his glass. 'We're pyroballogists that'll fire shot and shell into heaven itself if the devil's wearing a general's tail coat. Motivated by science we are, Nat'aniel, and damn the politics. Fighting men to be sure.'

Drinkwater was not sure if that was true of all the artillery officers mustered in *Explosion's* stuffy cabin, but it was certainly true of Lieutenant Thomas Tumilty whose desire to be throwing explosive shells at anyone unwise enough to provoke him, seemed to consume him with passion so that he sputtered like one of his own fuses.

'And I've some news for you personal like. Our friend Captain Martin has heard that our mortars are mounted. I'd not be surprised if he were to mention it to you . . .' Tumilty's eyes narrowed to slits and the hair on his cheeks bristled as he sucked in his cheeks in mock disapproval. He took another glass from the passing messman and turned away with an obvious wink as Captain Martin approached.

The commander's appearance as though on cue was uncanny, but Drinkwater dismissed the suspicion that Tumilty intended anything more than a warning.

'Well, Mr Drinkwater, itching to try your mortars at the enemy are you?'

'Given the opportunity I should wish to render you every possible assistance in my power, sir,' he said diplomatically.

'Were you not ordered to strike those mortars into your hold, Mr Drinkwater?' asked Martin, an expression of extreme dislike crossing his pale face.

'No sir,' replied Drinkwater with perfect candour, 'the existence of the mortar beds led me to suppose that the mortars might be shipped therein with perfect safety. The vessel would not become excessively stiff and they are readily available should they be required by any other ship. Struck into the hold they might have become overstowed by other . . .'

'Very well, Mr Drinkwater,' Martin snapped, 'you have made your point.' He seemed about to turn away, riled by Drinkwater's glib replies but recollected something and suddenly asked, 'How the devil did you get command of *Virago*?'

'I was appointed by the Admiralty, sir . . .'

'I mean, Mr Drinkwater,' said Martin with heavy emphasis, 'by whose influence was your application preferred?'

Drinkwater flushed with sudden anger. He appreciated Martin's own professional disappointments might be very great, but he himself hardly represented the meteoric rise of an admiral's élève.

'I do not believe I am anybody's protégé, sir,' he said with icy formality, 'though I have rendered certain service to their Lordships of a rather unusual nature.'

Drinkwater was aware that he was bluffing but he saw Martin deflate slightly, as though he had found the justification for his dislike in Drinkwater's reply.

'And what nature did that service take, Mr Drinkwater?' Martin's tone was sarcastic.

'Special service, sir, I am not at liberty to discuss it.' Martin's eyes opened a little wider, though whether it was at Drinkwater's effrontery or whether he was impressed, was impossible to determine. At all events Drinkwater did not need to explain that the special service had been as mate of the cutter *Kestrel* dragging the occasional spy off a French beach and no more exciting than the nightly activities on a score of British beaches in connection with the 'free trade'.

'Special service? You mean *secret* service, Mr Drinkwater,' Martin paused as though making up his mind. 'For Lord Dungarth's department, perhaps?'

'Perhaps, sir,' temporised Drinkwater, aware that this might prove a timely raising of his lordship's name and be turned to some advantage in his plan for Edward.

Real anger was mounting into Martin's cheeks.

'I am quite well aware of his lordship's activities, Drinkwater, I am not so passed over that . . .' he broke off, aware that his own voice had risen and that he had revealed more of himself than he had intended. Martin looked round but the other officers were absorbed in their own chatter. He coughed with embarrassment. 'You are well acquainted with his lordship?' Martin asked almost conversationally.

'Aye sir,' replied Drinkwater, relieved that the squall seemed to have passed. 'We sailed together on the *Cyclops*, frigate, in the American War.' Drinkwater sensed the need to be conciliatory, particularly as the problem of Edward weighed heavily upon him. 'I beg your pardon for being evasive, sir. I was not aware that his lordship's activities were known to you.'

Martin nodded. 'You were not the only officer to serve in his clandestine operations, Mr Drinkwater.'

'Nor, perhaps,' Drinkwater said in a low voice, the sherry making him bold, 'the only one to be disappointed.' He watched Martin's eyes narrow as the commander digested the implication of Drinkwater's remark. Then Drinkwater added, 'you would not therefore blame me for mounting those mortars, sir?'

For a second Drinkwater was uncertain of the result of his importunity. Then he saw the ghost of a smile appear on Martin's face. 'And you are yet known to Lord Dungarth?'

Drinkwater nodded. The knowledge that the lieutenant still commanded interest with the peer was beginning to put him in a different light in Martin's disappointed eyes.

'Very well, Mr Drinkwater.' Martin turned away.

Drinkwater heaved a sigh of relief. The antagonism of Martin would have made any plan for Edward's future doubly hazardous. Now, perhaps, Martin was less hostile to him. He caught Tumilty's eye over the rim of the Irishman's glass. It winked shamelessly. Drinkwater mastered a desire to laugh, but it was not the mirth of pure amusement. It had the edge of hysteria about it. Elizabeth had been right: he was no dissembler and the strain of it was beginning to tell.

Drinkwater returned to *Virago* a little drunk. The dinner had been surprisingly good and during it Drinkwater learned that it had been provided largely by the generosity of the artillery officers who had had the good sense to humour their naval counterparts. It was only later, slumped in his carver and staring at his sword hanging on a hook, that the irrelevant thought crossed his mind that it had not been cleaned after the fight with the French luggers. He sent for Tregembo.

When the quartermaster returned twenty minutes later with the old French sword honed to a biting edge on Willerton's grindstone he seemed to want to talk.

'Beg pardon, zur, but have 'ee looked at they pistol flints?'

'No, Tregembo,' Drinkwater shook his head to clear it of the effects of the wine. 'Do so if you please. I fancy you can re-knap 'em without replacing 'em.'

'There are plenty of flints aboard here, zur,' said Tregembo reproachfully.

Drinkwater managed a laugh. 'Ah yes, I was forgettin' we're a floating arsenal. Do as you please then.'

Tregembo had brought two new flints with him and took out the pull-through. He began fiddling with the brace of flintlocks. 'Do 'ee think we'll sail soon, zur?'

'I hope so, Tregembo, I hope so.'

'They say no one knows where we're going, zur, though scuttle-butt is that we're going to fight the Russians.' He paused. 'It's kind of confusing, zur, but they were our allies off the Texel in '97.'

'Well they ain't our allies now, Tregembo. They locked British

77

seamen up. As to sailing, I have received no orders. I imagine the government are still negotiating with the Baltic powers.'

Drinkwater sighed as Tregembo sniffed in disbelief.

'They say Lord Nelson's had no word of the fleet's intentions.'

'*They say* a great deal, much of it nonsense, Tregembo, you should know that.'

'Aye zur,' Tregembo said flatly in an acknowledgement that Drinkwater had spoken, not that he believed a word of what he had said. There followed a silence as Tregembo lowered the first pistol into the green baize-lined box.

'That volunteer, zur, the one you brought aboard t'other night. Have I seen him afore?'

Drinkwater's blood froze and his brain swam from its haze of wine and over-eating. He had not considered being discovered by Tregembo of all people. He looked at the man but he was nestling the second pistol in its recess. 'His face was kind of familiar, zur.'

Suddenly Drinkwater cursed himself for a fool. What was it Corneille had said about needing a good memory after lying? Tregembo had not left Petersfield when Edward called upon Elizabeth. It was quite likely that he had seen Edward, even that he had let him into the house. And it was almost certain that either he or his wife Susan would have learned that their mistress's visitor was the master's brother.

'Familiar, in what way?' he asked, buying time.

'I don't know, zur, but I seen him afore somewhere . . .' Drinkwater looked shrewdly at Tregembo. Edward's present appearance was drastically altered. Clothes and manners maketh the man and Edward had been shorn of his hair along with his self respect. He was also losing weight due to the paucity of the food and the unaccustomed labour. It was quite possible that Tregembo was disturbed by no more than curiosity. He might think he had seen Edward in a score of places, the frigate *Cyclops*, the cutter *Kestrel*, before he connected him with Petersfield. On the other hand he might remember exactly who Edward was and be mystified as to why the man had turned up before the mast aboard Drinkwater's own ship.

It struck Drinkwater that if the authorities got wind of what he had done he might only have Tregembo to rely on. Except Quilhampton, perhaps, and, with a pang, he recollected James Quilhampton was a party to the little mystery of Edward's note.

Drinkwater was sweating and aware that he had been staring at Tregembo for far too long not to make some sort of confession. He swallowed, deciding on a confidence in which truth might masquerade. 'You may have seen him before, Tregembo. Have you mentioned this to anyone else?'

Tregembo shook his head. 'No zur.'

'You recollect Major Brown and our duties aboard *Kestrel*?' Tregembo nodded. 'Well Waters is not unconnected with the same sort of business. I do not know any details.'

78

'But I saw him at Petersfield, zur. I remember now.'

'Ah, I see.' Drinkwater wondered again if Elizabeth had revealed Edward's relationship. 'His arrival doubtless perturbed my wife, eh? Well I don't doubt it, he was not expecting to find me absent.' Drinkwater paused; that much was true. '*Whatever* you have heard about this man Tregembo I beg you to forget it. Do you understand?'

'Aye zur.'

'If you can avoid any reference to him I'd be obliged.' Then he added as an afterthought, 'So would Lord Dungarth.'

'And that's why he is turned forrard, eh zur?'

Drinkwater nodded. 'Exactly.'

Tregembo smiled. 'Thank 'ee zur. You'll be a commander afore this business is over, zur, mark my words.'

Then he turned and left the cabin and Drinkwater was unaccountably moved.

Drinkwater turned in early. The effects of his dinner had returned and made him drowsy. He longed for the oblivion of sleep. A little after midnight he was aware of someone calling him from a great distance.

He woke slowly to find Quilhampton shining a lantern into his face.

'Sir! Sir! Bengal fires and three guns from the *London*, sir! Repeated by *St George*. The signal to weigh, sir, the signal to weigh . . .!'

'Eh, what's that?'

'Bengal fires and three guns . . .'

'I heard you, God damn it. What's the signal?'

'To weigh, sir.' Quilhampton's enthusiasm was wasted at this hour.

'Return on deck, Mr Q, and read the night orders again for God's sake.'

'Aye, aye, sir,' the crestfallen Quilhampton withdrew and Drinkwater rose to wash the foulness out of his mouth. It was not Quilhampton's fault. No-one in the fleet had had a chance to study the admiral's special signals and it boded ill for the general management of the expedition. Drinkwater spat disgustedly into the bowl set in the top of his sea chest. A respectful knock announced the return of the mate. 'Well?'

'The signal to unmoor, sir.'

'Made for . . .?'

'The line of battleships with two anchors down.'

'And how many anchors have we?'

'One sir.'

'One sir. The signal to weigh will be given at dawn. Call all hands an hour before. Have your watch rig the windlass bars, have the topsails loose in their buntlines ready for hoisting and the stops off the heads'ls.'

'Aye, aye, sir.'

Drinkwater retired to sleep. There was an old saying in the service. He prayed God it was true: all debts were paid when the topsails were sheeted home.

He did not know that an Admiralty messenger had exhausted three horses to bring Parker St Vincent's direct command to sail, nor that Lady Parker would return to London earlier than expected.

Chapter Eleven

Nadir

'What a God damn spectacle!' said Rogers happily as he watched the big ships weigh. The misfortunes of others always delighted him. It was one of his less likeable traits. Drinkwater shivered in his cloak, wondering whether his blood would ever thicken after his service in the Red Sea and how much longer they would have to wait. It was nine o'clock and the Viragos had been at their stations since daylight, awaiting their turn to weigh and proceed to sea through the St Nicholas Gat.

The signal to weigh had caused some confusion as no one was certain what the order of sailing was. Towards the northern end of the anchorage two battleships had run foul of each other, but already the handful of frigates and sloops had got away smartly, led out by the handsome *Amazon*, commanded by Edward Riou. Following them south east through the gatway and round the Scroby Sands, went the former East Indiaman *Glatton*, her single deck armed with the carronades which had so astonished a French squadron with their power, that she had defeated them all. Her odd appearance was belied by the supreme seamanship of the man who now commanded her. 'Bounty' Bligh turned her through the anchorage with an almost visible contempt for his reputation. Drinkwater had met Bligh and served with him at Camperdown. Another veteran of Camperdown, the old 50-gun *Isis* ran down in company with the incomparable *Agamemnon*, Nelson's old sixty-four. The order of sailing had gone by the board as the big ships made the best of their way to seaward of the sands. The 98-gun *St George*, with Nelson's blue vice-admiral's flag at the foremasthead was already setting her topgallants, her jacks swinging aloft like monkeys, a band playing on her poop. The strains of *Rule Britannia* floated over the water.

Despite himself Drinkwater felt an involuntary thrill run down his spine as Nelson passed, unable to resist the man's genius despite the cloud he was personally under. Even Rogers was silent while Quilhampton's eyes were shining like a girl's.

'Here the buggers come,' said Rogers as the other seventy-fours stood through the road; *Ganges*, *Bellona*, *Polyphemus*. Then came *Monarch*, Batter Pudding's father's flagship at Camperdown, and the rest, all setting their topgallants, their big courses in the buntlines ready to set when the intricacies of St Nicholas's Gat had been safely negotiated.

'*Invincible*'s going north sir,' observed Easton pointing to the Caister end of the anchorage where the cutters and gun brigs were leaving by the Cockle Gat.

'I hope he has a pilot on board,' said Drinkwater thinking of the treacherous passage and driving *Kestrel* through it years ago.

'Some of the storeships goin' that way too,' offered Quilhampton, aping Drinkwater's clipped mannerism.

'Yes, Mr Q. Do you watch for *Explosion*'s signal now.'

'Aye, aye, sir.'

'Martin's still playing at bloody commodore,' said Rogers to Easton in a stage whisper. The master sniggered. 'Hey look, someone's lost a jib-boom . . .' They could not make out the ship as she was masked by another but almost last to leave was Parker's *London*.

'The old bastard had trouble getting his flukes out of the mud,' laughed Rogers making an onomatopoeic sucking plop that sent a burst of ribald laughter round *Virago*'s poop.

'I hope, Mr Rogers, that is positively the last joke we hear about the subject of the admiral's nuptials,' said Drinkwater, remembering the plain-faced girl on whom he so relied. He might at least defend her honour on his own deck.

'In fact,' he added with sudden asperity, 'I forbid further levity on the subject now we are at sea under Sir Hyde's orders.'

Drinkwater put his glass to his eye and ignored Rogers who made an exaggerated face at Easton behind his back. Quilhampton laughed, thus missing the executive signal from *Explosion*.

Drinkwater had seen the bunting flutter down from the topgallant yardarm where the wind spread it for the bombs to see.

'Heave up, Mr Matchett. Hoist foretopmast stays'l!'

The anchor was already hove short and it was the work of only a few minutes to heave it underfoot and trip it. 'Anchor's aweigh, sir!'

'Tops'l halliards, Mr Rogers! Lee braces, there!' He turned to Mr Quilhampton who had flushed at missing the signal from *Explosion*. 'See those weather braces run, Mr Q.'

'Aye, aye, sir,' the boy ran forward to vindicate himself.

'Starboard stays'l sheet there! Look lively, God damn it!'

'Anchor's sighted clear, sir.'

Aloft the topsail parrels creaked against the greased topmasts as the yards rose. The canvas flogged, then filled with great dull crumps, flogged and filled again as the yards were trimmed. Drinkwater looked with satisfaction at the replaced mainyard.

'Steady as you go.'

'Steady as you go, zur.' *Virago* gathered way and caught up on *Zebra* which had not yet tripped her anchor.

'Port your helm,' Drinkwater looked round to see the order was obeyed. The big tiller was pushed over to larboard and *Virago* began to turn to starboard her bowsprit no longer pointing at *Zebra*.

'Trim that foreyard, Graham, God rot you! Don't you know your business?' bawled Rogers as the petty officers directed the stamping, panting gangs of men. Matchett was leaning outboard fishing for the anchor with the cat tackle.

'Course south east a half south.' Drinkwater looked to starboard and raised his hat. Aboard the *Anne Reed* he saw Tumilty acknowledge his greeting.

'Course south east a half south, zur,' reported Tregembo.

'Course south east a half south, sir,' repeated Easton, the sailing master. Drinkwater suppressed a smile. He almost felt happy. It was good to be under way at last, and upon his own deck at that. He did not want to look astern at the roofs and church towers of Great Yarmouth with their reminders of the rule of Law, which he so much admired yet had so recently disregarded.

The reflection made him search for his brother as the hands secured the deck and adjusted the sails to Rogers's exacting direction. He found him at last, in duck trousers and a check shirt, hauling upon the anchor crown tackle, a labour for unskilled muscles, supervised by Mr Matchett in the starboard forechains. The heaving waisters brought the inboard fluke of the sheet anchor in against its bill board and able seamen leapt contemptuously outboard to pass the lashings.

'You had better cast the lead as we pass the Gatway, Mr Easton, the tide will set us on the Corton side else, and I've no wish to go aground today.'

'Aye, aye, sir. Snape! Get your arse into the main chains with a lead!'

'Give her the forecourse, Mr Rogers. And you may have Quilhampton set the spanker when we come on the wind off the Scroby Sands.'

Drinkwater looked at his watch. It was eleven o'clock. A ship was coming up from the south and Drinkwater checked her number against the private signals. She was the *Edgar*, Captain George Murray, joining the fleet. He remembered Murray as the frustrated captain of the sluggish frigate *La Nymphe*, unable to get into action during the fight of St George's Day off the Brittany coast. With a shock Drinkwater realised that had been seven years earlier. It had been his first action in charge of a ship, the cutter *Kestrel* whose commander, Lieutenant Madoc Griffiths, lay sweating out the effects of malaria in his cabin.

At noon Drinkwater checked Easton's entry on the slate and stood down the watch below. Despite the confusion in the fleet Martin's little squadron was keeping tolerably good station. It was clear Martin wanted a post-captaincy out of this expedition.

'What course for the passage, sir?' asked Easton formally.

Drinkwater smiled wanly. The fleet was tired of uncertainty. 'I have only orders to stand towards the Naze of Norway, Mr Easton, as I told you yesterday.'

'Mushrooms, Mr Easton,' said Rogers cheerfully, 'that is all we are, mushrooms . . .'

'Mushrooms, Mr Rogers?' said Easton, frowning.

'Aye, mushrooms, Mr Easton. Kept in the dark and fed with bullshit.'

'But I tell you I am right, Bones.' The smell of rum hung in the heavy air.

Mr Jex had drawn the surgeon into the stygian gloom of *Virago*'s hold on the pretext of examining the quality of a barrel of sauerkraut. The familiar tone he used in addressing Lettsom only emphasised the purser's misjudgement of the surgeon's character. Listening to the exaggeratedly flippant remarks which Lettsom customarily used, Jex had assumed the surgeon might prove an ally. Part of Jex's desire to find a confidant was due to his isolation after the discovery of his conduct in the affair off the Sunk. Lettsom avowed an abhorrence of war and the machinations of Admiralty, a common attitude among the better sort of surgeon and a product of keeping educated men in a state of social limbo, mere warrant officers among compeers of far lesser intellect.

Jex had decided that since he could not escape the taint of cowardice he might as well assume a spurious conscientious objection. The rehabilitation of himself thus being complete in his own eyes, if in no-one else's, he now began to search for a means of furthering his own ends. But Jex's mind was expert in calculating, and the readiness and facility with which he did this was apt to blind him to his limitations in other fields. He was a man who considered himself clever when he was not. He was, therefore, a dangerous person to thwart, and Drinkwater had crossed him.

Mr Jex's stupidity now led him to believe that certain facts that had come his way were a providential sign that his new, Quakerish philosophy had divine approval, and that his deductive powers used in reaching his conclusion merely proved that he was a man of equal intellect with the surgeon, hence the familiar contraction of the old cognomen, 'Sawbones'.

It was unfortunate that a mind skilled in feathering its own nest and dividing the rations of unfortunate seamen to an eighth part (for himself) was a mind that delighted in nosing into the affairs of others. He had nursed a grievance against Lieutenant Drinkwater since he had been out-manoeuvred in the matter of his appointment. Drinkwater had intimidated him as well as humiliated him in his own eyes. Jex had not expected fate to be so kind as to put into his hands such weapons as he now possessed, but now that he had them it seemed that it was one more confirmation of his superior abilities.

It had started when he had been turned from his cot at one in the morning by an angry Mr Trussel. The gunner had brought a new recruit and Jex had let the dripping wretch know exactly what he thought of being roused to attend to the wants of waterborne scum. So vehement had he become that he had shoved his lantern in the face of the newcomer. Jex was incapable of analysing the precise nature of the expression he found there, but the man was not afraid as he should have been, only cold and shivering. Jex's suspicions were roused because the man did not quail before him.

Jex had seen the man immediately he came aboard, before his hair was cut and he had lost weight, while he was still dressed in a gentlemen's breeches. At that moment Jex did not recognise Edward, merely took note of him. And because Jex had taken note of him he continued to observe 'Waters'. Rogers had quartered Edward Drinkwater among the 'firemen', an action station for the most inept and inexperienced waisters whose duty was to pump water into the firehoses deployed by the purser.

There might have been no more to it had Jex not gone ashore for cabin stores at Yarmouth shortly before the order to sail. Being idly curious he had bought a newspaper, an extravagance he was well able to afford. Had he not purchased the paper he might never have made the connection between the new 'landsman volunteer' and the man he had seen in the Blue Fox, a man who had come into the taproom immediately Lieutenant Drinkwater had left the Inn.

The *Yarmouth Courier* reported: 'A foul double murder, which heinous crime had lately been perpetrated upon an emigrant French nobleman, the Marquis de la Roche-Jagu, and his pretty young mistress, Mlle Pascale Eugenie Vrignaud. The despicable act had been carried out in the marquis's lodgings at Newmarket. He had died from a sword cut in the right side of the neck which severed the trapezius muscle, the carotid artery and the jugular vein. Mlle Vrignaud had been despatched by a cut on the left temple which had rendered her instantly senseless and resulted in severe haemorrhage into the cranial cavity. Doctor Ezekiel Cotton of Newmarket was of the opinion that a single blow had killed both parties . . .'

Jex rightly concluded that the two lovers had been taken in the sexual act and that the murderer had struck a single impassioned blow. But it was the last paragraph that filled Mr Jex's heart with righteous indignation: 'A certain Edward Drinkwater had earlier been in the company of Mlle Vrignaud and has since disappeared. He is described as a man of middle height and thick figure, having a florid complexion and wearing his own brown hair, unpowdered.'

Mr Jex had embraced this news with interest, his curiosity and cunning were aroused and he remembered the man in the Blue Fox.

'I tell you I *am* right,' Jex repeated.

Lettsom looked up from the opened cask. 'There is nothing wrong with this sauerkraut, it always smells foul when new opened.'

Lettsom straightened up.

'To save 'em from scurvy
Our captain did shout,
You shall feed 'em fresh cabbage
And old sauerkraut.

'Make 'em eat it, Mr Jex, Mr Drinkwater's right . . .'

85

'No, no, Mr Lettsom. Damme but you haven't been listening. I mean this report in the paper here.' He thrust the *Yarmouth Courier* under Lettsom's nose. Lettsom took it impatiently and beckoned the lantern closer. When he had finished he looked up at the purser. Jex's porcine eyes glittered.

'You are linking our commander with the reported missing man?'

'Exactly. You see my point, then.'

'No, I do not. Do you think I am some kind of hierophant that I read men's minds.'

Jex was undettered by the uncomprehended snub.

'Suppose that the murderer . . .'

'Even that scurrilous rag does not allege that the missing man actually carried out murder.' The legal nicety was lost on Jex.

'Well suppose that he *was* the murderer, and *was* related to the captain.'

'Good heavens Mr Jex, I had no idea you had such a lively imagination.' Lettsom made to leave but Jex held him.

'And suppose that the captain got him aboard here under cover of night . . .'

'What precisely do you mean?' Lettsom looked again at the sly features of the purser.

'Why else would Lieutenant Drinkwater turn his own brother forrard? Eh? I'm telling you that the man Edward Waters is the man wanted for this murder at Newmarket.' He slapped the paper with the back of his hand. Lettsom was silent for a while and Jex pressed his advantage. Lettsom did not know that Drinkwater's acquisition of Jex's funds had poisoned the purser against his commander. Jex had writhed under this extortion, ignoring the fact that his own perquisites were equally immoral.

'Well, will you help me, then?' asked Jex revealing to Lettsom the reason for this trip into the hold and the extent of Jex's stupidity.

'I? No sir, I will not.' Lettsom was indignant. He made again to leave the hold and again Jex restrained him.

'If I am right and you have refused to help me you would have obstructed the course of justice . . .'

'Jex, listen to me very carefully,' said Lettsom, 'if you plot against the captain of a ship of war you are guilty of mutiny for which you will surely hang.'

Lettsom retired to his cabin and pulled out his flute. He had not played it for many weeks and instantly regretted his lack of practice. His was not a great talent and he rarely played in any company other than that of his wife. He essayed a scale or two before launching into a low air of his own composition, during which his mind was able to concentrate upon its present preoccupation.

Mr Lettsom was a man of superficial frivolity and apparent indifference which he had adopted early in his naval life as a rampart against the cruelty in the service. He had found it kept people at a distance and, with the exceptions of his wife and three daughters, he

86

liked it that way. The experience of living as a surgeon's mate through the American War had strangled any inherent feeling he had for the sufferings of humanity. In the main he had found his mess mates ignorant, bigotted and insufferably self-seeking; his superiors proud, haughty and incompetent and his inferiors brutalised into similar sub-divisions according to their own internal hierarchy.

To his patients Lettsom had applied the dispassionate results of his growing experience. He was known as a good surgeon because he had an average success rate and did not drink to excess. His frivolous indifference did not encourage deep friendship and he was usually left to his own devices, although his versifying brought him popular acclaim at mess dinners. He had rarely made any friends, most of his professional relationships were of the kind he presently enjoyed with Rogers, a kind of mutual regard based on respect overlaying dislike.

But Mr Lettsom's true nature was something else. His deeper passions were known only to his family. His wife well understood his own despair at the total inadequacy of his abilities, his resentment at the inferiority of surgery to 'medicine', his fury at the quackery of socially superior physicians. A long observation of humanity's conceit had taught him of its real ignorance.

In a sense his was a simple mind. He believed that humanity was essentially good, that it was merely the institutions and divisions that man imposed upon man that corrupted the metal. It was his belief that mankind could be redeemed by a few wise men, that the dissenting tradition of his grandfather's day had paved the way for the unleashing of the irresistible forces of the French Revolution.

Drinkwater had been right, Lettsom was a Leveller and a lover of Tom Paine. He did not share Drinkwater's widely held belief that the aggression and excesses of the revolution put it beyond acceptance, holding that man's own nature made such things inevitable just as the Royal Navy's vaunted maintenance of the principles of law, order and liberty were at the expense of the lash, impressment and a thousand petty tyrannies imposed upon the individual. A few good men . . .

He stopped playing his flute, lost in thought. If Jex *had* discovered the truth, Lettsom feared for Drinkwater. Despite their political differences the surgeon admired the younger lieutenant, seeing him as a man with humanist qualities to whom command came as a responsibility rather than an opportunity. Jex's evidence, if it was accurate, appeared to Lettsom as a kind of quixotic heroism in defiance of the established law. Drinkwater had hazarded his whole future to assist his brother and Lettsom found it endearing, as though it revealed the lieutenant's secret sympathy with his own ideals. With the wisdom of age Lettsom concluded that Drinkwater's subconscious sympathies lay exposed to him and he felt his admiration for the younger man increase.

He took up the flute again and began to play as another thought struck him. If the new landsman-volunteer was indeed Drinkwater's brother then Lettsom would not interfere and to hell with Jex. He did not find it difficult to condone such a crime of passion, particularly when it disposed of a marquis, one of those arrogant parasites that had brought the wrath of the hungry upon themselves and destroyed the peace of the world.

'Flag's signalling, sir.'

'Very well.'

'Number 107, sir.' There was a pause while Quilhampton strove to read the signal book as the wind tore at the pages.

'Close round the admiral, as near as the state of the weather and other circumstances will permit.'

'Very well.' The circumstances would permit little more than a token obedience to Parker's order. Since the early hours of Monday, 16 March, a ferocious gale had been blowing from the west south west. It had been snowing since dawn and become very cold. The big ships had reduced to storm canvas and struck their topgallant masts. At about nine o'clock the fireship *Alecto* had reported a leak and been detached with the lugger *Rover* as an escort.

Drinkwater ordered an issue of the warm clothing he had prudently laid in at Chatham as Lettsom reported most of the men afflicted with coughs, colds or quinsies. His own anxiety was chiefly in not running foul of another ship in the snow squalls that frequently blinded them. The fleet began to fire minute guns.

'Do you wish to reduce sail, sir?' asked Easton anxiously, shouting into his ear.

Drinkwater shook his head. 'She stands up well, Mr Easton, the advantage of a heavy hull.'

'Aye, aye, sir.'

Virago was a fine sea-keeper, bluff and buoyant. Though she rolled deeply it was an easy motion and Drinkwater never entertained any apprehension for her spars. Although at every plunge of her bowsprit much of it immersed she hardly strained a ropeyarn.

'She bruises the grey sea in a most collier-like style, Mr Easton, how was she doing at the last streaming of the log?'

'Six and a half, sir.'

'Tolerably good.'

'Yes sir.'

Two hours later the wisdom of not reducing sail was borne out. In a gap in the snow showers the *London* was again visible flying Number 89.

'Ships astern, or in the rear of the fleet, make more sail!'

'Aye, very well. We've no need of that but I wonder if those in the rear can see it.' Half an hour later Parker gave up the struggle.

'Number 106, sir, "Wear, the sternmost and leewardmost first and come to the wind on the other tack".'

'Oh, my God,' said Rogers coming on deck to relieve Easton, 'that'll set the cat among the pigeons.'

'That'll do, Mr Rogers,' said Drinkwater quickly, 'At least the admiral's had the foresight to do it at the change of watch when all hands should be on deck.'

And so the British fleet stood away from the Danish coast in the early darkness and the biting cold, uncertain of their precise whereabouts and still with no specific orders for the Baltic.

The cold weather continued into the next day while Parker fretted over his reckoning and hove-to for frequent soundings.

'I'll bet those damned pilots aboard *London* are all arguing like the devil as to where the hell we are,' laughed Rogers as he handed the deck over to Trussell who as senior warrant officer after the master kept a deck watch. It was eight in the morning and the gale showed little sign of abating, though the wind had veered a point. It was colder than the previous day and cracked skin and salt water boils were already appearing.

'Hullo, that's a new arrival ain't it Mr Rogers?' asked Drinkwater coming on deck. He indicated a seventy-four, looming out of the murk flying her private number and with a white flag at her mizen. Rogers had not noticed that the ship was not part of the fleet as they stood north east again under easy sail, the ships moving like wraiths through the showers.

'Er, ah . . . yes, sir,' he said flushing.

'*Defiance*, sir,' volunteered Quilhampton hurriedly, 'Rear Admiral Graves, sir, Captain Richard Retalick.'

'Thank you Mr Q.' Quilhampton avoided the glare Rogers threw at him and knew the first lieutenant would later demand an explanation why, if he was such a damned clever little wart, he had not informed the officer of the watch of the sighting.

The forenoon wore on, livened only by the piping of 'Up spirits', the miserable file of men huddled in their greygoes, their cracked lips, red-rimmed eyes and running noses proof that the conditions were abysmal. The only fire permitted aboard a vessel loaded with powder was the galley range and the heat that it dissipated about the ship was soon blown away by the draughts. The officers fared little better, their only real advantage being the ability to drink more heavily and thus fortify themselves against the cold. Mr Jex, whose duties rarely brought him on deck at all, took particular advantage of this privilege.

Edward Drinkwater had received an issue of the heavy-weather clothing that his brother had had the foresight to lay in against service in this northern climate. He had found it surprisingly easy to adapt to life below decks. A heavily built man who could afford to lose weight, his physique had stood up well in the few days he had been on board. His natural sociability and previous experience at living on his wits inclined him to make the best of his circumstances, while his connections with the turf and the stud had made him familiar with the lower orders of contemporary society as well as 'the fancy'. The guilt he felt for what he had done had not yet affected him and although he was periodically swept by grief for Pascale it was swiftly lost in that last image of her in life, her face ecstatic beneath her lover. He relived that second's reaction a hundred times a day, snatching up the sword and hacking it down in ungovernable fury in the turmoil of his imagination.

The rigorous demands of his duties combined with the need to be vigilant against exposing his brother, and hence himself, had left him little time to ponder upon moral issues. When turned below, his physical exhaustion swiftly overcame him and the fear of the law that had motivated his flight to Yarmouth evaporated on board the *Virago*. From his messmates he learned of the numbers of criminals sheltering in the navy, and that the service did not readily give up these living dead, could not afford to if it was to maintain its wooden ramparts against the pernicious influence of Republican France. Edward had relied upon his brother with the simple trust of the irresponsible and Nathaniel had not let him down. He did not know the extent to which Drinkwater had risked his career, his family, even his life. From what Edward had seen of the Royal Navy, the captain of a man of war was a law unto himself. He was fortunate in having a brother in such a position, and delivered his fate into Nathaniel's capable hands.

As to his altered circumstances, Edward was enough of a gambler to accept them as a temporary inconvenience. He was certain they would not last forever and from that sense of impermanence he was able to derive a certain satisfaction. His messmates took no notice of the quiet man amongst them, they lived cheek by jowl with greater eccentricities than his. But the gestures did not go unnoticed by Mr Jex.

'Come man, lively with that cask, damn it.' Mr Jex stood over the three toiling landsmen as they manoeuvred the cask clear of the stow, sweating with the effort of controlling it as the ship pitched and rolled. Mr Jex's rotund figure condescended to hold up a lantern for them as they finally succeeded in up-ending it.

'Open it up then, open it up,' he ordered impatiently, motioning one of the men to pick up the cold chisel lent by Mr Willerton. He watched Waters bend down to take the tool and dismissed the other two with a jerk of his head. Things were working out better than he had supposed. Waters grunted as he levered the inner hoop of the lid and Jex held the lantern closer to read the number branded into the top of the cask.

'Get the damn thing open then,' Jex was sweating himself now, suddenly worried at the notion of being alone in the hold with a murderer. He had to force himself to recover his fugitive mood of moral ascendancy. Circumstances again seemed to come to his aid. Waters staggered back appalled at the smell that rose from the cask of salt pork. Jex's familiarity with the stench ensured he reasserted himself.

'Not used to the stink eh? Too used to comfortable quarters,' Jex paused for emphasis, 'comfortable quarters *like the Blue Fox, eh,*

Mister Drinkwater?' Jex's tiny eyes glittered in the lamplight, searching Edward's face for the reaction of guilt brought on by his accusation.

But the purser was to be disappointed. That slight, emphatic pause had alerted Edward to be on his guard. The quick instinct that in him was a gambler's intuition, while in his brother showed as swift intelligence, caused him to look up in sharp surprise.

'You're mistaken, sir,' he said in the rural Middlesex accent of his youth, 'my name is Waters,' he grinned, 'I'm no relation to the cap'n, Mr Jex.' He shook his head as if in simple wonderment at the mistake and looked down at the mess inside the cask as though swiftly dismissing the matter from his mind.

Jex was non-plussed, suddenly unsure of himself, and yet . . .

Waters looked up. Jex was still staring at him. He shrugged. 'As for the Blue Fox, was that what you said? I don't know anything about such a place. Tavern is it? Strewth, if I could afford to live in a tavern I'd not be aboard here, sir.'

That much was true, thought Edward, as he strove to maintain a matter-of-fact tone in his voice though inwardly alarmed that he had been discovered.

But Jex was not satisfied. 'Landsman volunteer aren't you?'

'That's right, sir.'

'What did you volunteer for?'

'Woman trouble, Mr Jex, woman trouble.'

'I know,' began Jex, a sudden vicious desire spurring him to provoke this man to some act of insubordination that would have him at the gratings to be flogged by his own brother. But his intentions were disturbed by the arrival of Mr Quilhampton with a message that the purser was to report to Lieutenant Rogers without delay. He had lost his chance, and Edward was doubly vigilant to avoid the purser as much as possible, and even, if necessary, take matters into his own hands.

Drinkwater watched the brig beating up from the east with the alarm signal flying from her foremasthead. She reminded him of *Hellebore* and would pass close under *Virago*'s stern as she made for *London* to speak with the admiral.

'The *Cruizer*, sir, eighteen-gun brig, same as our old *Hellebore*.'

'I was just thinking that, Mr Trussel.' The two men watched her approach, saw her captain jump into the main chains with a speaking trumpet. Drinkwater had met James Brisbane in Yarmouth and raised his hat in salutation.

'Afternoon Drinkwater!' Brisbane yelled as his ship surged past. 'We sighted land around Boubjerg. We must be twenty leagues south of our reckoning!' He waved, then jumped inboard as his brig covered the last two miles to the flagship.

'God's bones!' Drinkwater muttered. Sixty miles! A degree of latitude, but it was no wonder, since they had seen neither sun, moon nor stars since leaving Yarmouth. It was equally surprising that the bulk of the fleet was still together.

A little later the flagship signalled, firing guns to emphasise the importance of the order. The fleet tacked to the north west and once more clawed its way offshore.

The following day the battleship *Elephant* arrived with the news that the *Invincible*, which they had last seen leaving Yarmouth Roads by way of the Cockle Gat, had been wrecked on the Haisbro Sand with the loss of most of her crew. As this intelligence permeated the fleet Drinkwater was overwhelmed with a sense of impending doom, that the whole enterprise was imperilled by the omens. And his fears for Edward and himself only seemed to lend potency to these misgivings.

That evening the weather showed signs of moderating. Shortly after dark as he sat writing up his journal by the light of a swaying lantern Drinkwater was disturbed by a knock at his cabin door. 'Yes?'

Mr Jex entered. He was flushed and smelt of rum. He held what appeared to be a newspaper in his hand.

'Yes, Mr Jex? What is it?' Jex made no reply but held out the paper to Drinkwater. Unsatisfied with the replies of Waters, Jex sensed the landsman's cunning was more than a match for him. And the purser was nervous of a man he suspected of murder. To himself he disguised this fear in the argument that it was really Lieutenant Drinkwater who was the target for his desire to settle a score. The rum served to restore his resolve to act.

Drinkwater bent over the print. As he read he felt as though a cold hand was squeezing his guts. The colour drained from his face and the perspiration appeared upon his forehead. He tried in vain to dismiss the image the description called to mind.

From somewhere above him came Jex's voice, filled with the righteous zeal of an archangel. 'I know the man you brought aboard in Yarmouth is your brother. And that he is wanted for this murder.'

A Turbot Bright

The cabin filled with a silence only emphasised by the creak of *Virago*'s fabric as she worked in the seaway. The rudder stock ground in the trunking that ran up the centre of the transom between the windows and stern chasers.

Drinkwater crossed his arms to conceal the shaking of his hands and leaned back in his chair, still staring down at the newspaper on the table. Its contents exposed the whole matter and Jex, of all people, knew everything. He looked up at Jex and was made suddenly angry by the smug look of satisfaction on the purser's pig-like features. His resentment at having been forced into such a false position by both Edward and this unpleasant little man before him combined with his weariness at trying to argue a way out of an untenable position. His anger boiled over, made worse by his awareness of the need to bluff.

'God damn it, sir, you are drunk! What the devil d'you think you are about, making such outrageous suggestions? Eh? Come, what are these allegations again?'

'The man Waters is your brother . . .'

'For God's sake, Mr Jex, what on earth makes you think that?'

'I saw you together in the Blue Fox, a house in which I have an interest.'

A piece of the jig-saw as to how Jex had discovered his deception was now revealed to Drinkwater. Even as he strove to think of some way out of the mess he continued to attack the purser's certainty. He barked a short, humourless and forced laugh.

'Hah! And d'you think I'd turn my brother forward, eh? To be started by Matchett and his mates?'

'If he had committed murder.' Jex nodded to the paper that lay between them.

Drinkwater leaned forward and put both hands on the *Yarmouth Courier*. 'Mr Jex,' he said with an air of apparent patience, 'there is no possible connection you can make between a man who claimed to be my brother whom you saw in a tavern in Chatham, the perpetrator of this murder and a pathetic landsman who volunteered at Yarmouth.'

'But the similarity of names . . .'

'A coincidence Mr Jex.' The eyes of the two men met as each searched for a weakness. Drinkwater saw doubt in the other man's

SKAGERRAK

SWEDEN

THE SKAW

KATTEGAT

VINGA BAY

BOUBJERG

JUTLAND

THE SOUND

ZEELAND'S REEF

GILLELEJE

COPENHAGEN

THE GREAT BELT

ZEELAND

THE LITTLE BELT

DENMARK 1801

R.M.W.

face, saw it break through the alcohol-induced confidence. Jex was no longer on the offensive. Drinkwater pressed his advantage.

'I will be frank with you, Mr Jex, for your misconstruction is highly seditious and under the Articles of War,' he paused, seeing a dawning realisation cross Jex's mind. 'I see you understand. But I will be frank as far as I can be. There is a little mystery hereabouts,' he was deliberately vague and could see a frown on Jex's brow now. 'I do not have to tell you that the liberal Corresponding Societies of England, Mr Jex, those organisations that Mr Chauvelin tried to enlist in ninety-one to foment revolution here while he was French ambassador, are still very active. They are full of French spies and you can rest assured that a fleet as big as ours in Yarmouth has been observed by many eyes including some hostile eyes that have doubtless watched our movements with interest . . .'

Drinkwater smiled to himself. Jex was a false patriot, a Tory of the worst kind. A place-seeking jobber, jealous of privilege, anxious to maintain the status quo and feather his own nest, even as he aspired to social advancement. To men of Jex's odious type fear of revolution was greater than fear of the pox.

'I cannot say more, Mr Jex, but I have had some experience in these matters . . . you may verify the facts with the quartermaster Tregembo, if you cannot take the word of a gentleman,' he added.

Jex was silent, his mind hunting for any advantage he might have gained from the web of words that Drinkwater was spinning. He was not sure where the area of mystery lay; with the man in the Blue Fox, the landsman Waters or the murder with its strange, coincidental surname. The rum was confusing him and he could not quite grasp where the ascendancy he had felt a few minutes earlier had now gone. He had meant to press Drinkwater for a return of his money, or at least establish some hold over his captain that he might turn to his own advantage. He had been certain of his arguments as he had rehearsed them in the spirit room half an hour ago. Now he was dimly aware of a mystery he did not understand but which was vaguely dangerous to him, of Drinkwater's real authority and the awesome power of the Articles of War which even a pip-squeak lieutenant might invoke against him. Jex's intelligence had let him down. Only his cunning could extricate him.

'I am not . . .'

'Mr Jex,' said Drinkwater brusquely, suddenly sick of the whole charade, 'you are the worse for drink. I have already confided in you more than I should and I would caution you to be circumspect with what I have told you. I am unhappy about both your motive and your manner in drawing this whole matter to my attention.' He stood up, 'Good night Mr Jex.'

The purser turned away as *Virago* sat her stern heavily in a trough. Jex stumbled and grabbed for the edge of the table.

Drinkwater suddenly grinned. 'Take your time, Mr Jex, and be careful how you go. After all if Waters is a murderer you may find yourself eased overboard one dark night. I've known it happen.' Drinkwater, who knew nothing of the purser's cowardice, had touched the single raw nerve that Jex possessed. The possibility of being killed or maimed had never occurred to him when he had solicited the post of purser aboard the *Virago*. Indeed there seemed little likelihood of the ship ever putting to sea again. Now, since witnessing the horribly wounded Mason die in agony, he thought often of death as he lay in the lonely coffin-like box of his cot.

Drinkwater watched the purser lurch from the cabin. He felt like a fencer who had achieved a lucky parry, turned aside a blade that had seemed to have penetrated his guard, yet had allowed his opponent to recover.

He did not know if Jex had approached Edward, and could only hope that Tregembo's explanation, which he was sure Jex would seek in due course, would not betray him. But it was the only alibi he had. He found his hands were trembling again now that he was alone. From the forward bulkhead the portraits of Elizabeth and Charlotte Amelia watched impassively and brought the sweat to his brow at the enormity of what he had done. He wondered how successfully he had concealed the matter behind the smokescreen of duty. What was it Lettsom had said about concealing inadequacy that way? He shrugged off the recollection. Such philosophical niceties were irrelevant. There was no way to go but forwards and of one thing he was now sure. He had no alternative but to carry out his bluff. There was no time to wait for a reply to his letter to Lord Dungarth.

He would have to land Edward very soon.

The following morning dawned fine and clear. The wind had hauled north westerly and the fleet made sail to the eastward. The little gun-brigs were taken in tow by the battleships. Soon after dawn the whole vast mass of ships, making six or seven knots, observed to starboard the low line of the Danish coast. First blue-grey, it hardened to pale green with a fringe of white breakers. At nine o'clock on the morning of March 19th the fleet began to pass the lighthouse on The Skaw and turned south east, into the Kattegat. The Danes had extinguished the lighthouse by night, but in the pale morning sunshine it formed a conspicuous mark for the ships as each hauled her yards for the new course. At one o'clock Parker ordered the frigate *Blanche* to proceed ahead and gain news of the progress of Nicholas Vansittart. He had left Harwich a fortnight earlier in the Hamburg packet with a final offer to Count Bernstorff, the Danish Minister.

After the hardships of the last few days the sunshine felt warm and cheering. First lieutenants throughout the fleet ordered their men to wash clothes and hammocks. The nettings and lower rigging of the ships were soon bright with fluttering shirts and trousers. The sight of the enemy coast to starboard brought smiles and jokes to the raw faces of the men. Officers studied its monotonous line through their glasses as though they might discern their fates thereby.

The sense of corporate pride that could animate British seamen, hitherto absent from Parker's fleet, seemed not dead but merely dormant, called forth by the vernal quality of the day. This reanimation of spirit was best demonstrated by Nelson himself, ever a man attuned to the morale of his men. As the wind fell light in the late afternoon he called away his barge and an inquisitive fleet watched him pulled over to the mighty *London*. One of his seamen had caught a huge turbot and presented it as a gift to the little one-armed admiral.

In a characteristically impetuous gesture beneath which might be discerned an inflexible sense of purpose, Nelson personally conveyed the fish to his superior. It broke the ice between the two men. When the story got about the fleet by the mysterious telegraphy that transmitted such news, Lettsom composed his now expected verse:

'Nelson's prepared to grow thinner
And give Parker a turbot bright,
If Parker will only eat dinner,
And let Lord Nelson fight.'

But Mr Jex had not shared the general euphoria as they passed the Skaw. He had slept badly and woke with a rum-induced hangover that left his head throbbing painfully. He had lost track of the cogent arguments that had seemed to deliver Lieutenant Drinkwater into his hands the previous evening. His mind was aware only that he had been thwarted. To Jex it was like dishonour.

Soon after the change of watch at eight in the morning as the curious on deck were staring at the lighthouse on the Skaw, Jex waylaid Tregembo and offered him a quid of tobacco.

'Thank 'ee, zur,' he said, regarding the purser with suspicion. 'Tregembo isn't it?'

'Aye, zur.' Tregembo bit a lump off the quid and began to chew it.

'You have known Lieutenant Drinkwater a long time, eh, Tregembo?' The quartermaster nodded. 'How long?'

'I first met Mr Drinkwater when he were a midshipman, aboard the *Cyclops*, frigate, Cap'n Henry Hope . . . during the American War.'

'And you've known him since?'

'No zur, I next met him when I was drafted aboard the *Kestrel* cutter, zur, we was employed on special service.'

'Special service, eh?'

'Aye zur, very special . . . on the French coast afore the outbreak of the present war.' A sly look had entered the Cornishman's eyes. 'I'm in Mr Drinkwater's employ, zur . . .'

'Ah yes, of course, then perhaps you can tell me if Mr Drinkwater has a brother, eh?' Tregembo regarded the fat, peculating officer and remembered what Drinkwater had said about Waters and what he had learned at Petersfield. He rolled the quid over his tongue:

'Brother? No zur, the lieutenant has no brother, Mr Jex zur.'

'Are you sure?'

'I been with him constant these past nine years and I don't know that he ever had a brother.'

'And this special service . . .'

'Aye zur, we was employed on the *Hellebore*, brig, under Lord Nelson's orders.' Tregembo remembered what Drinkwater had said to him and now that he had seen what Jex was driving at he was less forthcoming.

'Under Lord Nelson, eh, well, well . . . so Mr Drinkwater's highly thought of in certain quarters then?'

'Aye zur, he's well acquainted with Lord Dungarth.' Tregembo was as proud of Drinkwater's connection with the peer as Jex was impressed.

'It is surprising then Tregembo, that he is no more than a lieutenant.'

'Beggin' your pardon but 'tis a fucking disgrace . . . It's a long story, zur, but Mr Drinkwater thrashed a bugger on the *Cyclops* and the bastard got even with him in the matter of a commission . . .' A smile crossed Tregembo's face. 'Leastaways he thought he'd bested him, but he ended in the hospital at the Cape, zur.' He leaned forward, his jaw rotating the quid as he spoke. 'Men don't cross the lieutenant too successfully, zur, leastaways not sensible men.'

'Bloody wind's still freshening, sir, and I don't like the look of it.' Rogers held his hat on, his tarpaulin flapping round him as he stared to windward. The white streaks of sleet blew across the deck, showing faintly in the binnacle lamplight. Both the officers staggered as *Virago* snubbed round to her anchor, sheering in the wind, jerking the hull and straining the cable.

'Rouse out another cable, Sam,' Drinkwater shouted in Rogers's ear, 'we'll veer away more scope.'

The good weather had not lasted the day. Hardly had the fleet come to an anchor in Vingå Bay than the treacherous wind had backed and strengthened. Now, at midnight, a full gale was blowing from the west south west, catching them on a lee shore and threatening to wreck them on the Swedish coast.

Drinkwater watched the grey and black shapes of the hands as they moved about the deck. He was glad he had been able to provide them with warm clothing. Tonight none of them would get much sleep and it was the least he could do for them. They were half-way through bringing up the second cable when they saw the first rocket. It reminded them that out in the howling blackness, beyond the circumscribed limit of their visible horizon, other men in other ships were toiling like themselves. The arc of sputtering sparks terminated in a baleful blue glare that hung in the sky and shone faintly, illuminating the lower masts and spars of the *Virago* before dying.

'Someone in distress,' shouted Easton.

'Mind it ain't us, Mr Easton, get a lead over the side to see if we are dragging!'

Suddenly from forward an anonymous voice screamed: 'Starb'd bow! 'Ware Starb'd bow!'

Drinkwater looked up to see a pyramid of masts and spars and the faint gleam of a half-set topsail above a black mass of darkness: the interposition of a huge hull between himself and the tumbling wavetops that had been visible there a moment earlier.

'Cut that cable!' he shouted with all the power in his lungs. Forward a quick-witted man took up an axe from under the fo'c's'le. Drinkwater waited only long enough to see the order understood before shouting again:

'Foretopmast stays'l halliards there! Cast loose and haul away! Sheet to starboard!' There was a second's suspense then the grinding crunch and trembling as the strange ship drove across their bow, carrying away the bowsprit. She was a huge ship and there was shouting and confusion upon her decks.

'Christ! It's the fucking *London*!' shouted Rogers who had caught a glimpse of a dark flag at her mainmasthead. All Drinkwater was aware of were the three pale stripes of her gun decks and the fact that in her passing she was pulling *Virago* round to larboard. There was more shouting including the unmistakably patrician accents of a flagship lieutenant demanding through his speaking trumpet what the devil they were doing there.

'Trying to remain at anchor, you stupid blockhead!' Rogers bawled back as a final rendering from forward told where *Virago* had torn her bowsprit free of *London*'s main chains. The unknown axeman succeeded in cutting the final strands of her cable.

'We're under way, Easton, keep that God damn lead going.' Easton had a lantern in the chains in a flash and Quilhampton ran aft reporting the foretopmast staysail aloft.

'Sheet's still a-weather, sir . . .'

'Cast it loose and haul aft the lee sheet.'

'Aye, aye . . .'

Virago's head had been cast off the wind, thanks to *London*. Now Drinkwater had to drive her to windward, clear of the shallows under their lee.

'Spanker, Rogers, get the bloody spanker on her otherwise her head'll pay off too much . . .' Rogers shouted for men and Drinkwater jumped down into the waist. He wished to God he had a cutter like the old *Kestrel* that could claw to windward like a knife's edge. Suddenly *Virago*'s weatherly, sea-kindly bluff bows were a death trap.

'Mr Matchett! Will she take a jib or is the bowsprit too far gone?'

'Reckon I c'd set summat forrad . . .'

'See to it,' snapped Drinkwater. 'Hey! You men there, a hand with these staysails!' He attacked the rope stoppings on the mizen staysail and after two men had come to his aid he moved forward to the foot of the foremast where the main staysail was stowed. His hands felt effeminately soft but he grunted at the freezing knots until more men, seeing what he was about, came to his assistance.

'Halliards there lads! Hoist away . . . up she goes, lively there! Now we'll sail her out like a yacht!' He turned aft. 'Belay that main topsail, Graham, she'll point closer under this canvas . . .'

'Aye, aye, sir.'

'Cap'n, cap'n, zur.'

'Yes? Here Tregembo, I'm here!'

'Master says she's shoaling . . .'

'God's bones!' He hurried aft to where Easton was leaning outboard, gleaming wetly in the lamplight from where a wave had sluiced him and the leadsman. Drinkwater grabbed his shoulder and Easton looked up from the leadline. He shook his head. 'Shoaling, sir.'

'Shit!' he tried to think and peered over the side. The faint circle of light emitted by the lantern showed the sea at one second ten feet beneath them, next almost up to the chains. But the streaks of air bubbles streaming down-wind from the tumbling wave-caps were moving astern: *Virago* had headway. He recalled the chart, a shoaling of the bay towards its southward end. He patted Easton's shoulder. 'Keep it goin', Mr Easton.' Then he jumped inboard and made for the poop.

'Steer full and bye!'

Out to starboard another blue rocket soared into the air and he was aware that the sleet had stopped. He could see dark shapes of other ships, tossing and plunging with here and there the gleam of a sail as some fought their way to windward while others tried to hold onto their anchors. He remembered his advice to Quilhampton on the subject of anchors. He had lost one now, and although he had not lost the ship, neither had he yet saved her.

A moment later another sleet squall enveloped them. He looked up at the masthead pendant. *Virago* was heading at least a point higher without square sails and Matchett had succeeded in getting a jib up on what was left of the bowsprit. He wondered how much leeway they were making and tried looking astern at the wake but he could see nothing. He wondered what had become of the *London* and what old Parker was making of the night. Perhaps 'Batter Pudding' would be a widow before dawn. Parker would not be the first admiral to go down with his ship. He did not know whether Admiral Totty had survived the wreck of the *Invincible*, but Balchen had been lost with *Victory* on the Caskets fifty years earlier, and Shovell had died on the beach in the Scillies after the wreck of the *Association*. But poor Parker might end ignominiously, a prisoner of the Swedes.

'Quite a night, sir,' Rogers came up. He had lost his hat and his hair was plastered upon his head.

'Quite a night, Sam.'

'We've set all the fore and aft canvas we can, she seems to sail quite well.'

'She'll do,' said Drinkwater tersely, 'If she weathers the point, she'll do very well.'

'Old Willerton's been over the side on the end of the foretack.'

'What the devil for?'

'To see if his "leddy" is still there.'

'Well is it?' asked Drinkwater with sudden superstitious anxiety.

'Yes,' Rogers laughed and Drinkwater felt a sense of relief, then chid himself for a fool.

'Pipe "Up spirits", Sam, the poor devils deserve it.'

Virago did weather the point and dawn found her hands wet, cold and red-eyed, anxiously staring astern and out on either beam. Of the fifty-eight ships that had anchored in Vingå Bay only thirty-eight were now in company. They beat slowly to windward, occasionally running perilously close together as they tacked, grey shapes tossing in heavy grey seas on which was something new, something to add greater danger to their plight: ice floes.

Many of the absent ships were the smaller members of the fleet, particularly the gun-brigs, but most of the bombs were still in company and the *Anne Reed* made up under *Virago's* larboard quarter. Once they had an offing they bore away to the southward.

The wind shifted a little next day then, at one bell in the first watch, it backed south westerly and freshened again. Two hours later *Virago* followed the more weatherly ships into the shelter of the Koll. Drinkwater collapsed across his cot only to be woken at four next morning. The wind had increased to storm force. Even in the lee of the land *Virago* pitched her bluff bow into the steep seas and flung the spray over her bow to be whipped aft, catching the unwary on the face and inducing the agonising wind-ache as it evaporated. Rain and sleet compounded the discomfort and Drinkwater succeeded in veering a second cable onto his one remaining anchor. At daylight, instead of rigging out a new bowsprit, the tired men were aloft striking the topgallant masts, lowering the heavy lower yards in their jeers and lashing them across the rails.

Then, having exhausted themselves in self-preservation, the wind eased. It continued to drop during the afternoon and just after midnight the night-signal to weigh was made from *St George*. Nelson, anxious to prosecute the war in spite of, or perhaps because of, the disappearance of Parker, was thwarted before the fleet could move. The wind again freshened and the laboriously hove in cables were veered away again.

Nelson repeated the signal to weigh at seven in the morning and this time the weather obliged. An hour and a half later the remnants of the British squadrons in the Baltic beat out of Skalderviken and then bore away towards the Sound and Copenhagen.

By noon the gale had eased. *London* rejoined, together with some of the other ships. The flagship had been ashore on an uncharted shoal off Varberg castle and the *Russell* had had a similar experience attempting to tow off the gun-brig *Tickler*. Both had escaped. Less fortunate was the gun-brig *Blazer* which also ran ashore at Varberg and was captured by the Swedes.

The fleet was hove to when Parker rejoined to await the results of Vansittart's embassy. Just before dark the *Blanche* was sighted making up from the south. The news that she brought was eagerly awaited by men who had had a bellyful of shilly-shallying.

Chapter Thirteen

Councils of Timidity

There are many levels at which a man can worry and Drinkwater was
no exception. Over-riding every moment of his life, waking and
sleeping, was concern for his ship and its performance within so
large a fleet. Beneath this constant preoccupation lay a growing
conviction that the expedition had been left too late. In the two days
since *Blanche* rejoined the fleet a number of alarming rumours had
circulated. It was learned that Vansittart's terms had been rejected
by Count Bernstorff and the Danish government. Both Vansittart
and Drummond, the accredited British envoy to the Danish court,
had been given their passports and told to leave. Britons resident in
Denmark had been advised to quit the country while the Swedish
navy, already possessing its first British prize, the *Blazer*, was making belligerent preparations at Carlscrona. Worse still, the Russians
were reported cutting through the ice at Revel.

But it was the inactivity of their own admiral that most worried
the British. Every hour the Commander-in-Chief waited, robbed
them of surprise, and every hour the fleet lay idle increased the
gossip and rumour that spread from passing boat to gunroom to
lower deck. Vansittart had given Parker formal instructions to commence hostilities in one breath and warned him of the formidable
preparations made at Copenhagen in another. Drummond endorsed
the determination of the Danes and promised the hesitant Parker a
bloody nose. After the first conference aboard *London*, at which
Nelson was present, Parker had excluded his second-in-command
and Rear Admiral Graves from further consultation. Instead he
interviewed the pilots from the Hull Trinity House who were as
apprehensive as the admiral and informed Parker that they were
familiar with the navigation of The Sound alone, and could undertake no responsibility for the navigation of the Great Belt. Nelson,
who saw the Russians as the greatest threat, thought that defeat of
the Tsar would automatically destroy the Baltic Alliance, wished to
take a detachment of the fleet by the Great Belt and strike directly at
Revel. He had made his recommendations in writing and Dommett,
the captain of the fleet, had emerged from Parker's cabin, his face a
mask of agony, to reveal to the assembled officers on the *London*'s
quarterdeck that Parker had struck out every single suggestion made
by Vice-Admiral Nelson.

It was a story that had gone round the fleet like wildfire and, together with the rumour circulated from *Blanche* about Danish preparations, added to the feeling that they were too late.

Lieutenant Drinkwater was a prey to all these and other worries as he stood upon *Virago*'s poop on the freezing morning of March 26th. He was staring through his glass at a large boat flying the red flag of Denmark together with a white flag of truce, as it pulled through the fifty-two British ships anchored off Nakke Head at the entrance to The Sound.

Meanwhile in *London*'s great cabin, a confident young aide-de-camp with a message from Governor Stricker at Elsinore told Parker that if his guns were no better than his pen he had better return to England. There were two hundred heavy cannon at Cronbourg Castle, together with a garrison of three thousand men and Parker, used to the clear waters of the West Indies, was apprehensive of dark nights and fields of ice. Parker's hesitation was obvious to the young Danish officer and the worried countenances of *London*'s officers, as they waited in the cold, led him to conclude they shared their admiral's apprehensions.

Drinkwater began to pace *Virago*'s poop as the watch idled round the deck, needlessly coiling ropes and unenthusiastically chipping the scale off a box of shot set on the after mortar hatch. A low mumble came from them and exactly reflected the mood of the entire fleet.

Two days earlier, after conferring with Parker, Vansittart and Drummond had been sent home in the lugger *Kite*. Drinkwater had taken advantage of the departure of the lugger to send a letter to Lord Dungarth and the subject of that letter was the fundamental worry that underlay every thought of every waking hour. Since the interview with Jex, Drinkwater had striven to work out a solution to the problem of Edward. Sweating at the thought of his guilt, of the reception of his first letter to Dungarth sent by Lady Parker, and of Jex's knowledge, he had spent hours formulating a plan, considering every turn of events and of how each circumstance would be regarded by others. Now the constant delays denied him the opportunity to land Edward. The last few days had had a nightmare quality enhanced by the bad weather, the freezing cold and the continual nagging worries over the fleet itself.

For the first time in months he had a nightmare, the terrifying spectre of a white clad woman who reared over his supine body to the clanking of chains. With the illogical certainty of dreams she seemed to rise higher and higher above him, yet never diminished in size, while her Medusa head became the smiling face of someone he knew. He woke shivering yet soaked in sweat, his heart beating violently. Compelled by some subconscious urge he had risen in his night-shirt and struck a light to the cabin lantern and spread out the roll of canvas from the bottom of his sea-chest. Already the paint was cracking but, in the light of the lantern, it did not detract from the face that looked back at him: the face in his dream. The portrait was larger than the two now hanging on the forward bulkhead. It showed a young woman with auburn hair piled upon her head. Pearls were entwined in the coiffure that was at once negligent and contrived. Her creamy shoulders were bare and her breasts were just visible behind a wisp of gauze. The grey eyes looked directly out of the canvas and Drinkwater shivered, not from cold, but with the sensation of someone walking upon his grave. The lovely Hortense Montholon had been brought off a French beach in the last days of peace. For months she had masqueraded as an émigrée, sending information from England to her lover Edouard Santhonax in Paris. She had been returned to France by Lord Dungarth and married Santhonax on his escape following the battle of Camperdown.

Drinkwater had acquired the portrait by his capture of the French frigate *Antigone* in the Red Sea. She had been commanded by the same Santhonax and, though he had escaped yet again, Drinkwater had kept the canvas. It had lain in the bottom of his sea-chest, cut from its wooden stretcher and hidden from his wife, for it was unlikely that Elizabeth would understand its fascination. But to Drinkwater it symbolised something more than the likeness of a beautiful woman. The face of Hortense Santhonax was the face of the enemy, not the face of the tow-haired Danes but a manifestation of the force now consuming the whole continent of Europe.

He could not see it objectively yet, but the liberal allure of the French Revolution had long faded. Even those staunch republicans, the Americans, had disassociated themselves from the lawless disregard for order with which the French pursued their foreign policies or instructed their ragged, irresistible and rapacious armies. He remembered something Dungarth had said the night they landed Hortense upon the beach at Criel: 'Nine parts of humanity is motivated by a combination of self-interest and apathy. Only the tenth part hungers for power, and it is this which a prudent people guards itself against. In France the tenth part has the upper hand.' As he stood shivering in the dawn Drinkwater glimpsed the future in a flash. This rupture with Denmark, whatever its sinister motivations from the steppes, was a single symptom of a greater cancer, a cancer that fed upon a doctrinaire philosophy with a spurious validity. He was engaged in a mighty struggle between moderation and excess, and his spartan life had filled him with a horror of excess.

A wild knocking at his door caused him to roll the portrait up. 'What is it?'

'The admiral's made the signal to prepare to weigh, sir.' It was Quilhampton's voice. 'Wind is fresh westerly, sir, and it's eight bells in the middle watch.'

'Very well, call all hands, I'll be up directly.'

The day that followed had been a disaster. In a rising wind which caused problems to the smaller vessels in weighing their anchors, the fleet had got under way at daylight. Led by the 74-gun *Edgar* with her yellow topsides, they beat to the westward, along the north coast of the flat, featureless, coast of Zeeland. *Edgar*'s captain, George Murray, had recently surveyed the Great Belt and it was by this passage that Sir Hyde Parker had finally decided to pass into the Baltic. The Commander-in-Chief did not hold his determination very long. In the wake of *Edgar*, slightly inshore of the main battle fleet, the smaller ships tacked wearily to windward. Ahead of *Virago* were the seven bombs, astern of her the other tenders. At eleven o'clock while Drinkwater consulted his chart, listened to the monotonous chant of the leadsman and occasionally referred to the old, worn notebook left him years earlier as part of Blackmore's bequest, the *Zebra* struck the Zeeland's Reef.

Alarmed by the lookout's shout, Drinkwater watched *Zebra*'s fore topgallant go by the board and ordered *Virago* tacked at once. Soon after, *Edgar* had flown *Virago*'s pennant with the order to assist *Zebra* and he had sent away his boats with two spare spars to lash across their gunwhales in order to carry out her anchor.

He had watched Rogers pull away over the choppy grey sea and been forced to kick his own heels in idleness until, just before dark, the combined efforts of the bomb ships' boats succeeded in getting *Zebra* off the reef.

While Drinkwater had spent the afternoon at anchor, Parker had been told an even more alarming piece of news. Someone in the flagship had informed the Commander-in-Chief that greater risks would have to be run by taking the fleet through the Great Belt. Alarmed by this and the accident to *Zebra*, Parker countermanded his orders and the fleet was ordered to return to its anchorage off Nakke Head. *Virago*, escorting the *Zebra*, had once again dropped her anchor at midnight, and now, in the chilly sunshine of the following morning, Drinkwater looked across to where Mr Quilhampton and a party from *Virago* were helping the *Zebra*'s people get up a new fore topgallant mast.

On his own fo'c's'le Mr Matchett was putting the finishing touches to the gammoning of their own refitted bowsprit. Over the rest of *Virago* the mood of listless despair hung like a cloud.

At last Drinkwater saw the Danish boat leave *London*'s side and though during the afternoon reports came down to him where he dozed in his cabin, that Murray, Nelson, Graves and other officers were all visiting the flagship, nothing else happened.

Drinkwater woke from his sleep at about four o'clock. He could not afterwards explain it, but his mind was resolved over the problem of Edward. He would brook no further delay. He passed word for Quilhampton and Rogers.

'Ah, Mr Rogers, I wish you to have the long boat made ready an hour before daylight with a barrel of biscuit in it, together with water barricoes, mast and sail. I want a crew told off tonight, say six men, with Tregembo as leading hand. Mr Quilhampton will command the boat and I shall accompany it. In the unlikely event of our being absent when the signal is made to weigh, you are to take charge. I will give you that order in writing when I leave.'

'Very good, sir, may I ask . . .?'

'No, you may not.'

Rogers looked offended and turned on his heel. Drinkwater called him back.

'I do not want any of your irreverent speculation on this matter, Sam. Be pleased to remember that.'

'Aye aye, sir.' Drinkwater raised his eyebrows and stared significantly at Quilhampton.

'The same goes for you, Mr Q.'

'Yes sir.'

'Very well. Now pass word for the volunteer Waters to come aft and do you, Mr Q, mount a guard on my cabin and see we are not disturbed.'

Rogers opened his mouth to protest, thought better of it, and strode from the cabin. Drinkwater waited for Edward to appear, occupying the time by rummaging in a canvas bag he had had brought into the cabin by an inquisitive Mr Jex.

A knock at the door was followed by Mr Quilhampton's head. 'Waters is here now, sir.'

'Very well, show him in.'

Edward entered the cabin and stood awkwardly, looking around with a curious sheepishness. It suddenly struck Drinkwater that a month or two more might have made Edward into a seaman. Already he was lean and fit and had not been long enough on salt beef for it to have made much difference to him. But it was his attitude that most struck Drinkwater. Four months ago they had met as equals, now Edward had all the inherent awkwardness of one who felt socially inferior. The realisation embarrassed Drinkwater.

'How are you?' he asked too brusquely for Edward to perceive any change in their bizarre relationship.

'Well enough . . . sir.'

'How have you been treated?'

'The same as all your seamen,' Edward replied with a trace of bitterness, 'I have no complaints.'

Drinkwater bit off a tart rebuke and poured two glasses of blackstrap. He handed one to Edward then went to the door. 'Mr Q, I want a bowl of hot water from the galley upon the instant.'

'A bowl of hot water, sir?' He caught the gleam in Drinkwater's eye. 'Er, yes sir.'

'Sit down Ned, sit, down.' Drinkwater closed the door. 'Your circumstances are about to change. Whether 'tis for the better I cannot say, but listen carefully to what I tell you.' He paused to collect his thoughts.

'Jex, the purser, has tumbled you. He saw a cursed newspaper report about the murder and also saw you in the Blue Fox, at Chatham. You knew of this?'

107

Edward nodded. 'I did not know how he had found out, but he approached me . . .'

'You did not . . .?'

'Confess? Good God no! I merely acted dumb, as any seaman does in the presence of an officer.' The ghost of a smile crossed Edward's face. 'What did you do about Mr Jex?' The anxiety was now plain.

Drinkwater sighed. 'Bluffed, Ned, bluffed. Denied you were my brother, said the name of the suspected murderer was a coincidence then gave him to understand that there might be something of a mystery surrounding the whole affair, but that it was not his concern . . . come in!'

A heavy silence hung in the cabin as Quilhampton ushered in the messman with the bowl of water. Both rating and mate could scarcely disguise their curiosity. It would be all over *Virago* in a matter of moments that Waters, the landsman volunteer, was taking wine with *Virago*'s commander. But Nathaniel no longer cared. Perhaps some apparent unconcern would lend credibility to what he proposed. Edward did not seem to have noticed, but waited only for the intruders to leave before bursting out:

'What the hell d'you mean you told him there was something of a mystery . . .'

'God damn it, Ned, I've lied for you, risked my career, abused my position of command and maybe jeopardised my whole life for brotherly bloody affection! D'you not think a flat denial would only have increased Jex's inquisitiveness. Mr Jex is not to be counted among my most loyal officers, he is seeking to avenge a grudge. But he is not stupid enough to risk his suspicions against the Articles of War, nor bright enough not to be a little confused by what I have told him. Perhaps he will work it all through and conclude I have deceived him; if that is the case his malice will be thereby increased. But by that time you will be gone.'

Edward shook his head. 'I don't understand . . .'

'My shaving things are lying on the cabin chest there,' he indicated the cotton roll, 'do you shave while I talk . . . Now, I wrote from Yarmouth to Lord Dungarth. I was employed by him some years ago in secret operations on the French and Dutch coasts. He is a spy-master, a puppet-master he calls himself, and *may* be able to find you some employment . . .'

'What the devil did you say about me for God's sake?' asked Edward lathering himself.

'Only that a person known to me was anxious to be of service to his country, had asked for my protection and spoke fluent French. That this person might prove of some value for a patriotic service in a Baltic state. His lordship is intelligent enough to draw his own conclusions . . .'

'Especially if he reads the newspapers,' muttered Edward as the razor rasped down his tanned cheek. He swished the razor in water and turned to his brother.

'So I am to become a puppet, to dance to his lordship's string-pulling, eh?'

'You have scant reason for bitterness, Edward,' said Drinkwater sharply, 'I would have thought it preferable to dancing on the gallows.' Drinkwater mastered his anger at Edward's peculiar petulance and poured himself another glass of blackstrap.

'I am about to land you on the Danish coast. You should acquire a horse and make for Hamburg. The Harwich packet calls fortnightly and when the *Kite* left for England with the envoys she carried mails. Among them was a letter to Lord Dungarth stating that the person of whom I had written earlier would take his instructions from the packet master in the name of 'Waters'.

'And d'you think the security of these letters will be breached?'

'I doubt it. The second is hardly incriminating, the first I sent by special delivery. To be precise the Commander-in-Chief's wife.'

'Good God!'

'It is the best I can do for you Ned, for I must land you.' He had thought to say 'disencumber myself of you', but refrained.

'Yes, of course. How long must I wait in Hamburg?'

'I should give it two months . . . meet the Harwich packet when she berths.'

'After which this Lord Dungarth will have abandoned me much as you now wish to.' The two brothers stared at each other.

'That is right, Ned,' Drinkwater said quietly, 'And damned sorry I am for it.'

Edward shrugged. 'I need money.'

Drinkwater nodded and reached into his chest. 'You can take the money I took from you at Yarmouth, plus twenty sovereigns of mine. I should like to think that one day you were in a position to redeem the debt . . . as for clothes these will have to suffice.' He upturned a canvas bag. Shirts, pantaloons, shoes and a creased blue broadcloth coat fell out.

'A dead man's?'

'Yes, named Mason.'

'It seems you have thought of everything . . .'

Drinkwater ignored the sarcastic tone. 'You had better take his sword and his pistol. I have renewed the flint and there is a cartouche box with a spare flint and powder and ball for half a dozen rounds.' He watched Edward put on one of the shirts and try the shoes. They were a tolerable fit. 'If you are careful you have sufficient funds to purchase a horse and lodgings for your journey. I suggest you speak only in French. Once in Hamburg you must trust to luck.'

'Luck,' repeated Edward ironically, pulling on Mason's coat, 'I shall need a deal of that . . . and if she fails me, as she has done before, then I may always blow my brains out, eh? Nathaniel?' He turned to find his brother gone and the cabin filling with the grey light of dawn.

*   *   *

Drinkwater looked astern once at the dark shape of *Virago* as the first of the daylight began to illuminate the anchorage. A freezing wind blew in their faces as the boat, her sheets trimmed hard in, butted her way to the south eastwards, through the anchored ships. The only advantage to be had from the multitude of delays they had been subjected to in the past weeks was that a boat working through the anchorage was unlikely to attract much attention. There had been too much coming and going between the ships for any suspicions to be aroused.

The boat's crew were muffled against the cold. Beside him in the stern sat Edward, staring at the approaching shore and ignoring the curious looks of his former messmates. He had one hand on the rail and the other round Mason's canvas bag, sword and cocked hat.

The two brothers sat in silence. There had been no formal leave taking, Drinkwater having re-entered the cabin merely to announce the readiness of the boat.

Edward's ingratitude hurt Nathaniel. He could not imagine the emotions that tore his brother, how the comparison of their situations had seemed heightened by the social gulf that had divided them during Edward's short sojourn before the mast. Nor could Edward, to whom precarious existence had become a way of life, fully realise the extent to which Drinkwater had risked his all. And a man used to gambling and living upon his wits with no-one to blame but himself for his misfortunes usually casts about for a scapegoat. But this was lost on Drinkwater who charitably assumed the bleak prospect looming before his brother accounted for Edward's attitude.

Quilhampton tacked the boat seaward again in the growing light. The low coast of Zeeland was now clearly visible to the south of them and after half an hour they went about again and stood inshore where the tree-lined horizon was broken by the harder edges of roofs and the spire of Gilleleje. Drinkwater nudged Quilhampton and pointed at the village. Quilhampton nodded.

Forty minutes later they lowered the sail and got out the oars, running the boat on the sand in a comparative lee.

Drinkwater walked up the beach alongside Edward. Neither man said a word. Behind them Quilhampton stilled a speculative murmur among the boat's crew.

The two brothers strode past fishing boats drawn up on the beach. From the village a cock crowed and rising smoke told of stirring life. They saw a man emerge from a wooden privy who looked up in astonishment.

'I think I will take my leave now,' Edward said, his voice devoid of any emotion.

'Very well,' replied Nathaniel, his voice flat and formally naval.

Edward paused then gripped the canvas bag flung over his shoulder with both fists, avoiding the necessity of shaking hands. He nodded to his brother then turned and strode away. Drinkwater stood and watched him go. The man from the privy had reappeared

110

at the door of a neat wooden house. With him was a woman with yellow hair and a blue shawl wrapped about her shoulders. They stood staring at the approaching stranger. Edward made no attempt to conceal himself but walked up to them and raised his hat. The woman retreated behind her husband but after a few minutes, during which it was clear that Edward was making himself understood to the Dane, curiosity brought her forward again. Though the two looked twice at Drinkwater, Edward did not turn and after a moment Nathaniel walked back to the boat.

The wind before which *Virago*'s longboat returned was foul for the fleet to attempt The Sound. But the day proved more eventful than could have been expected as that dismal realisation permeated every wardroom and gun-room in the fleet. About ten in the morning the Commander-in-Chief began signalling various ships for boats. There followed hours during which, in a grey and choppy sea, the boats of the fleet pulled or sailed about, commanded by blue midshipmen with notes and orders, while the weary seamen toiled at the oars to invigorate their circulation.

The cold was bitter, following an unseasonal early spring, winter had reasserted itself. In England daffodils, new budded in the warmth of early March, now froze on the stem, an omen from the North that did not go unnoticed among the ignorant and neglected womenfolk who waited eagerly for news of the vaunted Baltic expedition.

But a new air gradually transformed the weary ships. The battleships hauled alongside the cumbersome flat-bottomed boats they had so laboriously towed or carried from England and lowered 24-pounder guns into them. Colonel Stewart's detachment of the 49th Foot improvised musket drill over the hammock nettings, while his riflemen were said to be ready to shoot the Tsar's right eye out. Even the bombs were part of this rejuvenation, the artillery detachments being ordered out of their tenders and on board the vessels they were to attend in action.

Mr Tumilty's rubicund, smiling face came over the side and the red haired Irishman pumped Drinkwater's hand enthusiastically.

'Why Mr Drinkwater, but I'd sure never like to see you naval boys try to do anything secret, 'tis for sure the whole population of Denmark has seen us cruising up and down the coast, by Jesus!' Drinkwater grinned, thinking of his own private secret expedition that had only been accomplished an hour or two earlier.

'I'm damned glad to see you, Mr Tumilty, but what's the cause of all this sudden activity?'

'Don't you know? Why, Admiral Parker has at last decided to let Lord Nelson have his way. The bombs are to join a squadron under his lordship's command. And for certain 'tis Revel or Copenhagen for us, m' dear fellow.'

'Are we to go with the bombs, then?'

'Aye, Nat'aniel. They say Nelson has been nagging the poor old admiral 'til he was only too glad to get rid of him.' Tumilty shivered and rubbed his hands. 'God, but it's cold. To be sure a man that'd go to sea for fortune would go to hell for pleasure . . .'

'Well, Mr Tumilty, do you go to see Mr Jex and give him my compliments and ask him to issue a greygoe to you, and sheepskins to your men. We should have enough.'

'That's mighty kind of you Nat'aniel, mighty kind. Sure an'it'll be hotter than the hobs of hell itself when we kindle those big black kettles you've got skulking beneath those hatches,' he added, rubbing his hands again, this time with enthusiasm.

'Beg pardon, sir, message from the admiral . . .' Drinkwater took the packet from Quilhampton and noted the boat pulling away from the ship's side. In his delight at welcoming Tumilty he had not seen it arrive.

He scanned the order: *The ships noted in the margin are* . . . Drinkwater looked down the list. There, at the bottom he found *Virago* . . . *to form a squadron under my command ordered forward upon a special service* . . . *The ships and vessels placed under my directions are to get their sheet and spare anchors over the side, ready for letting go at the shortest notice* . . . *commanding officers are to take especial notice of the following signals* . . . *No 14 to anchor by the stern* . . . It was signed in the admiral's curious, left-handed script: *Nelson and Brontë.*

'Mr Rogers!'

'Sir?'

'The vice-admiral is to shift his flag to *Elephant* this morning.'

'What the devil for?'

'She draws less than the *St George*, Mr Rogers. Do you direct the watch officers to pay particular attention to all signals from the *Elephant*. We are to form part of a detachment under Nelson . . .'

The sudden activity of the fleet and the disencumbering of Edward had coincided to throw off Drinkwater's depression. He suddenly felt ridiculously buoyant, a feeling shared by the impish Tumilty whose smile threatened to disappear into his ears.

''Twill be a fine music we'll be playing to these damned knaves, Mr Rogers, so it will, a fine *basso profundo* with the occasional crescendo to make 'em jump about like eejits.'

'Let's hope we're not too late, Mr Tumilty,' said Rogers who had not yet forgiven Drinkwater for his mysterious behaviour over Waters.

'Beg pardon, zur, but Mr Trussel sent me down with more orders just come, zur.'

'Thank you Tregembo.' Drinkwater took the packet and broke the wafer.

'Beg pardon, zur, but may I speak, zur?'

'What is it?'

''Tis well-known about the ship that the man we landed yesterday was a spy, zur.'

112

Drinkwater looked at the Cornishman. They both understood.

'Mr Jex approached me some days ago, zur. It cost him two plugs of tobacco to learn you ain't got no brother, zur.'

'Thank you.'

'Now, with your permission, zur, I'll see to your sword and pistols, zur.'

'They are all right, thank you Tregembo, I have not used them since last you attended to them.'

'I'll look at them, just the same.'

Drinkwater bent over the new orders. It was a general instruction to the bomb vessels to place themselves under the orders of Captain Murray of the *Edgar*. It was anticipated that they would be used against the fortress at Cronbourg. A note was included from Martin. The commander's crabbed script drew Drinkwater's attention to the fact that it was suspected that *Zebra* had suffered some damage on the Zeeland's Reef and he might yet be able to render Drinkwater a service. Drinkwater fancied he could read the unwritten thought that lay behind that fatuous phrase, that he, Nathaniel Drinkwater, was an intimate of Lord Dungarth. Drinkwater wondered what Martin would do if he knew that the lieutenant, with whom he was currently currying favour, had just assisted a murderer to escape the noose.

Late in the afternoon the brig *Cruizer* was ordered forward to send in a boat to make a final demand of Governor Stricker at Cronbourg as to his intentions if the British fleet attempted to pass The Sound. It revealed to all, including the Danish commander, that Parker was still vacillating.

The following morning, Saturday March 28th, the wind hauled westerly and the temperature rose. The sun shone and the fleet weighed, setting all sail to the royals in an attempt to enter and pass The Sound. But the wind fell light and the contrary current held up the lumbering battleships so that Parker, learning from Brisbane of the *Cruizer* that Stricker had laughed in his face, could not risk his ships drifting under the heavy guns of the fortress. Once again the fleet anchored and in *Virago*'s cabin that night they debated how long it took to wear an anchor ring through the shank.

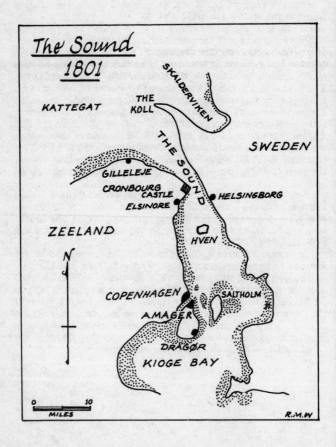

PART THREE

Lord Nelson

'It is warm work; and this day may be the last to any of us at a moment. But mark you! I would not be elsewhere for thousands.'

NELSON, COPENHAGEN, 2 April, 1801

Chapter Fourteen   29–30 March 1801

The Sound

'Two guns from the flagship, sir.'

'Very well, what o'clock is it?'

'It wants a few minutes of midnight, sir; wind's freshened a little from the west.'

Drinkwater struggled into his greygoe and hurried on deck. He looked up at the masthead pendant and nodded his approval as Rogers reported the hands mustering to weigh.

'Sheet home the topsails, Mr Rogers, and have headsails ready for hoisting. Mr Easton!'

'Sir?'

'Have you a man for the chains?'

'All ready.'

'Very well.'

'One thing we *can* do is weigh the bloody anchor in the middle of the night,' offered Rogers in a stage whisper.

'*Virago* 'hoy!'

'Hullo?' Drinkwater strode to the rail to see the dim shape of a master's mate standing in the stern of a gig.

'Captain Murray desires that you move closer inshore towards Cronbourg Castle, sir. The bombs are to prepare to bombard at daylight!'

'Thank you.' Drinkwater turned inboard again. 'Can you make out *Edgar* in this mist?'

'Aye, sir, just, she's hoisted lanterns.'

Drinkwater saw the flare of red orpiment from the *Edgar*'s stern.

'Bengal light, sir, signal to weigh.'

'Very well. Mr Matchett!'

'Sir?'

'Heave away!'

Virago filled her topsails as the anchor came a-trip and the water began to chuckle under her round bow. Keeping a careful watch to avoid collision Drinkwater conned the old ship south-eastwards in the wake of the *Edgar*. On either beam dark shapes with the pale gleam of topsails above indicated the other bombs creeping forward ready to throw their fire at the intransigent Danes. Then, barely an hour after they had got under way, the wind shifted, backing remorselessly and beginning to head them.

'Topsail's a-shiver, zur,'

'Brace her hard up, Mr Easton, God damn it!'

'Hard up, sir, aye, aye . . . it's no good sir, wind's drawing ahead.'

The concussion of guns from the darkness ahead and the dark rose glow of twin Bengal lights together with a blue rocket signalled the inevitable.

'Main braces, Mr Easton, down helm and stand by to anchor!'

Once again the anchor splashed overboard, once again *Virago*'s cable rumbled through the hawse pipe and once again her crew clambered aloft to stow the topsails, certain in the knowledge that tomorrow they would have to heave the cable in again. They were nowhere near close enough to bombard as Murray intended.

All morning Drinkwater waited for the order to weigh as the light wind backed a little. During the afternoon the rest of the ships worked closer inshore and by the evening the whole fleet had brought to their anchors four miles to the north west of Cronbourg castle. Drinkwater surveyed the shore. The dark bulk of the fortress was indistinct but the coast of Zeeland was more heavily wooded than at Gilleleje. The villages of Hellebaek and Hornbaek were visible, the latter with a conspicuous church steeple looking toylike as the sun westered to produce a flaming sunset. It picked out not only the villages of Denmark but small points of metallic fire and the pink planes of sunlit stone where the guns of the Swedish fortress at Helsingborg on the opposite side of The Sound peered from their embrasures.

Men lingered on deck in silence watching the Danish shore where figures could be seen on foot and horseback. Here and there a carriage was observed as the population of Elsinore came out to look at this curiosity, the heavy hulls of the British ships, the tracery of their masts and yards silhouetted against the blood red sunset. It seemed another omen, and to the Danes a favourable one. The image of those ships reeking in their own blood-red element was not lost on Drinkwater who wrote of it in his journal before turning again to the stained notebook he had consulted when the fleet had made for the Great Belt.

The book was one of several left him after the death of Mr Blackmore, the old sailing master of the *Cyclops*. Drinkwater had been his brightest pupil on the frigate and the old man had left both his notebooks and his quadrant to the young midshipman. The notebooks had been meticulously kept and inspired Drinkwater to keep his own journal in considerable detail. Blackmore had carried out several surveys and copied foreign charts, particularly of the Baltic, an area with which he had been familiar, having commanded a ship in the Scandinavian trade.

Drinkwater looked at the chartlet of The Sound. The ramparts of Cronbourg were clearly marked together with the arcs of fire of the batteries and a note that their range was no more than one and a half miles. The Sound was two and a half miles wide and the fleet could not hope to pass unscathed if they received fire from both Helsingborg and Cronbourg.

Drinkwater was familiar with the current. It had frustrated them already, usually running to the north but influenced by the wind with little tidal effect. The Disken shoal formed a middle ground but should not present any problem to the fleet. It was the guns of Cronbourg that would do the damage, those and the Swedish cannon on the opposite shore.

Drinkwater went on deck before turning in. It was bitterly cold again with a thin layer of high cloud. Trussel was on deck.

'All quiet, Mr Trussel?'

'Aye sir, like the grave.'

'Moonrise is about two-fifteen and the almanac indicates an eclipse.'

'Ah, I'd better warn the people, there's plenty of them as still believes in witchcraft and the like.'

'As you like, Mr Trussel.' Drinkwater thought of his own obsession with Hortense Santhonax and wondered if there were not something in old wives' tales. There were times when a lonely man might consider himself under a spell. He thought, too, of Edward, and where he might be this night. Trussel recalled him.

'To speak the truth, Mr Drinkwater, I'd believe any omen if it meant making some progress. This is an interminable business, wouldn't you say?'

'Aye, Mr Trussel, and the Danes have been well able to observe every one of our manoeuvres.'

'And doubtless form a poor opinion of 'em, what with all the shilly shallying. I've never seen so much coming and going even when the Grand Fleet lay at St Helen's. Why your little boat-trip t'other morning went unremarked by anyone.'

The point of Trussel's chat emerged and Drinkwater smiled.

'Indeed, Mr Trussel, that was the point of it.'

'The point of it, sir . . .?' said Trussell vaguely.

'Come, what is the rumour in the ship, eh? Ain't it that the mysterious fellow we took aboard at Yarmouth is, in truth, a spy?'

'Aye, sir. That's what scuttlebutt says, but I don't always hold that scuttlebutt's accurate.'

'But in this case it is, Mr Trussel, in this case it most certainly is. Good night to you . . .'

In his coffin-like cot Mr Jex lay unsleeping. He felt a growing sense of unease at the quickening pace of events. The fruitless comings and goings of the last week, the weary handling of ground tackle and sails had scarcely affected him since he did no special duty at such times. True the bad weather had confined him sick and miserable in his cabin but he had at least a measure of satisfaction in abusing and belabouring his steward, a miserable, cowed man who was loved by no-one. But even Jex had overcome his sickness eventually and the

119

prolonged periods at anchor had pacified his internal disquiet. Like his Commander-in-Chief, Jex did not wish to pass the fortress at Cronbourg, but whereas Parker was merely excessively cautious, Jex was a coward. He found it increasingly difficult to concentrate upon his columns of figures, even when they showed a rise in the fortunes of Hector Jex to the extent of yet wiping out the amount extorted by Lieutenant Drinkwater. Instead he found unbidden images of muti-lated bodies entering his mind; of bloody decks strewn with limbless corpses, of the surgeon's tubs filled with arms and legs.

Lieutenant Rogers's bloodthirsty yarns lost nothing in the telling and Jex's disgrace in the action with the luggers had left him a prey to the cruel and merciless wit of his brother officers. Rogers's lack of either tact or compassion only fuelled the constant references to Jex's cowardice so that the purser conceived a hatred for the first lieuten-ant that began to exceed that he already felt for his commander.

As for the latter, Jex had felt a hopelessness at having been out-manoeuvred yet again by Mr Drinkwater. The ostentatious depar-ture of Waters from the ship had seemed to him to prove the accuracy of Drinkwater's assertions about the mysterious landsman. All Jex could do was hope to determine whether or not a real murder had taken place at Newmarket, and whether or not the Marquis de la Roche-Jagu really existed. He could not himself conceive that it would have been reported without it being known in Newmarket whether or not the event had actually taken place. And it was this desire to live long enough to prove the arrogant Mr Drinkwater wrong that was constantly undermined by the growing horror of premature death.

Even as he lay there, a deck below the anchor watch who mar-velled at the lunar eclipse, he saw himself dead; torn apart by cannon shot, his bowels spilling from his paunch.

Drinkwater stood in the sunshine and looked round the deck. He had done all he could to move *Virago* forward to a position where she might assist the seven bomb vessels if they required it, yet remain out of range of the guns of Cronbourg with her vulnerable cargo of explosives and combustibles.

He looked beyond the masts of the bomb vessels at their target. Anchored in a line, just outside the known arc of fire of the Danish guns they were preparing to bombard the castle.

Despite the fact that he had already trodden the soil of Denmark, his preoccupation with Edward's plight had so far blinded him to a full realisation of the enemy's country. To date he had seen it as a series of landmarks to take bearings of, a flat coast with hidden, offshore dangers and a population amply warned of their approach. This morning he realised the alien nature of it. Weighing at daylight the bombs with the battleship *Edgar* and the frigate *Blanche* had taken up the positions attempted the previous day. The castle of Cronbourg loomed before them, an edifice of unusual aspect to

English eyes, used to the towers of the Norman French. The red-brick walls, towers and cupolas with their bright green copper roofs had a fantastic, even fairy-like quality that seemed at first to totally disarm Sir Hyde Parker's fears.

But even as they let their anchors go at six in the morning of March 30th the Danish flag was hoisted in the north westerly breeze that set fair for the passage of The Sound. The white cross on a red, swallow-tail ground had the lick of a dragon's tongue about it, as it floated above the fortress, over the roofs of the town of Elsinore.

The men had breakfasted at their stations and Lettsom had come on deck to see for himself the progress of the fleet. Easton was pointing out the landmarks.

'The town is Helsingør, Mr Lettsom, which we call Elsinore, the castle is called Cronbourg, or Cronenbourg on some charts.'

'Then that is Hamlet's castle, eh? Is that so Mr Drinkwater?'

'I suppose it is, Mr Lettsom.'

'And they tell me you had an eclipse last night.'

'I think 'twas the moon that had an eclipse. Happily it had no effect upon us.'

'Quite so, sir.' Lettsom paused for a moment. ' "The moist star, upon whose influence Neptune's empire stands, Was sick almost to doomsday with eclipse . . ." Hamlet, gentlemen, Act One . . .'

'Sick to doomsday with anchoring more like, Bones,' put in Rogers.

Lettsom ignored the first lieutenant and produced another quotation: ' "But look, the morn, in russet mantle clad, Walks o'er the dew of yon high eastern hill . . ." '

'But it ain't high, Mr Lettsom, thus proving Shakespeare did not know the lie of the land hereabouts.'

'True, sir, but there's such a thing as poetic licence. And here, if not the dawn, is Mr Jex.'

The assembled officers laughed as the purser came on deck, and the surgeon, in fine form now he had the attention of all, continued his thespian act.

'Good morning Mr Jex,' he said, then added darkly, ' "here is a beast that wants discourse of reason".'

Bewildered by the laughter, yet conscious that he was the cause of it, Jex looked sullenly round.

' "A dull and muddy-metalled rascal", eh, Mr Jex?' Even Lettsom himself was scarce able to refrain from laughter and Jex was roused to real anger.

'Do you mind your manners, Mr Lettsom,' he snarled, 'I've given you no cause to abuse me.'

' "Use every man after his desert and who would 'scape whipping?" '

'Why,' laughed Rogers unwilling to let Lettsom have all the fun, 'both you and your eighth man would qualify there, Mr Jex . . .'

Laughter spread along the deck among the seamen who well understood the allusion to Jex's corruption.

'Aye, "be thou as chaste as ice, as pure as snow, thou shalt not escape calumny."'

'Hold your God damn tongue . . .' burst out Jex, the colour mounting to his face at this public humiliation.

'Gentlemen, gentlemen,' Drinkwater temporised, 'I beg you to desist . . . Mr Jex, I assure you the surgeon meant no offence but merely wished to air his knowledge of the Bard. I am by no means persuaded his powers of recall are accurate . . .'

'Sir!' protested Lettsom but Drinkwater called their attention to the fleet.

'Let us see whether aught is rotten in the state of Denmark shall we?'

'Mr Drinkwater, you o'erwhelm the powers of my muse,' grinned Lettsom, 'I shall betake myself to my cockpit and sulk like Achilles in his tent.'

The surgeon and purser were instantly forgotten as glasses were lifted to watch the fleet weigh from the anchorage and begin the approach to Copenhagen through the sound.

Led by *Monarch*, the foremost ship of Lord Nelson's division, the ships of the line stood south eastwards in brilliant sunshine. It presented a magnificent spectacle to the men watching from the huddle of bomb ships that waited eagerly to play their part in the drama of the day. The wind had settled to a fine breeze from the north north westward, as *Monarch* approached Cronbourg. They could see her topmen racing aloft to shake out the topgallants from their stoppings.

'*London*'s signalling, sir, "General bombs, commence the bombardment".'

'Thank you, Mr Easton. Mr Rogers, have the crews in the boats ready to render assistance, and Mr Tumilty, perhaps you will give us the benefit of your opinion in the action.'

'I shall be delighted, Nat'aniel. Mark *Zebra* well, I hear she took a pounding on the reef t'other day and, though I believe her to be well built, if Bobbie Lawson overloads his mortars I think she may be in trouble.'

'Is Captain Lawson likely to over-charge his mortars, Tom?'

'To win the five guineas I wagered that he couldn't sustain one round a minute for more than half an hour he may become a mite careless, Nat'aniel, so he may . . .'

Drinkwater laughed just as the first bomb fired. 'That's *Explosion*,' snapped Tumilty, suddenly concentrating. The concussion rolled over the water towards them as they saw *Explosion*'s waist billow clouds of smoke.

'She certainly lives up to her name.'

'They'll remark the fall of shot before anyone else fires,' said Tumilty informatively. They could see the arc of the shell reach its apogee and then they were distracted as the batteries at Cronbourg opened a rolling fire. For a moment *Monarch*'s hull disappeared behind a seething welter of splashes, then behind the smoke of her own discharge as first she, and then successive ships astern returned the fire of the castle. It was six forty-five in the morning.

For the next hour the air was rent by the explosions of the guns. The deep rolling of British broadsides was answered by the heavy fire from Cronbourg. Nearer, the powerful and thunderous bark of the ten- and thirteen-inch mortars enveloped the lower masts of the bomb vessels in heavy clouds of smoke. No signals came from the bombs and the Viragos were compelled to stand idle, but it afforded them a rare and memorable sight.

'No fire from the Swedes, sir,' said Rogers, '*Monarch*'s inclining to their side of the channel.'

Parker's centre division was abeam of them now, all the ships setting their topgallants but keeping their main courses in the buntlines so as to hamper neither the gunnery nor the conning of the battlefleet through The Sound.

''Tis a fine sight, Nat'aniel,' said Tumilty, 'at moments like this one is almost persuaded that war is a glorious thing.'

'Sadly, Tom, that is indeed true. See the *Elephant*, the two-decker with the blue flag at her foremasthead, that's Nelson's flagship, see how he holds his fire. That's the contempt of Old England for you, by God!'

'If that's war on the English style, wait until you see that Irish version, by Jesus,' Tumilty grinned happily, ''Tis not your cold contempt, but your hot-tempered fury that puts the enemy to flight . . .'

They both laughed. 'There goes the old *Isis*. See Mr Q, that is quite possibly the last time you'll see a fifty in the line of battle . . . included here for her shallow draught I imagine.'

Beyond the battleships, on the Swedish side of The Sound the smaller vessels were under way. The gun-brigs and the frigates towing the flat-boats, the sloops and the fire-ships *Otter* and *Zephyr*, the tenders and cutters all stood southward, sheltered by the rear division of Admiral Graves. Only *Blanche* and *Edgar* remained to cover the bomb vessels and at fifteen minutes to eight the rear repeating frigate hoisted a string of bunting.

'*Jamaica* signalling, sir, "Repeated from flag, bombs to cease fire and approach the admiral".' Mr Quilhampton closed the signal book.

'That's a touch of the naval Irish, Mr Tumilty,' said Rogers nudging the artillery officer. 'It means Parker wants us to play chase.'

'Is that a fact, Mr Rogers,' said Tumilty calling his non-commissioned officer to the break of the poop while Drinkwater and Rogers bawled orders through their trumpets to get *Virago* under way.

The order was obeyed with alacrity. Topmen raced aloft to shake out the topsails while the fo'c's'le party set to with their spikes at the windlass. At the fiferails there was much heaving as sheets were belayed and halliards manned.

'Now Hite,' asked Tumilty, leaning over the rail and addressing the bombardier who had a watch and tablet in his hands, 'what did you make it?'

'Mr Lawson was engaged for thirty-seven minutes, sir, both mortars in use and by my reckoning he threw forty-one shells . . .'

Tumilty whistled. 'Phew, he must have been working them poor artillerymen like devils, eh Hite?'

'Yes sir.'

'An' I've lost five guineas, devil take it!'

'You've lost your wager then?' asked Drinkwater as he strode forward to get a better view of the fo'c's'le party.

'To be sure an' I have.'

'You look damned cheerful about it.'

'An' why shouldn't I look cheerful? An' why shouldn't *you* look cheerful seeing as how you stand to benefit from it.'

'Me? Hoist away there, Mr Q. Lively there with the cat-tackle, Mr Matchett. Steer south east, Mr Easton . . . how should I be delighted in your misfortune, Tom?'

'Well I'll put up another five that says *Zebra* will be unfit for the next bombardment and *Virago* will stand in the line.'

Drinkwater looked curiously at the little Irishman before turning his attention again to getting *Virago* under way and taking station in the rear of the line of bomb vessels.

Standing across to the Swedish side the squat little ships left the Danish shore as the frustrated guns of Cronbourg fell silent.

By nine o'clock they were clear of The Narrows and at noon anchored with the rest of the fleet off the island of Hven.

'I wonder what damage the mortars did, Tom.'

Tumilty shrugged. ''Tis not what execution they did to Elsinore or Cronbourg that should interest you, Nat'aniel, but what damage they did to *Zebra*.'

Chapter Fifteen   30 March–1 April 1801

Copenhagen Road

'Christ, but it's bloody cold again.' Rogers stamped upon the deck and his breath was steaming in the chilling air. It was not yet dark but the brief warmth of the sun had long gone. Pancakes of ice floated slowly past the ship and Lettsom, invigorated by the air's freshness after a day spent below and well muffled in sheepskins, watched curiously from the rail.

'I don't think I can stand much more of this blasted idling in ignorance Lettsom, stap me if I can!'

'Happen you have little choice,' answered Lettsom straightening up.

'No,' growled Rogers with angry resentment.

'I suppose you want to know what those two ships learnt . . .'

'Yes, *Amazon* and *Cruizer* went forward with the lugger *Lark*; her master's familiar with the approaches to Copenhagen. Someone said they thought Nelson was in the lugger but . . .' he shrugged resignedly. 'Bollocks to them; I suppose they'll tell us in good time when they want us to get shot.'

'How is our commander taking the delay, he seems an active man?'

'Drinkwater? He's a strange cove. He was promoted in '99 but because of some damned administrative mix-up he lost the commission. He took it blasted well; if it'd been me I'd have made an unholy bloody row about it.'

'I don't doubt it,' said Lettsom drily, 'I think our Mr Drinkwater something of a stoic, though an oddity too. What d'you make of this spy business?'

Rogers shrugged. 'What is there to make of it? As I said Drinkwater's a strange cove. Been mixed up in the business since before the war; ask Tregembo if you want to know about our commander. Lying old buzzard will tell you tales as tall as the main truck; about the young midshipman who slit the gizzard of some Frog and took the m'sieur's sword for his pains, or retook an American prize after her crew over-powered the prize crew. All in all it's a bloody mystery why our Nathaniel ain't commanding this bloody expedition against the festering Tsar . . . Let's face it, Bones, he couldn't make a worse mess of it than that old fool Parker and *he's* got Lord Nelson to prod his reluctant arse for him.'

'True, Mr Rogers, but it does seem that Mr Drinkwater was

specially selected for his discretion in landing this spy fellow. I'd say he'd achieved that with a fair degree of success, wouldn't you?'

'Yes, I suppose . . . hey, what's that going on alongside *Cruizer*?' Rogers whipped the night-glass from its rack and stared hard at the grey shape of the brig half a mile away and partially hidden from them behind *Blanche*. 'By God, she's getting under way!'

Lettsom stared into the gathering darkness and had to confess he could see nothing remarkable.

'There man, are you blind? Damned good surgeon you'll make if you can't see a bloody brig getting under way with her boats alongside.'

'No, I can't see a thing. D'you want me to tell the captain on my way below?'

'Yes, I'd be obliged to you.' Rogers turned away. 'Hey fo'c's'le there! Can't you see anything unusual on the starboard beam. Keep your blasted eyes peeled, God damn it, unless you want a Danish guard-boat coming alongside to piss in your ear while you're asleep up there . . .'

'Aye, aye, sir.' Lettsom heard the aggrieved tone in the response.

In the cabin he told Drinkwater of the news of *Cruizer*.

'Thank you Mr Lettsom, pray take a seat. Will you take a glass and a biscuit with me? I daresay we will know what's amiss tomorrow morning, in the meantime a glass to keep the cold out before turning in would be a good idea, eh?'

'Indeed it would, sir, thank you.'

'Mr Lettsom, I don't care much for doggerel, but I hear that you command a superior talent upon the flute. Would you oblige me with an air?'

'With the greatest of pleasure, Mr Drinkwater. Are you familiar with the work of Lully?'

'No. Pray enlighten me.'

The fleet had moved south from Hven at daybreak. They were now anchored within sight of the roofs and spires of Copenhagen, at the northern end of Copenhagen Road. Another council of war had been held aboard *London* to which the artillery officers were summoned. Quilhampton returned from delivering Tumilty to the flagship with news for Drinkwater.

'*Amazon* and *Cruizer*, sir, they've been forward with the *Lark*, lugger. Lord Nelson's reconnoitred the Danish position, so one of the mids aboard *London* told me.'

Drinkwater nodded. 'Doubtless we'll learn all the details when he returns. I'm obliged to you Mr Q.' Drinkwater reached for the old notebooks of Blackmore and pored over the chart, lost in thought.

The Danish capital of Copenhagen straddled a narrow strait between the easternmost part of Zeeland and the smaller island of Amager. The strait formed the inner harbour and ran through the heart of the city. To the east the sea formed a large open roadstead separated from the main part of The Sound by the low, sandy island of Saltholm which supported little but a few huts and a quantity of marram grass. But the roadstead was deceptive. In addition to the shoals that lined the shores of Amager and Saltholm, which converged at the southern end off Dragør in The Grounds, a large elliptical mud-bank split the roadstead in two. Called the Middle Ground it divided the area into two navigable channels. The westernmost one, which from the British fleet's present anchorage led first towards, and then southwards past Copenhagen, was called the King's Deep. The easternmost which ran due south close to the Saltholm shore, and out of range of the guns at Copenhagen, was known as the Holland Deep.

The problem in attacking Copenhagen would be whether to enter the King's Deep from the north, which might bottle the ships up at the southern end with an unfavourable wind preventing them returning through the Holland Deep, or assembling at the southern end and forcing a passage to the north through the King's Deep when the wind changed.

Drinkwater was suddenly disturbed by the opening of his door and the gleam of gold coins flung across the chart before him. He looked up in astonishment. Tumilty's usually florid face was blue with cold and a large dewdrop depended from his nose. But his expression was one of utter joy.

'There's my stake in the wager, Nat'aniel, and sure it is that I've just as cheerfully parted with another five to Captain Lawson for his superior pyroballogy from the *Zebra*, so I have.'

'And what of *Zebra*, Tom?' asked Drinkwater cautiously.

'Would you believe they've strained the thirteen-inch mortar bed mortal bad! And would you believe that they've sprung a garboard on the reef, and while it ain't what her commander would call serious, what with the hands pumping for an hour a watch, but further concussions of her mortars might let the whole o' the Baltic into her bilge?'

'And *Virago*?' asked Drinkwater rising to pour two glasses of blackstrap.

'Nothing firm yet, Nat'aniel. Flag officer's minds don't leap to decisions with the same facility as that of your humble servant's, but 'tis only a matter of time until expedience itself must recommend *Virago* to fill the breach, an' there's me money as an act of faith.' He lifted the glass to his lips giving one of his heavily conspiratorial winks.

Drinkwater digested the news. 'What did you learn of the plans for the rest of the fleet?'

'Oh, Parker's increased the size of Nelson's detachment by adding *Edgar* and *Ganges*.'

'That makes twelve line of battle ships. D'you think he means Nelson to make the attack?'

Tumilty nodded. 'Certain of it . . . Fremantle is put in charge of those damned flat boats and there are some additional signals. Here, 'tis all in these orders.'

Tumilty tossed the papers onto the table. He added conversationally, '*Isis* lost seven men passing Cronbourg when one of her old guns blew up.' He emptied his glass, helped himself to another and went on, 'Nelson, it seems, went ahead yesterday afternoon in a lugger . . .'

'The *Lark*.'

'Just so; then last night Brisbane took the *Cruizer* and laid a couple of buoys at the north end o' the Holland Deep. D'you know where that is?'

Drinkwater pointed at the charts before him. Tumilty peered over his shoulder. 'Ah, and yesterday Nelson saw the Danes hacking down beacons off Dragør . . .'

'Here, at the southern end of the Channel leading to Copenhagen from the south. If we'd gone by the Great Belt we'd have had to pass the cannon at Dragør and as you see there is less room than through The Sound.'

'Just so, just so . . . apparently the whole operation is now in jeopardy because the beacons and buoys have been removed from the approach channels. There's a line of forts and floating batteries along the waterfront at Copenhagen and they command the approaches from the north or south. In their front lies a shoal . . .'

'Here,' Drinkwater pointed. 'The Middle Ground, between the flats round Saltholm and Copenhagen itself.'

'Nelson wants to attack from the south, waiting for a southerly wind so that he may have a breeze to carry himself north if he's forced to disengage. The position looks formidable enough . . .'

'And if it ain't buoyed . . .' Drinkwater's voice tailed off and a remote look came into his eyes. Then he suddenly slapped his hand down upon the papers.

'God's bones, why the deuce did I not think of it before . . . where the devil's Lord Nelson now?'

'Nelson? Why he's still on the *London*, or perhaps the *Elephant* . . . hey, where are you going?'

Drinkwater flung open his cabin door and shouted 'Have a boat ready for me at once there!' then re-entering the cabin he reached for his cloak, hat and sword.

'I'm off to see Nelson.'

'What about your orders?' Tumilty pointed to the packet lying unopened on the desk.

'Oh damn them! We ain't going anywhere until those channels are buoyed out!'

Nelson's barge was returning alongside *Elephant* as *Virago*'s boat approached. The barge had not left the battleship's side, although the admiral had gone on board by the time the *Virago*'s boat bumped alongside and a tall lieutenant jumped across into the barge, teetered

128

for a second upon a thwart, grabbed a tossed oar for support, and with a muttered 'By your leave,' flung himself at the manropes and scaled the side of the *Elephant*.

Touching his hat to the quarterdeck and announcing himself to the astonished marine sentry at the entry port Drinkwater collared a passing midshipman and looked round. The tail of a posse of officers was disappearing under the poop and Drinkwater guessed they followed Nelson into his cabin.

'His lordship, cully, upon the instant . . .' he growled at the boy.

Nelson was dismissing the entourage of officers, rubbing his forehead and pleading fatigue as Drinkwater pushed through them.

'What is your business, sir?' Drinkwater found himself confronted by a tall man in the uniform of a senior captain. The midshipman had melted away.

'By your leave sir, a word with his lordship . . .'

'What the devil is it, Foley?'

'An officer who requests a word with you.' Foley half turned and Nelson appeared in the doorway of the great cabin.

'My lord, I beg a moment of your time . . .'

Nelson was frowning. 'I know you!'

'I entreat your lordship to permit me to assist in the surveying and buoyage duties attending the fleet's approach to Copenhagen . . .' he felt Foley's hand upon his arm.

'Come sir, this is no time . . .'

'No, wait, Foley.' Nelson's one good eye glittered, though his face was grey with fatigue. 'Let us hear what the lieutenant has to say.'

'I was employed during the last peace in the buoy yachts of the Trinity House . . .'

'The Trinity House has provided us with pilots who do not share your enthusiasm, Mr, er . . .?'

'Drinkwater, my lord. You misunderstand me. These men are from the Trinity House at Hull, unfamiliar with the techniques of buoy-laying. The buoy yachts of the London House are constantly about the matter.'

There was a pause, then Nelson asked: 'Have I not seen you somewhere before, Mr Drinkwater?'

'Aye, my lord, at Syracuse in ninety-eight. I was first of the brig *Hellebore* . . .'

'The *Hellebore*?' Nelson frowned.

'You sent her to the Red Sea to warn Admiral Blankett of French intentions in Egypt.'

'Ah, I recollect. And all to no avail, eh, Mr Drinkwater?' Nelson smiled wearily.

'Not at all, my lord, we destroyed a French squadron and brought home a fine French thirty-eight.'

'Ah . . .' Nelson smiled again, the wide, mobile mouth that betrayed the wild passion of his nature showed too that he was still a man of no great age.

'Mr Drinkwater,' he said after a moment's consideration in the rather high-pitched Norfolk accent that he never attempted to disguise, 'your zeal commends you. What ship are you in?'

'I command the bomb-tender *Virago*, my lord. She has two mortars mounted and an artillery lieutenant as keen to use 'em as myself . . .' he held the admiral's penetrating gaze.

'The ruddy Irishman that was at this morning's conference aboard *London*, eh?'

'The same, my lord.'

'I shall take note of your remarks and employ you and your ship as seems most desirable. I will acquaint Captain Brisbane of the *Cruizer* of your familiarity with the matter now urgently in hand. In the meantime, I must ask you to excuse me, I am most fearfully worn out . . . Foley be a good fellow and see Mr Drinkwater off . . .'

'Thank you, my lord.' Drinkwater withdrew, never having thought to have an admiral ask to be excused, nor such a senior post-captain to escort him to his boat.

'I hope you are able to make good your claims, Mr Drinkwater,' remarked Foley.

'I have no doubt of it, sir.'

'The admiral's condescension is past the tolerable limits of most of us,' the captain added with a touch of irony, handing over the importunate Drinkwater to the officer of the watch.

But Drinkwater ignored the gentle rebuke. He felt the misconstruction placed upon his presence with Lady Parker at Yarmouth was now effaced. He had glimpsed that Nelson touch at Syracuse and now he knew it for what it really was. In contrast with the tradition of self-seeking that had divided and bedevilled fleet operations for generations, Nelson was destined to command men united in purpose, whose loyalty to each other overrode petty considerations of self. They might not triumph before the well-prepared defences of Copenhagen but if they failed they would do so without disgrace. In the last words of Edmund Burke, if die they must, they would die with sword in hand.

'Now gentlemen,' Drinkwater looked round the circle of faces: Rogers, the assembled warrant officers, the red-faced coat of Tumilty, the thin visage of Quilhampton. 'Well gentlemen, we are to split our forces. Mr Tumilty is to continue his preparations with his party under the direct command of Mr Rogers who will assume command of the ship in my absence. The three watches will be taken by Messrs Trussel, Matchett and Willerton who will also attend to those other duties as may from time to time be required of them. Messrs Easton and Quilhampton will provide themselves with the materials on this list and select a boat's crew which is to be adequately wrapped up against the cold. Mr Lettsom, you and Mr Jex will serve additionally to your established duties to second those other officers as they require it, or as Mr Rogers or myself deem it

130

necessary. This is a time for great exertion, gentlemen, I do not expect to have to recall anyone of you to your duty but there will be little rest in the next few days until the matter presently resolved upon is brought to a conclusion. What that conclusion will be rests largely upon the extent of our endeavours. Is that understood?'

There was a chorus of assent. 'Very well, any questions?'

'Aye sir.' It was Matchett, the boatswain.

'Yes?'

'Are we to stand in the line of bombs, sir, as I've heard?' Drinkwater shot a glance at Tumilty whose innocent eyes were studying the deckhead.

'I cannot tell you at present, Mr Matchett.' A murmur of disappointment ran through the little assembly. 'All I can say is that I represented our case to Lord Nelson himself not an hour since . . .'

There was a perceptible brightening of faces. 'That is all, gentlemen.'

'Sir! Beg pardon, sir.'

'Yes, what is it?' Drinkwater turned from the boatswain to Mr Quilhampton.

'For this surveying, sir, the tablet and board . . .'

'Yes?'

'Well, sir, I can hold a pencil in my right hand but . . .' Quilhampton held up the hook that terminated his left arm.

'Damn it, I had clean forgot, accept my apologies, Mr Q . . .' Drinkwater tore his mind off the instructions he was giving to Matchett and rubbed his forehead.

'Why don't 'e see Mr Willerton, sir. Carpenter'd knock him up a timber claw to hold anything, sir.'

'See to it, Mr Q, obliged to you Mr Matchett, now to the matter of these buoys. I want as many nets as you can knock up, about a fathom square, use any old rope junk but the mesh must be small enough to stop a twenty-four pound ball from escaping. Fit the boat up with coils of ten fathoms of three inch rope, enough for as many nets as you make. Then I want some of those deal planks left over from fitting the magazines, you know, the ones that Willerton has been hiding since Chatham, and small stuff sufficient to square lash 'em into a cross. No, damn it we'll nail 'em. Then I want a dozen light spars, boat-hook shafts, spare cannon ramrods, that sort of thing, all fitted with wefts of bunting. Get the duty watch cracking on that lot at once.'

'How many balls to each net, sir?'

'Four'll be too heavy to manhandle over the gunwhale, better make it three.'

'Then we can make the nets a little smaller, sir.'

Drinkwater nodded, 'See to it then.' He turned aft and caught sight of the purser. 'Oh, Mr Jex!'

'Sir?'

'Mr Jex, Mr Tumilty has asked me that it be specially impressed upon you that your party of firemen be adequately trained in the use of pump and hoses. When we go into action their efforts are required throughout the period the mortars are in use.'

'When we go into action sir?' Jex queried uncertainly. 'But I thought that the matter was not yet . . .'

'I hope that we will soon know . . . ah, Mr Willerton are you able to help Mr Q? You have little time . . .'

Drinkwater did not see the pale face of Mr Jex staring with disbelief at his retreating figure.

Half an hour later Drinkwater reported to Brisbane aboard *Cruizer*.

'Now see here, Drinkwater, what we achieved last night in the way of buoying the channel was little enough.' Brisbane leant over the sheet of cartridge paper spread upon the table in *Cruizer*'s cabin. On it the brig's master, William Fothergill, had pencilled in the outline of the islands of Saltholm and Amager. Upon the latter stood the city of Copenhagen. Also drawn in were the approximate limits of the shallow water.

'We are attempting to find out the five fathom line which will gives us ample water for Nelson's squadron. Happily for us the tidal range hereabouts is negligible, although a strong southerly wind will reduce the water on the Middle Ground . . .'

'So I understand, sir.'

'Last night we sounded for the eastern limit of the Holland Deep, here, along the Saltholm shore and laid four buoys . . .'

'What are you using for buoys, sir?'

'Water casks weighted with three double-headed shot, why?'

'With respect, sir, though adequate, the casks may be difficult to see, particularly if the sea is covered with sea-smoke as has been the case the last three mornings. May I suggest planks or short spars lashed or nailed in a cross with a hole drilled for a light pole. Ropes stoppered at the ends of the plants and drawn together to a becket at the base of the pole will afford a securing for the mooring and assist the pole to remain upright. If the pole carries a weft or flag I believe you will find this method satisfactory . . .'

'Damn good idea, sir,' put in Fothergill, 'and if necessary a lantern may be hung from the pole.'

'Quite so.' The three meen straightened up from the chart smiling.

'Very well, Mr Drinkwater, so be it. Now Mr Fothergill is about to ink in what we have done so far and then this chart will go across to Captain Riou aboard *Amazon*. From now on all surveying reports are to be returned to *Amazon* where this chart is to be completed. I understand they have a squad of middies and clerks making copies for all the ships as the information comes in.'

The meeting closed and Drinkwater urged his oarsmen to hurry back to *Virago*. Already his active mind was preparing itself for the coming hours. Away to the southward of them *Amazon* was anchored off Saltholm, together with the *Lark* and the other brig, *Harpy*, and the cutter *Fox*. Boats were out with leadsmen, their cold crews struggling through the floes of ice that reminded them all that further to the eastward the pack was breaking up and every day brought the combination of a Russian fleet closer. Even before they reached *Virago*, *Cruizer* was underway again with Lord Nelson on board to reconnoitre the enemy position.

It was late afternoon on the 31st before Drinkwater and his two boats pulled away from *Virago*'s side. Astern of them each towed the materials for two buoys, dismantled and lashed together so as not to inhibit the efforts of the oarsmen. Each boat was heavily laden with nets of round shot in the bilges, small barricoes of water under the thwarts and each oarsman had his feet on a coil of rope and a cutlass. The oars were double-banked with two spare men huddled in the bow. All, officers and men alike, were muffled in sheepskins and woollen scarves, mittens and assorted headgear. All had had a double ration of spirits before leaving the ship and two kegs of neat rum were stowed under the stern sheets of each boat. Mr Jex had protested at the extravagance but had been quietly over-ruled by Drinkwater.

Quilhampton sat in the stern next to his commander. His new left hand had been hurriedly fashioned from a lump of oak and was able to hold both a tiller and a notebook.

'It's good enough for the present,' Quilhampton had said earlier, and added with a grin, 'and impervious to the cold.'

Drinkwater felt the pressure of the crude hand against his arm as Quilhampton swung the boat to avoid an ice floe. On his own hands he wore fur mitts over a pair of silk stockings. Experiment had shown he could manage a pencil by casting off the mittens on their lanyard, and using his fingers through the stockings.

They headed for *Amazon*, reaching the frigate an hour after sunset, and Drinkwater reported to Captain Edward Riou. Not many years older than Drinkwater himself, Riou had made his reputation ten years earlier when he had saved the *Guardian* after striking an iceberg in the Southern Ocean. His remarkable energy had not deserted him and he had given up command of a battleship to carry out his special duties in the frigate *Amazon*. He fixed his bright, intelligent eyes on Drinkwater as the latter explained his ideas for buoying the edges of the shoals.

'You will find Brisbane has anchored *Cruizer* at the north end of the Middle Ground with lights hoisted as a mark for all the boats out surveying. I have instructed the masters and officers now out sounding to anchor their boats on the five fathom line until relieved by the launches carrying the buoys, but I admit the superiority of your suggestion. In view of your experience then, you should take your boats to the southern end of the Holland Deep and establish the run

133

of the Middle Ground to the southward. It is essential that both limits of the Deep are buoyed out by the morning and, if possible, that its southernmost extension is discovered. Lord Nelson desires to move his squadron south tomorrow and to make his attack upon the Danish line from a position at the southern end of the Middle Ground.'

Virago's two boats lay gunwhale to gunwhale in the darkness. While Quilhampton supervised the issue of rum, Drinkwater gave Easton his final instructions.

'We steer west by compass, Mr Easton, until you find five fathoms, when you are to drop your anchor and show a light. I will pull round you to establish the general trend of the bottom at a distance of sixty or seventy yards. If I am satisfied that we've discovered the edge of the bank I will pull away from you to the south south east until I am approximately a cable southward, then I will turn west and sound for the five fathom line and signal you with three lights when I am anchored. If your bearing has not altered greatly we may reasonably assume the line of the bank to be constant between the two boats. If there is a great change it will show the trend of the bank towards the east or west and we will buoy it. Do you understand?'

'Perfectly sir.'

'Very well, now we will lay a buoy at the first point to determine the starting position, so make ready and take a bearing from *Cruizer* when it is laid.'

'Aye, aye, sir.'

'Very well, let's make a start. Give way, Mr Q.'

The night was bitterly cold and the leadsmen were going to become very wet. The wind remained from the north and the sea, though slight, was vicious enough for the deep boats, sending little patters of freezing spray into their faces so that first they ached intolerably and then they numbed and the men at the oars became automata. Just within sight of each other the two boats pulled west, the boat-compasses on the botton boards lit by lanterns at the officers' feet. Forward the leadsman chanted, his line specially shortened to five fathoms so as not to waste time with greater depths.

Drinkwater kneaded the muscle of his right upper arm which was growing increasingly painful the longer they remained in this cold climate. The knotted fibres of the flesh sent a dull ache through his whole chest as the hours passed and he cursed Edouard Santhonax, the man who had inflicted the wound.

The shout of 'Bottom!' was almost simultaneous from the two boats and Drinkwater nodded for Quilhampton to circle Easton's boat, listening to his leadsman while the splash over the bow of the other boat indicated where Easton got his anchor overboard. Drinkwater picked up the hand-bearing compass. He would need the shaded lantern to read it but they were roughly west of Easton now.

'Five, five, no bottom, five, four, three, shoaling fast, sir!'

'Very well, bring her round to the northward,' he said to Quilhampton, staring at the dark shape of the other boat which had swung to the wind.

'Three, three, four, three, four, three . . .'

'Bring her to starboard again, Mr Q.' The oars knocked rhythmically against the thole pins and spray splashed aboard.

'. . . three, three, four, four, five . . . no bottom sir, no bottom . . .' He looked back at Easton and then at the boat compass. Easton was showing a light now; presumably he had made his notes and could afford to exhibit the guttering lantern on the gunwale.

'Head south, now, Mr Q, pass across his stern so we can hail him.'

'Aye, aye, sir.'

'Everything all right, Mr Easton?'

'Aye, sir. We anchored to the buoy sinker and have almost readied the first buoy . . .' The sound of hammering came from the boat.

'Keep showing your light, Mr Easton. Head south south east, Mr Q, pull for three minutes then turn west.'

Beside him Quilhampton began to whisper, 'One, and two, and three, and four . . .'

Drinkwater kept his eyes on the light aboard Easton's boat. Presently he felt the pressure of the tiller as Quilhampton turned west. He listened to the headsman's chant.

'No bottom, no bottom, no bottom . . . no bottom, five!'

'Holdwater all! Anchor forrard there!'

A splash answered Quilhampton's order, followed by the thrum of hemp over a gunwhale. 'Oars . . . oars across the boat . . .'

The men pulled their looms inboard and bent their heads over their crossed arms. Backs heaved as the monotonous labour ceased for a while. Drinkwater took a bearing of Easton's feeble light and found it to be north by east a half east.

'Issue water and biscuit, Mr Q.' He raised his voice. 'Change places, lads, carefully now, we'll have grog issued when we lay the first buoy. Well done the leadsman. Are you very wet Tregembo?'

'Fucking soaked, zur.' There was a low rumble of laughter round the boat.

'Serves 'ee right for volunteerin',' said an anonymous voice in the darkness and they all laughed again.

'Right, we wait now, for Mr Easton. Give him the three lights Mr Q.'

Quilhampton raised the lantern from the bottom boards and held it up three times, receiving a dousing of Easton's in reply, but then the master's lantern reappeared on the gunwale and nothing seemed to happen for a long time. A restive murmur went round the boat as the perspiration dried on the oarsmen and the cold set in, threatening to cramp ill-nourished and overexerted muscles.

'I daresay he's experiencing some delay in getting the buoy over,' said Drinkwater and, a few moments later, the light went out. Five minutes afterwards Easton was hailing them.

'We tangled with a boat from *Harpy*, sir. He demanded what we were doing in his sector.'

'What did you say?'

'Said we were from *Virago* executing Lord Nelson's orders, he used the password "Westmoreland" to which I replied "Northumberland".'

'Did that satisfy him?'

'Well he said he'd never heard of *Virago*, sir, but Lord Nelson sounded familiar and would we be kind enough to find out how far to the south this damned bank went.'

'Only too happy to oblige . . . sound round me then carry on to the south . . .'

'D'you think the Danes'll attack us, sir?' asked Quilhampton.

'To be frank I don't know; if 'twas the French doing this at Spithead I doubt we would leave 'em unmolested. On the other hand they seem to have made plenty of preparations to receive us and may wish to lull us a little. Still, it would be prudent to keep a sharp lookout, eh?'

'Aye, sir.'

They waited what seemed an age before the three lights were shown from Easton's boat then they continued south, the men stiff with cold and eager to work up some warmth. After sounding round the master's boat they left it astern, the lead plopping overboard as the oars thudded gently against the thole pins.

As the leadsman found the five fathom line the boat was anchored to the net of round shot on its ten fathom line and Drinkwater had the oars brought inboard and stowed while they prepared the buoy. Hauling alongside the four planks and two spars the men pulled them aboard, dripping over their knees, and cast off the lashings.

'Do you make sure the holes in the planks coincide before you nail 'em, Mr Q, or we're in trouble . . .'

They hauled the awkward and heavy planks across the boat in the form of a cross and, holding the lantern up, aligned the holes. Nailing the planks proved more difficult than anticipated since the point at which the hammer struck was unsupported. Eventually the nails were driven home and spunyarn lashings passed to reinforce them.

The four arm bridle was soon fitted and the awkward contraption manoeuvred to take the pole up through its centre. Eventually, as Easton completed pulling round them and set off for the south, they bent their anchor line to the bridle and prepared to cast off.

'Three lights, sir,' reported Quilhampton.

'Yes,' said Drinkwater, holding up his hand compass, 'and I fancy the bank is trending a little to the westward. Very well,' he snapped the compass shut, 'cast off from the buoy!'

He looked astern as they pulled away. The thin line of the spar soon disappeared in the darkness but the weft streamed out just above the horizon against the slightly lighter sky.

They laboured on throughout the small hours of the night,

celebrating their success from time to time in two-finger grog. The trend to the east did not develop although Easton laid a second buoy before the bank swung southward again.

Drinkwater's boat was on its fifth run towards the west and already the sky was lightening in the east when Drinkwater realised something was wrong.

'Oars!' he commanded and the men ceased pulling, their oars coming up to the horizontal. He bent over the little compass and compared its findings with the steering compass in the bottom of the boat. Easton's boat was well on the starboard quarter. Ahead of them he thought he could see the low coast of Amager emerging from the darkness, but he could not be sure. The boat slewed as an ice floe nudged it.

'I believe we've overshot the bank, Mr Q. Turn north, and keep the lead going forrard there!'

'Aye, aye, zur!'

As the daylight grew it became clear that they had misjudged their distance from Easton and over-run the tail of the bank for some distance, but after an anxious fifteen minutes Tregembo found the bottom.

As they struggled to get their second buoy over, Easton came up to them.

'Don't bother to sound round me, Mr Easton, this is the tail of the bank all right.'

'Well done, sir.'

'And to you and your boat. You may transfer aboard here, Mr Easton, with your findings. Mr Q you will take Mr Easton's boat back to the ship.'

'Aye, aye, sir.'

'Buoy's ready, zur.'

'Very well, hold on to it there . . .' The boats bumped together and Easton and Quilhampton exchanged places. 'A rum issue before we part, eh?'

The men managed a thin cheer and in the growing light Drinkwater saw the raw faces and sunken eyes of his two boats' crews. The wind was still fresh from the north west and it would be a hard pull to windward for them. A heavy ice floe bumped the side of the boat. 'Bear it off Cottrell!'

There was no move from forward. 'Cottrell! D'you hear man?'

'Beg pardon, sir, but Cottrell's dead sir.'

'Dead?' Drinkwater stood up and pushed his way forward, suddenly realising how chilled and cramped his muscles had become through squatting over his lantern, chart and compasses. He nearly fell overboard and only saved himself by catching hold of a man's shoulder. It was Cottrell's and he lolled sideways like a log. His face was covered by a thin sheen of ice crystals and his eyes stared accusingly out at Drinkwater.

'Get him in the bottom.' Drinkwater stumbled aft again and sat down.

'Can't sir, he's stiff as a board.'

Drinkwater swore beneath his breath. 'Shall I pitch 'im overboard sir?'

He had not liked to give such an order himself. 'Aye,' he replied, 'Poor old Jack . . . We have no alternative, lads.'

'He weren't a bad old sod, were 'e?'

There was a splash from forward. The body rolled over once and disappeared. A silence hung over the boat and Quilhampton asked 'Permission to proceed sir?'

'Carry on, Mr Q.'

'Zur!' Tregembo's whisper was harsh and urgent.

'What the devil is it?'

'Thought I saw a boat over there!'

Tregembo pointed north west, in the direction of Copenhagen. Drinkwater stood unsteadily. He could see a big launch pulling to the southward. It might be British but it might also be Danish. He thought of recalling Mr Quilhampton who was already pulling away from them but if the strange boat had not yet seen them he did not wish to risk discovery of the buoy that marked so important a point as the south end of the Middle Ground. Perhaps they could remove the weft, the bare pole would be much more difficult to see . . .

He rejected the idea, knowing the difficulty of relocating the bank and the buoy themselves, particularly in circumstances other than they had enjoyed tonight.

In the end he decided on a bold measure. 'Let go the buoy!'

He grabbed the tiller and leaned forward to peer in the compass. 'Give way together!' He swung the boat to the north west.

Heading directly for Copenhagen they could scarcely avoid being seen from the big launch. It was vital that observers in the approaching launch did not see the spar-buoy at the southern end of the Middle Ground.

The men were tired now and pulling into the wind after labouring at the oars all night was too much for them. Adding to their fatigue was a concentration of ice floes that made their progress more difficult still. After a few minutes it was obvious that they had been seen from the launch. Drinkwater swung the boat away to the north east, across the Middle Ground, drawing the pursuing launch away from the southernmost buoy. From time to time he looked grimly over his shoulder. He closed his mind to the ironic ignominy of capture and urged the oarsmen to greater efforts. But they could see the pursuing launch and knew they were beaten.

'Hang on, sir, that's one of them damned flat boats!'

'Eh?' Drinkwater turned again, numb with the cold and the efforts of the night. He could see the boat clearly now.

'Boat 'hoy! "Spencer"!' Drinkwater cudgelled his brain for the countersign given him by Riou.

138

' "Jervis"!' he called, then, turning to the boat's crew, 'Oars!' The men rested.

The big boat came up, pulled by forty seamen who had clearly not spent the night wrestling with leadlines and ice floes.

'What ship?' A tall lieutenant stood in her stern.

'*Virago*, Lieutenant Drinkwater in command.'

'Good morning, Lieutenant, my name's Davies, off to reconnoitre the guns at Dragør. There's a lot of you fellows out among the ice. Did you take us for a Dane?'

'Aye.'

'Ah, well, sir, 'tis All Fool's day today . . . Good morning to you.'

The big boat turned away. 'Well I'm damned!' said Drinkwater and, as if to further confound him the wind began to back to the westward. 'Well I'm damned,' he repeated. 'Give way, lads, it's time for breakfast.'

Chapter Sixteen 1 April 1801

All Fool's Day

Drinkwater's tired oarsmen pulled alongside *Amazon* as the frigate got under way. Riou complied with Drinkwater's request that his boat be allowed to return to *Virago* under the master and that he remain on board to give his findings to Fothergill.

Before passing off the quarterdeck into the cabin where Fothergill and other weary officers were collating information, Riou asked, 'How far south did you get, Mr Drinkwater?'

'I found the southern end of the bank, sir, and marked it with a spar buoy.'

'Excellent. I have recalled *Cruizer* as you see. Lord Nelson joins us and we are taking *Harpy*, *Lark* and *Fox* through the Holland Deep . . .'

'Sir . . .' A midshipman interrupted them. 'Begging your pardon, sir, but Lord Nelson's barge is close, sir . . .'

'Excuse me . . .' Drinkwater went aft as Riou stepped to meet the vice-admiral at the entry. He was soon lost in a mass of plotting and checking, working alongside Fothergill as the findings of the night were carefully laid on the master chart. For an hour they worked in total concentration as *Amazon* made her way southwards. When they emerged on the quarterdeck to take a breath of air they both looked astern. A master's mate came up to Fothergill to brief him as to what had been going on.

'*Cruizer*'s reanchored off the north end of the Middle Ground with *Harpy* a mile south and *Lark* a further mile to the south of her.'

'The admiral don't trust our buoys, eh?' smiled Fothergill, exhausted beyond protest.

'Don't trust the fleet not to see 'em or run 'em down, more likely.'

'The mark vessels are to hoist signals to indicate they are to be passed to starboard,' offered the master's mate helpfully.

Drinkwater heard his name called by Captain Riou. 'Sir?'

The admiral smiled. 'Morning, Drinkwater. I understand you found the end of the Middle Ground.' Nelson crossed the deck just as it canted wildly. The vice-admiral fell against Drinkwater who caught him, surprised at the frail lightness of his body.

Amazon had approached too closely to the Saltholm shore to avoid the occasional ranging shot ricochetting from the Danish batteries two miles away, and while Riou resolutely set more canvas and pressed the frigate over the mud, Nelson turned to a group of unhappy looking men in plain coats who Drinkwater realised were the pilots from the Trinity House at Hull. He remembered Nelson's poor opinion of their enthusiasm.

'There gentlemen,' he quipped, 'a practical demonstration of the necessity of holding to the channel.' The admiral turned again to Drinkwater, calmly ignoring Riou's predicament of getting *Amazon* into deeper water.

'The southern end of the shoal Mr Drinkwater . . .?'

'Marked, my lord, with a spar buoy.'

'Good.' The admiral paused then turned to a group of officers all heavily bedecked with epaulettes. 'Admiral Graves, Captains Dommett and Otway, may I present Mr Drinkwater, gentlemen, Lieutenant commanding the bomb *Virago*.'

Drinkwater managed a stiff bow.

'Mr Drinkwater has laid a spar buoy on the south Middle Ground . . .' There was a murmur of appreciation that was without condescension.

'Will a spar buoy be sufficient, my lord? If the division is to use it as a mark for anchoring may I suggest a more substantial mark.' It was Rear Admiral Graves and Dommett nodded.

'I concur with Admiral Graves, my lord.'

Nelson turned to the remaining captain. 'Otway?'

'Yes, my lord, I agree.'

'By your leave, my lord . . .'

'Yes, Drinkwater, what is it?'

'There is great movement of ice coming down from the south east, I observed the spar buoys were merely spun by the floes whereas I fear a larger object like a boat . . .'

'Oh, I doubt that, Drinkwater,' put in Captain Otway, 'a boat is a more substantial body with a stem to deflect the floes, no a boat, my lord, with a mast and flag . . .'

'And a lantern,' added Graves.

Drinkwater flushed as Nelson confirmed the opinion. 'Very well then, a boat it shall be. Don't be discouraged Mr Drinkwater, your exertions have justified you in my opinion, and Captain Dommett will write you orders to have your bomb vessel in the line when we attack the Danes.'

'Thank you, my lord.'

'And now will you be so kind as to direct Fothergill that when he returns to *Cruizer* he is to have one of the brig's boats placed in accordance with our decision.'

Drinkwater slept in a chair in *Amazon*'s wardroom as the frigate reached the en ' of the Holland Deep, sighted his spar buoy and turned north to order *Fox* anchored south of *Lark*. Nelson had concluded there was ample room to anchor his division off the southern end of the Middle Ground out of range of the Danish guns. The wind had veered again and *Amazon* had to beat laboriously back

141

through the Holland Deep to report to Sir Hyde Parker. This delay enabled Drinkwater to sleep off most of his exhaustion.

He was pulled back to *Virago* with Fothergill who handed him his copy of the chart before leaving for *Cruizer* and his own trip south to replace Drinkwater's buoy.

'The cartography isn't up to your own standard, Mr Drinkwater, but it'll serve.'

Drinkwater unrolled the corner of the chart. 'A midshipman's penmanship if I ain't mistaken,' he grinned at Fothergill. 'Your servant, Mr Fothergill . . .' Reaching up for the manropes he hauled himself up *Virago*'s side, the chart rolled in his breast.

'Welcome back, sir,' said Rogers.

'Thank you. Where's Mr Tumilty?'

'Here, sir, here I am Nat'aniel . . .'

'I owe you five guineas, Tom . . .'

'You do? By Jesus, what did I tell 'ee, Mr Rogers, that's five from you too . . .' Tumilty burst into a fit of gleeful laughter. 'An' it's All Fool's Day so it is.'

'All ready, Mr Drinkwater?' Drinkwater leaned over the rail to look down at Nelson in his barge. He was an unimpressive sight, his squared cocked hat at a slouch and an old checked overcoat round his thin shoulders.

'We await only your signal to weigh, my lord.'

'Very good. Instruct that Irish devil to make every shot tell.'

'Aye, aye, my lord.' Nelson nodded to his coxswain and the barge passed to the next ship in his division.

An hour later the greater part of the British force placed under Lord Nelson's orders stood to the southward, leaving the two three deckers, *St George* and *London*, four seventy-fours and two sixty-fours with Sir Hyde Parker at their anchorage at the north end of the Middle Ground. Passing slowly south under easy sail between the lines of improvised buoys and the anchored warning vessels Drinkwater was able to steady his glass on the horizon to the westward.

Preoccupation with other matters had not given him leisure to study the object of all their efforts, the city of Copenhagen. Above its low stretch of roofs the bulk of the Amalienbourg Palace was conspicuous. So were several fantastic and exotic spires. That of Our Saviour's church had a tall elongated spire with an exterior staircase mounting its side, while that of the Børsen was equally tall and entwined by four huge serpents.

But in the foreground the fortress of Trekroner, the Three Crowns, and the batteries of the Lynetten that lay before them, guarded the approaches to the city and combined with the line of blockships, cut down battleships, floating batteries, frigates and gun vessels to form a formidable defensive barrier. The enemy was only a little over two miles away, just out of range, though an occa-

142

sional shot was fired at the British as they boldly crossed the Danish front.

Nelson made few signals to his ships. At half past five he ordered the *Ardent* and *Agamemnon* to take the guard duty for the night and shortly after eight in the evening, the wind falling light and finally calm, the last ship came to her anchor in the crowded road. This was *Cruizer*, withdrawn from her station as a mark vessel.

As *Virago* came to her own anchor at about six-fifteen, Nelson made the signal for the night's password.

'Spanish jack over a red pendant. What does that signify, Mr Q?'

'Er . . . "Winchester", sir.'

'Very well. Pass word I want all the officers to dine with me this evening within the hour. I anticipate further work later in the night.'

'Aye, aye, sir.' It would scarcely be a 'dinner' since the galley stove was now extinguished and Tumilty and Trussel had begun to make their preparations for action, but Jex could hustle up something and Drinkwater wished to speak to them all.

He looked down into the waist in the gathering dusk. A party of artillerymen under the bombardier, Hite, were scouring the chamber of the after mortar to remove any scale. He wondered how the soldiers had got on between decks for there was little enough room for them all. They had slung their hammocks in the cable tier and he did not think either Tumilty or Rogers had spared much effort on their welfare.

At eight, just as *Virago*'s officers sat down to dinner, shells were reported coming over from howitzer batteries ashore, but the activity soon died away. Mr Quilhampton, shivering on the poop and excluded from the meal, recorded in *Virago*'s log various signals passed from the *Elephant* by guard boat and rocket. Mostly the signals concerned the direction of boats from the brigs and gun vessels as the admiral made his final dispositions. The bomb vessels were left largely alone.

But it was not for long. While Mr Tumilty was expatiating on the forthcoming employment of his beloved mortars, Mr Quilhampton had his revenge for missing dinner.

'Beg pardon, sir, but a boat's alongside from the flagship. His lordship's compliments and would you be kind enough to attend him at once.'

Drinkwater stood. 'It seems you must excuse me gentlemen. Please do not disturb yourselves on my account, but I would recommend that you rested. There is likely to be warm work for us tomorrow.' A cheer went up at this and only Jex remained silent as Quilhampton added:

'It is exceeding cold, sir . . .'

'I think I can manage, Mr Q, thank you,' Drinkwater replied drily.

Drinkwater scrambled down into the waiting boat. In his pocket he had stuffed notebook, pencil and bearing compass. As he settled alongside the unknown midshipman he observed the truth of Mr Quilhampton's solicitude. It was bitterly cold and the ice floes were even more numerous than they had been previously. The current, too, was strong, sweeping them northwards towards The Sound. The wind had died away to a dead calm. Above the surface of the sea the low wisps of arctic 'sea-smoke' almost hid the boat itself, though it was clear at eye level.

They crossed *Elephant*'s stern. The windows were a blaze of light with the shadows of movement visible within.

'Admiral's dining with the captains of the fleet, sir,' explained the midshipman, swinging the boat under the two-decker's quarter and alongside her larboard entry.

Drinkwater reported to the officer of the watch who conducted him to the ante-room. A number of officers were gathered there, mostly wearing the plain blue coats of sailing masters. There was a group of pilots who looked more worried than when Drinkwater had last seen them. From beyond the doors leading into the *Elephant*'s great cabin came the noise of conviviality.

A man in lieutenant's uniform detached himself from a small knot of masters and came over to Drinkwater with his hand extended.

'Evening. John Quilliam, third of *Amazon*.'

'Evenin'. Nathaniel Drinkwater, in command of *Virago*.' They shook hands.

'Captain Riou spoke highly of you after your visit to *Amazon* the other day.'

Drinkwater blushed. 'That was exceedingly kind of him.' He changed the subject. 'I trust your frigate was not damaged by the grounding?'

'I imagine she may have lost a little copper, but she'll do for today's work . . .' Quilliam smiled as a burst of cheering came from the adjacent room.

'Take no notice of that, Drinkwater, his lordship'll not let it interfere with tonight's business.'

'Which is . . .?'

'There is a little dispute about the water in the King's Deep. The pilots incline to the view that it is deeper on the Middle Ground side. Briarly, master of the *Bellona*, opposes their view, while Captain Hardy and Captain Riou are undecided. The Admiral has two boats assembled, one for Briarly and myself, the other for Hardy and you . . .'

'Me?'

Quilliam smiled again but any explanation as to why Drinkwater had been specially selected was lost as the double doors of the cabin were opened by an immaculate, pig-tailed messman and a glittering assembly of gold-laced officers emerged. They were all smiling and shaking hands, having dined well and in expectation of lean commons on the morrow. Drinkwater recognised Admiral Graves and Captain Foley, familiar too was 'Bounty' Bligh of the *Glatton*,

Edward Riou and George Murray of the *Edgar*, but the remainder were largely unknown to him. At the rear of the group the short, one-armed admiral, his breast ablaze with orders and crossed by the red ribbon of the Bath, had his left hand on the elbow of a tall post-captain who ducked instinctively beneath the deckhead beams.

'Ah, Quilliam,' said his lordship, catching sight of the two lieutenants, 'is all made ready?'

'Aye, my lord.'

'And you have briefed Lieutenant Drinkwater?' Quilliam nodded. 'Very good. Captain Hardy, I commend these two officers to you and I rely upon you to find out the truth of the matter.'

'Very well, my lord,' the tall captain growled and turned to the two lieutenants. 'Come gentlemen . . . Mr Briarly, let us make a start.'

They climbed down into the boats and were about to leave *Elephant*'s side when Nelson's high-pitched voice called down to them.

'Are your oars muffled?'

'Yes my lord.'

'Very well. Should the Danish guard boat discover you, you must pull like devils, and get out of his way as fast as you can.'

There was a murmur of enthusiastic assent from the seamen at the oars.

'Good luck then.'

Hardy, captain of the *St George* anchored eight miles to the north, had brought his own boat. A bright young midshipman leant against the tiller. He was muffled in an expensive bearskin coat provided by an indulgent parent well acquainted with the fleet's destination weeks earlier.

'I've had a long pole prepared for sounding, Mr Drinkwater, it'll make less noise than a lead.'

'Aye, aye, sir.'

Drinkwater wondered how close to the enemy they were to go that they needed to take such a precaution. They pulled in silence for a few minutes and Drinkwater noted their course by the light of the shaded lantern on the bottom boards.

'This north-going current is damned strong . . .'

'About two knots, sir.'

'Did you lay the mark on the south end of the Middle Ground?'

'Yes, sir. I laid a buoy on it and Lord Nelson ordered the buoy substituted by a boat.'

'Let us hope we can find it in the dark.'

They did find it. After half an hour of pulling east and then west after finding five fathoms, they discovered the set of the current was considerable and had misled them. But, having established the bearing of the moored boat from the admiral's lights hung in *Elephant*'s rigging, they began to move away.

145

'May I suggest we pull round the mark boat, sir, in order to establish that it has not substantially dragged and still marks the south end of the shoal.'

Hardy grunted approval and Drinkwater directed the midshipman while a man dipped the long pole overboard like a quant and peered at the black and white markings painted on it.

'It seems to be holding sir. I was worried because I only laid moorings for a spar buoy. I think Mr Fothergill must have laid a proper anchor.'

''Tis no matter, Mr Drinkwater. Time in reconnaissance is seldom wasted.'

They pulled west, losing the edge of the bank and swinging across the King's Channel that ran north, parallel to the Amager shore, the waterfront of Copenhagen and the defensive line of the Danish guns. The water deepened rapidly and the call came back that there was 'No bottom' until it gradually began to shoal on the Amager side.

Hardy swung the boat to the north while a man forward with a boat hook shoved the ice aside and the oarsmen struggled to pull rhythmically despite the floes that constantly impeded their efforts.

'There seems to be between six and eight fathoms in the main channel, sir,' Drinkwater said in a low voice after crouching in the boat's bottom and consulting his notebook. He was by no means certain of their exact position, but his line of bearing from *Elephant* was still reasonably accurate. 'The Middle Ground seems to be steep-to, with gentler shoaling on the Amager shore.'

Hardy leaned over his shoulder and nodded. 'Now I think you had better shutter that lantern and wrap canvas round it . . . not a word now, you men. Pull with short easy strokes and let the current do the work . . . Mr Fancourt . . .' Hardy pointed to larboard and the midshipman nodded. Drinkwater looked up and it took some minutes for his eyes to adjust again after the yellow lamplight.

Then he saw the enemy, dark, huge and menacing ahead of them. The southernmost ship of the Danish line was an old battleship. The spars that reared into the night sky showed that she had been cut down and was not rigged to sail, but two tiers of gun ports could just be made out and she was moored head and stern to chains.

Perfect silence reigned, broken only by the occasional plash and dribble as Hardy himself wielded the sounding pole. They could hear voices that spoke in a totally unfamiliar tongue, but they were not discovered. They were so close as they sounded round the enemy vessel that they thought there must have been times when the upper end of the pole appeared above the enemy's rail.

Greatly daring, Hardy pulled once more across the channel while Drinkwater scribbled the soundings down blind, hoping he could sort out his notes later. Satisfied at last, Hardy turned to the midshipman.

'Very well, Mr Fancourt, you may rejoin the admiral.'

* * *

Six bells rang out on *Elephant*'s fo'c's'le and the sentries were crying 'All's well!' as Hardy's boat returned alongside. Drinkwater followed Hardy under the poop and into the brilliantly lit great cabin. Briarly and Quilliam had returned ahead of them. Clustered round the master-chart that now carried much greater detail than when Drinkwater had last seen it were Nelson, Riou and Foley.

Nelson looked up. 'Ah, Hardy, you are back . . . Mr Briarly, oblige these two with a glass . . . right, what have you for us, Hardy?'

Drinkwater slopped the rum that Briarly handed him. He was shaking from the cold and though the cabin was not excessively warm, the candles seemed to make it very hot after the hours spent in the boat. He swallowed the rum gratefully and slowly mastered his shivering. There was clearly a dispute going on over the comparative depths.

'Call the pilots,' said Nelson at length. After a delay the elderly men entered the cabin. They too had dined and drunk well and spoke in thick Yorkshire accents. Drinkwater listened to the debate in progress round the chart-table. He helped himself to a second glass of rum and began to feel better, the alcohol numbing the ache in his arm. At last Nelson suppressed further argument.

'Gentlemen, gentlemen, it seems that the greater depth of water is to be found on the Middle Ground side of the King's Deep, yet, if what Captain Hardy says holds good for the length of the Channel, some danger will attend holding too strictly to that assertion, for the rapid shoaling on that side will give little warning of the proximity of the bank. Foley, we must include some such reference in the orders. Masters must pay attention to the matter and remark the leadsmen's calls with great diligence. I see little risk to the fleet if this injunction is remembered. Mr Drinkwater's buoy at the southern end of the Middle Ground is the keystone to the enterprise. Gentlemen I wish you good night . . .'

Drinkwater returned to *Virago* in a borrowed boat. His mind was woolly with fatigue and Nelson's rum. But the ache in his arm had almost gone, together with his worries over Nelson's opinion of him.

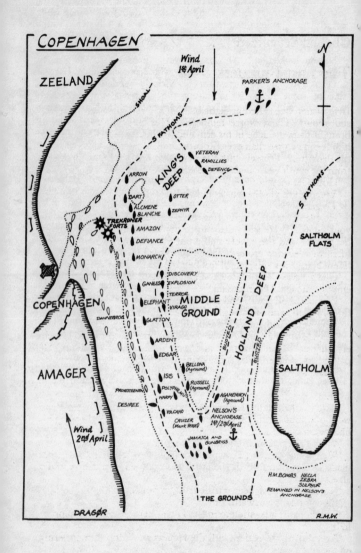

The Last Blunders

Drinkwater was called at eight bells in the middle watch. He was sour-mouthed and worse tempered. The chill in his cabin had brought back the ache in his arm and the insufficient sleep had left him feeling worse than ever. Rogers came in, having just taken over the deck from Trussel, with the news that the wind had sprung up from the south east. 'It seems our luck has changed at last, sir.'

'Huh! Get me hot water . . .'

'Tregembo's got the matter in hand . . .'

'Tregembo?'

'He spent yesterday sponging your best uniform and sharpening your sword. There was a deal of activity last night. *Blanche* dragged her anchor and there were numerous boats pulling about.' Rogers lifted the decanter from its fiddle and poured a generous measure. 'Here Nat, drink this, you'll feel better.' He held out the glass.

'God's bones!' Drinkwater shuddered as the raw spirit hit his empty stomach. 'Thanks Sam.'

'I've called all hands and got the galley stove fired up to fill 'em full of burgoo and molasses for ballast.'

'Very good. Did you enjoy your dinner?'

'Yes, thank you. Old Lettsom trilled us some jolly airs and Matchett sung us "Tom Bowling" and some other stuff by Dibdin.' He paused and seemed to be considering something.

'What is it?'

'Jex, sir . . .'

'Oh?'

'Acted rather oddly. Left us abruptly in the middle of dinner and we found him sitting on the bowsprit, tight as a tick and crying his bloody eyes out.'

'What time was this? Did any of the men see?'

'Well some did, sir. It happened about ten last night. Lettsom made us put him to bed, though I was inclined to put him under arrest . . .'

'No, no. You have been a trifle hard on him, Sam.'

'Bloody man's a coward, sir . . .'

'That's a stiff allegation to make. D'you have evidence to support it?'

'Aye, during the action with the luggers we found him cowering on the spare sails.'

'Why didn't you report him then?' asked Drinkwater sharply, getting up. Rogers was silent for a moment.

'Saw no point in bothering you . . .'

'Kept damned silent for your own purposes, more like it,' Drinkwater suddenly blazed. 'Jex is the worst kind of purser, Sam, but I had the measure of the man and now you have goaded him to this extreme . . .' Drinkwater fell silent as Tregembo knocked and entered the cabin. He brought a huge bowl of steaming hot water and put it down on the cabin chest, then he bustled about, laying out Drinkwater's best uniform and clean undergarments.

'You're worse than a bloody wife, Tregembo,' said Drinkwater partially recovering his good temper as the rum spread through him.

'Very well, Mr Rogers,' he said at last, 'let us forget the matter. As long as he stands to his station today we'll say no more about any aspect of it.'

'Aye, aye, sir,' replied Rogers woodenly, leaving the cabin.

After Tregembo had left Drinkwater stripped himself, decanted a little water with which to shave then lifted the bowl of water onto the deck. For a few shuddering moments he immersed as much of himself as he could, dabbing half-heartedly with a bar of soap and drying himself quickly. Bathing and putting on clean underwear was chiefly to reduce infection of any wounds he might suffer but, in fact, it raised his morale and when he stepped on deck in the dawn, his boat cloak over two shirts and his best coat, he had forgotten the labours of the night.

He paced the poop in the growing light, looking up occasionally at the masthead pendant to check the wind had not shifted. He could scarcely believe that after all the delays, disappointments and hardships, the wind that had played them so foul for so long should actually swing into the required quarter as if on cue.

Tregembo approached him with a crestfallen look. 'Mr Drinkwater, zur.'

'Eh? What is it Tregembo?'

'Your sword, zur, you forgot your sword.'

'Ah . . . er, yes, I'm sorry, and thank you for attending to it yesterday.'

Tregembo grunted and handed the weapon over. Drinkwater took it. The leather scabbard was badly worn, the brass ferrule at the end scratched. The stitching of the scabbard was missing at one point and the rings were almost worn through where they fastened to the sling. He half drew the blade. The wicked, thin steel glinted dully, the brass hilt was notched and scored where it had guarded off more than a few blows and the heavy pommel, that counterbalanced the blade and made the weapon such a joy to handle, reminded him of a slithering fight on the deck of a French lugger when he had consigned a man to oblivion with its weight. The thought of that unknown Frenchman's murder made him think of Edward and he looked at the horizon to the north west, where the spires of

150

Copenhagen were emerging from the night. He could see the line of the Danish ships, even pick out the tiny points of colour where their red ensigns already fluttered above the batteries. He buckled on the sword.

A feeling that something was wrong entered his head and it was some time before he detected its cause. The boat marking the southern end of the Middle Ground was missing.

It was clear Nelson had not slept. Drinkwater learned afterwards that he had laid down in his cot and spent the night dictating. He reported the missing mark only to hear that Nelson had already been informed and had sent for Brisbane to move *Cruizer* onto the spot and anchor there as a mark.

'Thanks to you and Hardy we have the bearing from *Elephant* so Brisbane should have no very great trouble.'

'Yes, my lord.'

'Come, Drinkwater, help yourself to some coffee from the sideboard there . . .'

'Thank you, my lord.'

'There should be something to eat, I shall be sending for all captains shortly so you may as well wait. Ah Foley . . .' Drinkwater did as he was bid, breakfasted and tried not to eavesdrop on Nelson's complex conversations with a variety of officers, secretaries and messengers who seemed to come into the cabin in an endless procession.

At seven o'clock every commander in Nelson's division had assembled on board the *Elephant*. Among the blue coats the scarlet of Colonel Stewart and Lieutenant-Colonel Brock commanding the detachment of the 49th Foot made a bright splash of colour, while the dull rifle-green of Captain Beckwith's uniform reflected a grimmer aspect of war.

Apart from the council aboard the flagship the British fleet seethed with activity. Drinkwater had little choice but to trust to the energies of Rogers and Tumilty in preparing the *Virago* for action, but he was learning that as a commander in such a complex operation as that intended by Nelson, it was more important to comprehend his admiral's intentions. Boats swarmed about the ships. On the decks of the battleships red-coated infantrymen drilled under their sergeants and were inspected by the indolent subalterns. Mates and lieutenants manoeuvred the big flat-boats into station while on every ship the chain slings were passed round the yards, the bulkheads knocked down, the boats not already in the water got outboard and towed astern, the nettings rigged and the decks sanded. Officers frequently glanced up at the masthead to see if the wind still held favourable.

Nelson explained his intended tactics by first describing the Danish line of defence:

'The enemy has eighteen vessels along the western side of the King's Deep. They mount some seven hundred guns of which over half are estimated to be above twenty-four pounds calibre. At the northern end, the line is supported by the Trekroner Forts. It is also supported by shore batteries like the Lynetten . . .' Each officer bent over his copy of the chart and made notes. Nelson went on, '. . . the force of the batteries is thought to be considerable and may include furnaces for heating shot. The Trekroner also appears to be supported by two additional heavy blockships.

'The channel into the port, dockyard and arsenal lies behind the Trekroner Forts and joins with the King's Channel just north of the forts. It is thought to be closed by a chain boom and is covered by enfilading fire from batteries on the land. Other ships, a seventy-four, a heavy frigate and some brigs and smaller vessels are anchored on this line.

'Batteries are also mounted on Amager, supporting the southern end of the line. In all the Danish defences extend four miles.'

The admiral paused and sipped from a glass of water. Drinkwater thought his face looked grey with worry but a fierce light darted from his one good eye and he watched the expressions of his captains as if seeking a weakness. He cleared his throat and went on.

'Each of you will receive written orders as to your station in the action from my secretary as you leave. These are as concise as possible and written on card for ease of handling. However it is my intention to explain the general plan to avoid needless confusion.

'As you have already been made aware, all the line of battleships are to have their anchors ready for letting go by the stern. They will anchor immediately upon coming abreast of their alloted target. *Edgar* will lead with Mr Briarly temporarily serving in her. Fire may be opened at your discretion. Captain Riou in *Amazon* is to take *Blanche*, *Alcmène*, *Arrow* and *Dart* and co-operate with the van in silencing the guns commanding the harbour mouth, or as other circumstances might require. The bomb vessels will take station outside the line of battleships and throw their shells into the dockyard and arsenal. Captain Rose in the *Jamaica*, frigate, is to take the gun-brigs into position for raking the line at its southern end, thus discouraging reinforcement of the floating batteries from the shore. Captain Inman in *Désirée* will also take up this station. Captain Fremantle with five hundred seamen will concert his action with Colonel Stewart and the 49th Regiment to embark in the flat-boats and storm the Trekroner Forts as soon as their fire is silenced.' Nelson looked round the assembly. 'It looks formidable to those who are children at war,' he said smiling inspiringly, 'but to my judgement, with ten sail of the line I think I can annihilate them.' There was a murmur of agreement. 'That is all. Are there any questions? Very well then. To your posts, gentlemen, and success to His Majesty's Arms.'

The captains, commanders and lieutenants-in-command filed out, collecting their written instructions as directed and Drinkwater, looking for his boat among the throng of craft pressing alongside *Elephant*'s flanks, found himself button-holed by Mr Briarly of the *Bellona*.

'Hold hard, sir. I ask you for your support for a moment. Lord Nelson has sent for masters and these damned pilots. They are still arguing about the approach to the King's Deep. You know Fothergill's boat is missing this morning?'

'Aye, it must have been driven off station by an ice floe, I warned . . .'

Briarly nodded. 'I heard,' he broke in impatiently, 'Look, Mr Drinkwater, you seem to have the admiral's ear, can you not persuade him that although there may be greater water on the Middle Ground side it is so steep-to that a small miscalculation . . .'

'Mr Briarly, his lordship has appointed you to lead the fleet in *Edgar*, surely the rest will follow.' Drinkwater was getting anxious about preparations aboard *Virago*.

'I was out this morning at first light, if each ship steers with . . .' he pointed out some conspicuous marks to Drinkwater which ensured a lead through the King's Deep.

'Are you certain of that?'

'Positive.'

'And will tell the admiral so?' Briarly nodded. 'Then I am certain you will carry the day, Mr Briarly. I am sure you do not need my assistance and I beg you let me return to my ship . . .'

'Morning, Drinkwater.' Drinkwater turned to find Martin at his other elbow.

'Good morning sir,' Drinkwater said absently, fishing in his pocket and remembering he had left his pocket compass in his greygoe. He would have liked to check the bearing of *Cruizer* to ensure Brisbane had anchored her in the correct place. Briarly had already gone to try and brow-beat the pilots.

'You are to be in the battle, Drinkwater,' said Martin, 'thanks to my good offices.'

'Yours sir?' Drinkwater looked up in astonishment. Martin nodded.

'I put in a good word for you the other day when I attended Lord Nelson.'

Drinkwater choked back an insubordinate laugh. 'Ah . . . I see . . . er, I'm greatly obliged to you sir.' And then he added with irresistible impishness, 'I shall inform Lord Dungarth of my obligation to you.'

Martin further astonished him by failing to see the implied sarcasm. 'I'd be vastly pleased if you would my dear fellow, vastly pleased.'

It was only when he was being pulled back to *Virago* that he remembered he had failed to take a bearing of the *Cruizer* from the *Elephant*.

'The admiral's just hoisted Number 14, sir,' reported Rogers as Drinkwater returned once again to *Virago*. ' "Prepare for battle and for anchoring with springs on the anchors and the end of the sheet cable taken in at the stern port." '

'Very well.'

'The ship is cleared for action, sir.'

'Very well, I shall make my rounds now. Mr Easton! Mr Easton be so good as to attend the flagship's signals. Here,' he handed his instruction card to the master, 'Study that. I do not anticipate weighing until after the line of battle ships.'

Drinkwater led the way below with Rogers following. In the cabin space the bulkheads had been hinged up so that the after carronades and stern chasers could be fired if necessary. 'Only the gun captains and powder monkeys to remain with these guns, Mr Rogers. All other men to be mustered on deck as sailtrimmers, firemen or for Mr Tumilty's shell hoists . . .'

'Aye, aye, sir.'

Drinkwater looked at the place where his table had so long stood. Beneath it the previously locked hatch to the magazine had been removed. An artillery private armed with a short fusil stood guard over it.

'Mr Trussel and Bombardier Hite are below, sir. The felt curtains are well doused and Mr Tumilty is satisfied.'

Two men emerged carrying a box each. 'Mr Willerton's powder boxes, sir, checked for leaks and found correct.' Drinkwater remembered Tumilty's strictness on this point. A leaking powder box laid a gradual powder train directly from the deck to the magazine.

'Very well.' He nodded encouragingly at the men and reascended to the poop, striding the length of the waist alongside the carronades.

'Same arrangement for the waist batteries, Mr Rogers . . .'

'Aye, aye, sir.'

Drinkwater climbed onto the fo'c's'le where Matchett had his party of veteran seamen at the senior station. 'You will have the anchor ready?'

'Aye, sir. With a spring upon it sir, as soon as it's weighed and sighted clear.'

'Very good, Mr Matchett. Leave the spring slack when we anchor again. It is the line of battle ships his lordship wished to anchor by the stern to bring them swiftly into action and avoid the delays and risks in being raked as they swing. We shall most likely anchor by the head.'

'Aye, aye, sir.'

'Good luck, Mr Matchett . . . Mr Willerton what the devil are you up to?'

Willerton appeared suddenly from the heads with a pot of red paint in his hand and his eyes innocently blue in the sunshine that was now breaking through the cloud.

'Attending to my leddy, sir, giving her a nice red tongue and lips to smack at the Frogs, sir.'

Drinkwater smiled. 'They ain't Frogs, Mr Willerton, they're Danes.'

'All the same to 'er leddyship, sir.'

Drinkwater burst out laughing and turned aft, nodding to the men waiting by the windlass. 'You may heave her dead short, my lads.'

Dropping below by the forward hatch he ran into Lieutenant Tumilty who was no longer his usual flippant self but wore an expression of stern concentration. He was also uncharacteristically formal.

'Good morning sir. My preparations are all but complete. If you wish I will show you the arrangements I have made.' They walked aft through the hold where *Virago*'s four score seamen had lived and messed, past the remaining cables and the space cleared for the artillerymen.

At the after end a hatch opened into the stern quarters giving access to the magazine under Drinkwater's cabin. Tumilty held out his arm.

'No further sir, without felt boots.'

'Of course,' said Drinkwater, almost colliding with Tumilty.

'Hite and Trussel are filling the carcases, the empty shells, with white powder. Hobbs here is sentry and will assist if the action goes on long . . .' Drinkwater nodded at another artillery-man who carried not a fusil, in such dangerous proximity to the magazine, but a truncheon. 'Once filled, the shells come through here to the after shell room.' Tumilty turned forward, indicating the huge baulks of timber below the after, thirteen-inch, mortar that formed a cavity in which the shells were lodged. Above his head a small hatch had been opened, admitting a patch of light below.

'We, or rather Rogers's men, whip up the charged shells through that hatch to the mortar above . . .'

'What about fuses?' asked Drinkwater.

'As you see the shells are all wooden plugged for storage. I cut the fuses on the fo'c's'le. It's clear of seamen once Matchett quits fooling with his anchors; he'll be busy aft here, whipping up the shells. I rig leather dodgers to protect the fuses from sparks. The sergeant or myself will cut the fuses. This controls the time of explosion. Time of flight, and hence range, is decided by the charge in the chamber of the mortar. As I was saying, the fuse is of special composition and burns four tenths of an inch per minute. A thousand yard flight takes 2.56 seconds, so you see, Nat'aniel, 'tis a matter for a man of science, eh?'

'Indeed, Tom, it is . . . what of the ten-inch shells forward?'

'They go up in shell hooks. Now, I've had all hands at mortar stations twice in your absence and they all know what to do. I think we'll take it easy to begin with but we should be firing more than one shell a minute from each gun when we get the range.'

'What about the dangers of fire? I understand they're considerable . . .'

'Mr Jex's party are well briefed. We've wet tarpaulins handy to go over the side, buckets and tubs o' water all over the deck and in the tops . . . sure an' 'twill be like nothing you've ever seen in your life, Nat'aniel,' Tumilty smiled, recovering some of his former flippancy.

'Sir! Sir!' Quilhampton scrambled over a pile of rope and caught hold of Drinkwater's arm. 'Beggin' your pardon, sir, but Mr Rogers says to tell you that the admiral's hoisted Number 66 and the preparative, sir, "General order to weight an' the leeward ships first." '

'Thank you, Mr Q, I'll be up directly.'

Drinkwater arrived on the poop, reached in his tail pocket and whipped out his Dollond glass. Already the fleet was in motion. On their larboard bow, just beyond the bomb vessel *Volcano*, the lovely *Agamemnon* was hoisting her topsails. *Edgar* was already under way, her yards being braced round and the canvas stiffening with wind. Water appeared white at her bow and somewhere a shout and three cheers were called for. Several of the ships cheered their consorts as the naval might of Great Britain got under way. Drinkwater's fatigue, aches, pains and worries vanished as his heart-beat quickened and the old familiar exciting tingle shot down his spine.

They might be dead in an hour but, by God, this was a moment worth living for! He tried to mask his idiotic enthusiasm and turned aft to begin pacing the poop in an effort to repress his emotions and appear calm.

Bunting rose and broke from *Elephant*'s yard arms as hard-pressed signalmen sweated to convey Nelson's last minute orders to the ships. Happily in the confusion none applied to the bomb vessels.

'*Agamemnon*'s in trouble, sir,' remarked Rogers, nodding in the direction of the sixty-four.

'Damned current's too much for her, she ain't got enough headway . . .'

'She'll fall athwart *Volcano*'s hawse if she ain't careful . . .'

'And ours by God! Veer cable Mr Matchett, veer cable!' They could see men on *Volcano*'s fo'c's'le hurriedly letting out cable as the battleship tried to clear the little bomb vessel while the current set her rapidly north.

They watched helplessly as the big ship crabbed awkwardly across their own bow, failed to weather the mark vessel, *Cruizer*, and brought up to her anchor on the wrong side of the Middle Ground. Within minutes a flat-boat was ordered to her assistance, to carry out another anchor and enable her to haul herself to windward.

Edgar, with Mr Briarly at the con, began to draw ahead unsupported and bunting broke out again from *Elephant*'s yards as Nelson ordered *Polyphemus* into the gap, followed by the old *Isis*. Drinkwater watched the next ship with some interest.

Bellona followed *Isis*, crossing close to *Cruizer*'s bowsprit as she turned into the King's Deep. Drinkwater wondered if her pilot could see his marks and transits through the smoke of *Edgar*'s fire as she engaged the *Provesteenen*, the most southerly Danish ship round which he and Hardy had sounded the night before. Beyond *Isis* Drinkwater could see *Désirée* which had got under way early and was already anchored and swinging to her spring to open a raking fire on the *Provesteenen*.

Russell, an old Camperdown ship and well-known to Drinkwater, was close behind *Bellona*, and *Elephant*'s topmen were aloft as the admiral's flagship moved forward to take station astern of *Russell*. *Ardent* and Bligh's *Glatton* were setting sail.

'*Bellona*'s not following in the wake of *Isis*,' remarked Easton.

'God's bones,' muttered Drinkwater, 'I think they are ignoring Briarly's advice.' *Bellona* appeared to have inclined to a slightly more easterly course than the first ships. As they watched a sudden gap opened up between *Isis* and *Bellona*. 'What the devil . . .?'

'*Bellona*'s aground!' remarked Drinkwater grimly, 'hit the damned Middle Ground and look, by heaven, *Russell*'s followed him!'

'That'll set the cat among the bloody pigeons,' said Rogers.

The Meteor Flag

To the watchers on *Virago* nothing was known of the little drama on *Elephant*'s quarterdeck as Nelson took over the con of the battleship personally. Overhearing the pilots advising the master to leave the grounded *Bellona* and *Russell* to larboard the admiral ordered the helm put over the other way, leaving the stricken ships to starboard and averting complete catastrophe. All Drinkwater, Rogers and Easton could see were the leading British ships under their topsails, moving slowly north enveloped in a growing cloud of smoke as gun after gun in the Danish line bore on them. Tumilty and Lettsom had joined the knot of officers on the poop and the *Virago*'s rail was crowded with her people as they watched the cannonade.

Following *Elephant* were *Glatton, Monarch, Defiance* and *Ganges*, weathering the south end of the Middle Ground, while Riou's frigates, led by *Amazon*, were in line ahead for the entrance to the King's Deep.

Rose's little gun-brigs each with their waspish names: *Biter, Sparkler, Tickler*, were shaking out their topsails; seemingly as anxious to get among the enemy fire as their larger consorts. Fremantle's flat-boats were also active, three or four of them clustered around *Agamemnon*'s bow assisting in carrying out her anchors, and converging on *Bellona* and *Russell* who were under fire from the *Provesteenen* and howitzer batteries on Amager.

'Hullo, old Parker's on the move.' The levelled telescopes swung to the north where the Commander-in-Chief's division was beating up to re-anchor at the north end of the Middle Ground.

'I wonder if he can see *Bellona* and *Russell* aground?' asked Easton.

'He'll have a damned fit if he can, two battleships out of the line is going to have quite an effect on the others,' offered Rogers.

'Your fire-eating brothers in Christ will have their whiskers singed, Mr Rogers,' said Lettsom philosophically. 'Here is a quatrain for you:

'See where the guns of England thunder
Giving blow for mighty blow,
Who was it that made the blunder,
Took 'em where they couldn't go?'

Rogers burst out laughing and even Drinkwater, keenly observing the progress of the action, could not repress a smile. He walked across to the deck log and looked at Easton's last entry: '10 o'clock, van ships

158

engaged, cannonade became general as line of battle ships got into station.'

To the north of them most of Parker's squadron were reanchoring. But four of his battleships were beating up towards Copenhagen against wind and current to enter the action.

Astern of the bomb vessels, *Jamaica* and the gun brigs were having a similar problem. The crowded anchorage had not allowed all the ships to get sufficiently to the south to weather the Middle Ground in the wind now blowing, and though Drinkwater thought that the shallow draught gun-brigs could have chanced slipping inside *Cruizer*, it was clear that Parker's caution was now epidemic in the fleet.

'*Explosion*'s signalling, sir, "Bombs General, weigh and form line of battle."'

The noise of the cannonade reached Mr Jex as he bent down in the hold. He was outboard of the great coils of spare cable, in the carpenter's walk against the ship's side. He had left the deck on the pretext of checking the sea inlet cock. From here water was drawn on deck by the fire engine, to spout from the two hoses his party had laid out on the deck. The spigot had been opened hours earlier and Jex merely crouched over it. His fear had reduced him to a trembling jelly. He could hear above the still distant sound of cannon the distinct chuckle of water alongside a hull under way: *Virago* was going into action.

For five minutes Jex huddled terrified against the ship's side before recovering himself. Standing uncertainly he began to make his way towards the spirit room.

Drinkwater stared through the vanes of his hand compass at the main mast of *Cruizer*.

'Damn! She won't weather *Cruizer*, Mr Easton, can you stretch the braces a little?'

Easton looked aloft then shook his head. 'Hard against the catharpings, sir.'

Rogers came and stood anxiously next to Drinkwater as he continued to stare through the brass vanes. He was swearing under his breath.

'Keep her full and bye, Tregembo!' Drinkwater could feel the sweat prickling his armpits. He took his eye off *Cruizer* for a second and saw how the stern of the grounded Russell was perceptibly nearer.

'*Hecla*'s having the same trouble, Nat,' Rogers muttered consolingly.

'That's bloody cold comfort!' snapped Drinkwater, suddenly venomous. Were they to go aground ignominiously after all their tribulations? He snapped the compass vanes shut and pocketted the little instrument.

'Set all sail, Mr Rogers, and lively about it!'

Rogers did not even bother to acknowledge the order. 'Tops there! Aloft and shake out the t'gallants! Fo'c's'le! Hoist both jibs . . .'

Easton had jumped down into the waist and was chivvying the waisters onto the topgallant halliards.

'Get those fucking lobsters to tail on, Easton. You there! Aloft and let fall the main course . . .'

The loose canvas flopped downwards, billowed and filled. *Virago* heeled a little more. Here and there a knife flashed to cut a kink jammed in a sheave but the constant days of battling with gales, of making and reducing sail now brought its own dividends and the Viragos caught something of the urgency of the hour.

The bomb vessel increased her speed, leaning to leeward with the water foaming along her side.

'Up helm and ease her a point.' Drinkwater had not taken his eyes off *Cruizer*'s stern. Suddenly the men looked up from coiling the ropes to see the brig's stern very close as they sped past, with a row of faces watching the old bomb vessel going into action.

Brisbane raised his hat, 'Tally ho, Drinkwater, by God! Tally ho and mind the mud!'

Drinkwater felt the thrill of exhilaration turn to that of fear as the deck heaved beneath his feet.

'God damn and blast it!' screamed Rogers, beside himself with angry frustration, but suddenly they were free and a ragged cheer broke from those who realised that for an instant their keel had struck the Middle Ground.

In a moment they could bear up for the battle . . .

'Larboard bow, sir!' Drinkwater looked up. Coming round *Cruizer*'s bow was *Explosion*, just swinging before the wind to make her own approach to her station. Drinkwater could not luff without colliding or losing control of *Virago*, neither dare he bear away for a little longer since *Russell* was indicating the bank dangerously close to his starboard side. He resolved to stand on, aware that Martin was screeching something at him through a trumpet.

'Damn Captain Martin,' he muttered to himself, but a chorus of 'Hear, hear!' from Rogers and Easton indicated the extent of his concentration. Martin was compelled to let fly his sheets to check *Explosion*'s headway.

'Up helm, Tregembo . . . reduce sail again!'

Astern Martin was still shouting as *Explosion*, closely followed by *Volcano, Terror* and *Discovery* weathered the *Cruizer* and the Middle Ground.

'For what we are about to receive, may we be truly . . . Jesus!' A storm of shot swept *Virago*'s deck. They had left astern *Désirée*, anchored athwart the Danish line with a spring straining on her cable, and *Polyphemus* was drawing onto the larboard quarter. She too was anchored, though by the stern. As *Virago* crossed the gap between *Polyphemus* and the next anchored ship, the *Isis*, a broadside from *Provesteenen* hit her, cutting up the rigging and sails and wounding the foremast. On their own starboard side they had already passed *Russell*,

160

flying the signal for distress and with flat-boats heaving out cables from her bow and stern while cannon shot dropped all round them. As they passed *Bellona* a terrific bang occurred and screams rent the air.

Beside Drinkwater Lieutenant Tumilty wore a seraphic smile. 'Gun exploded,' he explained for the benefit of anyone interested. *Bellona*'s guns were returning the Danish fire and Drinkwater looked ahead. From this close range the enemy defences took on a different aspect. From a distance the exiguous collection of prames, radeaus, cut down battleships, floating batteries, transports and frigates had had a cheap, thread-bare look about them, compared with the formal naval might of Great Britain with its canvas, bunting and wooden walls. But from the southern end of the King's Deep it looked altogether different. Already *Bellona* and *Russell* were of little use, although both returned fire and strove throughout the day to get afloat again. Against the remaining ships the massed cannon of the Danish defences looked formidable. Spitting fire and smoke, the blazing tiers of guns were the most awesome sight Drinkwater had ever seen.

The gaps between the British ships were greater now, occasioned by the loss of *Bellona* and *Russell* from the line. Shot whined over the decks, ripping holes in the sails and occasionally striking splinters from *Virago*'s timber.

There was a scream as the bomb vessel received her first casualty, an over-curious artilleryman who spun round and fell across the ten-inch mortar hatch while his shattered head flew overboard.

The Danes were defending their very hearths, and kept up the gunfire by continually sending reinforcements from the shore to relieve their tired men, and sustain the hail of shot against the British.

Virago's fore topgallant was shot away as she passed *Edgar*, engaged against the *Jutland*, an old, cut down two-decker. Rogers leapt forward, temperamentally unable to remain inactive for long in such circumstances. He began to clear the mess while Drinkwater concentrated upon the calls of the leadsman in the starboard chains. Beyond *Jutland* the odd square shapes of two floating batteries and a frigate were firing at both *Edgar* and the next ship ahead, Bligh's *Glatton*. The former East Indiaman which had once compelled a whole squadron to surrender to her deadly, short range batteries of carronades was keeping up a terrific fire. Most of her effort was concentrated on her immediate opponent, another cut-down battleship, the *Dannebrog*, flagship of the Danish commander, Commodore Olfert Fischer. But *Virago* did not pass unmolested, three more men were wounded and another killed as the storm of shot swept them.

'Bring her to starboard a little, Mr Easton, and pass word to Mr Matchett, Mr Q, to watch for my signal to anchor; we are almost on our station abeam the admiral.'

The two officers acknowledged their orders.

Drinkwater studied *Elephant* for a moment. He could see the knot of glittering officers on her quarterdeck in the sunshine. Beyond the flagship lay the *Ganges* and then a gap, filled with boats pulling up and down the line. Just visible in the smoke were *Monarch* and Graves's flagship *Defiance*, and somewhere ahead of them, in the full fire of the heavy batteries of the Trekroner Forts, were Riou and his frigates.

'Bring the ship to the wind, Mr Easton.' *Virago* began to turn. 'You may begin your preparations, Mr Tumilty.' As they had closed *Elephant* the Irishman had been observing his targets and taking obscure measurements with what looked like a pelorus.

To his astonishment Tumilty winked. 'And now, my dear Nat'aniel, you'll see why we've brought all this here.' Leprechaun-like he hopped onto the foredeck and began to bawl instructions at his artillerymen.

Drinkwater felt the wind on his face and dropped his arm as the main topsail flogged back against the mast. 'Bunt lines and clew lines there! Ease the halliards! Up aloft and stow!' Rogers paused, looking along the deck to see his orders obeyed. 'You there, up aloft . . . Bosun's mate, start that man aloft, God damn it, and take his name!'

Virago's anchor dropped just as the leadsman called 'By the mark five!'

'Perfect, by God,' Drinkwater muttered to himself, pleased with his positioning, and suddenly thinking of Elizabeth in his moment of self-conceit.

'How much scope, sir?' Matchett was crying at him from forward.

'Half a cable, Mr Matchett,' he called through the speaking trumpet. He felt *Virago* tug round as her anchor bit and she brought up. She lay quietly sheering a few degrees in the current.

'Brought up, sir,' reported Easton, straightening up from taking a bearing.

'Very well, Mr Easton.' Drinkwater looked round. Astern of them *Terror* was turning into the wind to anchor while *Explosion* and *Discovery* continued past *Virago*. Of *Volcano* there was no sign, though Drinkwater afterwards learned she had been ordered to anchor and throw shells against the howitzer battery on Amager at the southern end of the line.

He raised his hat to Martin as the commander went past, partly out of bravado, partly to mollify the touchy man. To the south the confusion caused by the groundings had resulted in *Isis* anchoring prematurely to cover *Bellona* and *Russell*. The consequence of this was a dangerous extension of the line of battleships north of the *Elephant* with the lighter frigates absorbing enormous punishment from the Trekroner Forts, the Lynetten, Quintus and other batteries, plus the guns of the inner line commanded by Steen Bille. The whole area was a mass of smoke and fire while Parker's three relieving battleships, *Ramilles, Defence* and *Veteran* were making no apparent headway to come to Riou's assistance.

'Mr Drinkwater! I'm ready to open fire if you can steady the ship a little.'

Drinkwater turned his attention inboard. Rogers had a gang of men aft, their arms extended above their heads where they prepared to whip up the shells; groups of artillerymen, stripped to their braces in the biting wind, clustered round the mortars which, looking like huge, elongated cauldrons pointed their blunt, ineffective looking muzzles out to starboard, at the sky over Copenhagen.

'Mr Easton, let fall the mizzen topsail and keep it backed against the mast. Fire as you will, Mr Tumilty.'

'Thank 'ee, sir, and will you be kind enough to observe the fall o' shot?'

Drinkwater nodded. Tumilty hopped back to the fo'c's'le where he bent behind the leather dodger then walked aft beside the sergeant to the thirteen-inch mortar. Tapping the prepared fuse into the first shell Tumilty saw the monstrous ball, more than a foot in diameter and which contained ten pounds of white gun powder, safely into the chamber of the mortar. He had already loaded the powder he judged would throw the carcase over the opposing lines of ships into the heart of the Danish capital.

Handing the linstock to his sergeant he leaped up onto the poop and pulled his telescope from his pocket. '*Festina lente*, eh Nat'aniel . . . Fire!'

The roar was immense, drowning the sound of the guns of the fleets, and white smoke rolled reeking over them.

'Mark it! Mark it!' yelled Tumilty, his glass travelling up and then down as a faint white line arced against the blue sky to fall with increasing speed onto the roofs of the city.

At the mortar bed the artillerymen crowded round, swabbing out the chamber of the gun. The elevation remained unchanged, being set at forty-five degrees.

Drinkwater stared at the arsenal of Copenhagen trying to see where the shell burst. He saw nothing.

'Over, by Jesus,' said Tumilty happily, 'and at least the fuse was not premature.' Drinkwater watched him fuss round the mortar again as the whipping up gang began to work. The ten inch had been readied but Tumilty held its fire until he was satisfied with the performance of the after mortar.

Although he felt the deck shudder under the concussion and gasped as the smoke and blast passed over him, Drinkwater was ready for the next shot. The carcase descended on the arsenal and Drinkwater saw it burst as it hit the ground.

'A little short Mr Tumilty, I believe.' The landing of the third shot was also short but at his next Tumilty justified his claim to be the finest pyroballogist in the Royal Artillery. The explosion was masked by the walls of the arsenal but Tumilty was delighted with the result and left the poop to supervise both mortars from the waist.

Dutifully Easton and Drinkwater reported the fall of the shells as well as they could. From time to time Tumilty would pause to traverse his mortar-beds but he maintained a steady fire. Beneath his feet Drinkwater was aware that *Virago* had suddenly become a hive of activity. All the oddities of her construction had been built for this

163

moment: the curious hatches, the fire-screens, the glazed lantern niches; the huge futtocks and heavy scantlings; the octagonal hatches. Mr Trussel and Bombardier Hite received instructions from Tumilty and made up the flannel cartridges in the filling room. The artillery sergeant cut fuses on the now deserted fo'c's'le. In the waist seamen and soldiers scurried about as they carried shells, fuses, cartridges and buckets of water with which to douse the hot mortars. Orchestrating the whole was Lieutenant Tumilty, his face purple with exertion, his active figure justifying his regiment's motto as he seemed everywhere at once like some hellish fiend.

As they fired over the main action Drinkwater was able to see something of the progress of the battle. Already damage to the British ships was obvious. Several had lost masts and others flew signals of distress. Amongst the splashes of wide cannon shot the flat-boats and boats of the fleet pulled about, coolly carrying out anchors. Through this hail of shot Brisbane sailed the *Cruizer* from her now redundant duty of marking the south end of the Middle Ground, the length of the line to Riou's support. Of the Danish line Drinkwater could see little beyond those hulks and prames on his beam. One appeared to have got out of the line and several seemed to strike their flags, but as they had reappeared the next time he looked he could not be sure what was happening. *Terror, Explosion* and *Discovery* were throwing shells into Copenhagen. Neither *Hecla, Zebra* nor *Sulphur* appeared to have weathered the Middle Ground and got into the action.

'Fire! Fire!' Drinkwater swung round. A flicker of flames raced along the larboard rail but Rogers was equal to it. 'Fire party, hoses to the larboard waist!'

Drinkwater looked in vain for Jex, but his men were there, dragging an already pulsing hose towards the burning spars lying on the rail.

'Part-burnt wads, Nat'aniel,' shouted Tumilty unconcerned, identifying the cause of the fire.

'Where the devil's Mr Jex?' Drinkwater called out, frowning.

'Don't know, sir,' replied Rogers, as he had men cutting the lashing round the spars and levering them overboard. A shot whined over his head and he ducked.

'Mr Easton!'

'Sir!'

'Find Jex!'

'Aye, aye, sir.'

But Easton had not left the poop when Jex appeared through the smoke that billowed back from the ten-inch mortar forward. He was drunk and in his shirt-sleeves. 'I hear the cry of fire!' he shouted, holding up his hands above his head and staggering over a ring-bolt. 'Here I am you bastards, at my fucking action station, God rot you all . . .'

Men turned to look at the purser as he reached the after mortar and was again engulfed in the smoke of discharge. He emerged to the astonished onlookers like a theatrical wraith, his face flaccid, his

164

cheeks wet with tears. Drinkwater was aware of a sniggering from the men at the shell-hatch.

'Bastards, you're all bastards . . .' Jex flung his arms wide in a gesture that embraced them all.

'Mr Jex . . .!' Drinkwater began, his jaw dropping as Jex's right arm flew off, spun round and slapped a topman across the face. The astonished man put up his hands and caught the severed limb.

'Cor! Pusser's give me back me bleeding eighth . . .'

The grotesque joke ended the brief hiatus on *Virago*'s deck. Jex looked stupidly at his distant arm then down at the gouts of his blood as it poured from the socket. He began to scream and run about the deck.

Rogers felled him with one end of a burning royal yard he was heaving overboard. Jex fell to the deck, his legs kicking and his back arching, the red stain growing on the planking.

'Jesus Christ,' muttered Easton watching, fascinated.

At last Jex grew still. Jumping down from the rail having tossed overboard all the burning spars Rogers pointed to the body and addressed two seamen standing stock still beside a starboard carronade.

'Throw that damned *thing* overboard.'

Then Tumilty's after mortar roared again.

'Mr Drinkwater, sir! The Commander-in-Chief is signalling, sir!'

'Well Mr Q, what is it?'

'Number 39, sir: "Discontinue the action," sir.'

' "Discontinue the action"? Are you certain? Drinkwater raised his Dollond glass and levelled it to the north. *Ramilles*, *Veteran* and *Defence* were still clawing to windward and he could see *London* still at anchor, with her blue admiral's flag at the main. And there too were the blue and white horizontal stripes of Number 3 flag over the horizontal red, white and blue of Number 9.

'Mr Easton, what o'clock d'you have?'

'Twenty minutes after one, sir.'

'You must log receipt of that signal, Mr Easton . . . Mr Matchett . . . where the devil's the bosun?'

'Here sir.'

'Prepare to weigh.'

'Aye, aye, sir.' Drinkwater looked again at the *London*. There was no mistaking that signal. It was definitely Number 39.

'Cease fire, Mr Tumilty . . . Mr Rogers, disperse the hands to their stations for getting under way . . .' Drinkwater looked anxiously about him. Disengagement was going to be difficult. The battleships had only to cut their cables, they were already headed north and would soon be carried out of the action but the bombs had to weigh and turn. *Virago* could not turn to larboard, away from the Danish guns, because of the Middle Ground upon whose edge she had been anchored. To turn to starboard would put the ship under a devastating raking fire. Drinkwater swallowed. If he weighed immediately he might obtain a little shelter behind the battleships but he ran two risks in doing so. The first was that with the prevailing current he might run foul of one of the bigger ships; the second was that too precipitate a departure from the line of battle could be construed as cowardice.

'What the devil d'you want me to cease fire for?' Tumilty's purple face peered belligerently through the smoke.

'The Commander-in-Chief instructs us to abandon the action, damn it!'

'What the bloody hell for?'

'Do as you're told, Tumilty!' snapped Drinkwater.

'Beg pardon, sir, Flag's only acknowledged the signal . . .'

'Eh?' Drinkwater looked where Quilhampton pointed. *Elephant* had not repeated Parker's order. He looked astern and saw *Explosion* had repeated Number 39.

'What the bloody hell . . .?'

'Can you see *Defiance*, Mr Q?' Quilhampton stared over the starboard quarter and levelled the big watch-glass.

'I can't be sure, sir, but I *think* Admiral Graves has a signal hoisted but if he has it ain't from a very conspicuous place . . .'

'Not very conspicuous . . .?' Drinkwater frowned again and returned his attention to the *Elephant*. Nelson had signalled only an *acknowledgement* of sighting Number 39 to Parker but not repeated it to his ships, and Number 16, the signal for Close Action, hoisted at the beginning of the battle, still flew.

Drinkwater tried to clear his head while the concussion of the guns went on. Nelson was clearly not eager to obey. From Parker's distant observation post it must be obvious that Nelson was in trouble. *Bellona* and *Russell* were aground, both flying conspicuous signals of distress; there was a congestion of ships at the southern end of the line which, combined with the presence of some bombs and the gun-brigs still in the southern anchorage, suggested that something had gone dreadfully wrong with Nelson's division. *Agamemnon*, after repeated efforts to kedge round *Cruizer*, had given up and sent her boats to the assistance of the fleet while *Cruizer*, the mark vessel, had abandoned her station to support Riou.

Parker could see the northern end of the line more clearly. Frigates engaged with prepared positions presaged disaster, while his three battleships were clearly going to be unable to relieve Riou as they were still too far off.

'Pusillanimous Parker's lost his bloody nerve, eh?' said Rogers levelling a glass alongside Drinkwater.

'I think,' said Drinkwater, 'he's giving Nelson the chance to get out while he may. But I think he little appreciates what bloody chaos there will be if Nelson tries to disengage at this juncture . . .'

'Well Nelson ain't moving!' Rogers nodded across at *Elephant*.

'No.' Drinkwater paused. 'Tell Matchett to veer that cable again, Sam . . . Mr Tumilty! Re-engage!' A cheer went along *Virago*'s deck and the next instant her waist filled with smoke and noise as the mortars roared.

166

'Flag to *Virago*, Number 214, for a "Lieutenant to report on board the Admiral," sir,' said Quilhampton diligently.

'Very well, pass word to Lieutenant Rogers, Mr Q.' Quilhampton went in search of the first lieutenant who had disappeared off the poop. Astern of them *Explosion* hauled down Number 39.

It was twenty minutes before Rogers returned. Rogers was elated.

'By God, sir, you should see it from over there, Nelson himself claims it's the hottest fire he's ever been under and the Danes are refusing to surrender. They're striking, then firing on the boats sent to take 'em . . .'

'What did the admiral want?' cut in Drinkwater.

'Oh, he remarked that *Virago*'s shells were well directed and could we drop some into the Trekroner Forts.'

'Mr Tumilty!' Drinkwater shrieked through the din. He beckoned the Irishman onto the poop. 'His lordship wants us to direct our fire at the Trekroner Forts.'

Tumilty's eyes lit up. 'Very good. I'll switch the ten-inch to firing one pound shot, that'll shake the eejits if they haven't got casemates over there.'

Tumilty took ten minutes and four careful shots to get the range. The Trekroner Forts were at extreme range and the increased charge of twice the amount of powder used to reach the arsenal made *Virago* shake to her keel.

The one-pound shot arrived in boxes, and stockingette bags of them were lifted into the forward mortar, one hundred to a shot. Drinkwater found the trajectory of these easier to follow than the carcases as they spread slightly in flight.

For half an hour *Virago* kept up this bombardment until Quilhampton reported a flag of truce flying at *Elephant*'s masthead. All along both lines the fire began to slacken and an air of uncertainty spread over the fleet.

Looking northwards Drinkwater saw *Amazon* leading the frigate squadron towards Parker's anchored ships and rightly concluded that Riou, unable to see Nelson's signal for close action, had obeyed Parker's order to withdraw. It was only later that he learnt Riou had been cut in two by a round shot an instant after giving the order.

Desultory firing still rippled up and down the line as observers saw boats of both nations clustered round *Elephant* flying flags of truce. As the sun westered it appeared some armistice had been concluded, for Nelson made the signal to his ships to make sail. A lieutenant was pulled across to the line of bomb vessels to order them to move nearer the Trekroner Forts and remain until the admiral sent them further orders.

'That will bring the whole city in range,' grinned the smoke-grimed Tumilty.

'I think, gentlemen,' said Drinkwater shutting the Dollond glass with a snap, 'that we are to be the ace of trumps!'

Ace of Trumps

'Oh, my God!' Drinkwater peered down into the boat alongside *Virago*. By the lantern light he could see the body of Easton lying inert in the stern sheets.

'Where's the other boat? Mr Quilhampton's boat,' he demanded, suddenly, terribly anxious.

'Here sir,' the familiar voice called as the cutter rounded the stern. There were wounded men in her too.

'What the devil happened?'

'*Elephant* ordered us to carry out a cable, sir, and then, when we had done that, Captain Foley directed us to secure one of the Danish prizes . . .'

'Foley?'

'Yes, sir. Lord Nelson returned to *St George* when *Elephant* grounded trying to get away to the north . . .'

'Go on . . .'

'Well sir, we approached the prize about two o'clock and the bastards opened fire on us . . .'

Drinkwater turned away from the rail to find Rogers looming out of the darkness.

'Get those men out, Mr Rogers, and then take a fresh crew and get over the *Monarch*.'

'The *Monarch*, sir?'

'I sent Lettsom over there earlier tonight, she was in want of a surgeon.'

'Bloody hell.'

Drinkwater did what he could while he waited for the surgeon's arrival. It was little enough but it occupied the night and he emerged aching into the frozen dawn. It was calm and a light mist lay over the King's Deep.

The hours of darkness had been a shambles. After the exertions of the previous nights and the day of the battle, Drinkwater was grey with exhaustion. The British ships had not extricated themselves from the battle without difficulty. In addition to *Elephant*, *Defiance* had gone aground. *Monarch*, which had been badly damaged in the action and suffered fearful loss of life, had become unmanageable and run inshore only to collide with *Ganges*, run aground and come under the renewed fire of the Danes. Fortuitously the impact of *Ganges* drove *Monarch* off the mud and both ships got away in the growing night. One of the Danish ships had exploded with a fearful concussion and the air was still filled with the smell of burning.

Drinkwater had worked his own ship across the King's Deep during the evening, answering *Elephant*'s signal for a boat to attend her cables and *Monarch*'s for a surgeon. *Virago* was now anchored closer to the city, commanding the Trekroner Forts with her still-warm mortars and in company with *Explosion, Terror* and *Discovery*.

A rising sun began to consume the mist revealing that the majority of the British fleet had joined Sir Hyde Parker at the north end of the Middle Ground. Lettsom returned with Rogers, whose boat's crew had worked like demons. To the south *Bellona* and *Russell* had gone, the former by picking up *Isis*'s cable and hauling herself off. *Désirée*, too, seemed to have got off. Nearer them *Defiance* was still fast, but by the time Drinkwater sent the hands to breakfast she too was under way.

Shutting the magazines and exhorting his officers to use the utmost caution bearing in mind the weary condition of the men, Drinkwater had the galley range fired up and all enjoyed a steaming burgoo. Drinkwater was unable to rest and kept the deck. The excitement and exertions of the last hours had driven him beyond sleep and, though he knew reaction must come, for the moment he paced his poop.

The Danish line presented a spectacle that he would never forget. From his position during the battle Drinkwater's view had been obscured by smoke. He had been able to see only the unengaged sides of the British ships and had formed no very reliable opinion of the effects of the gunfire. But now he was able to see the effect of the cannonade on the Danish vessels.

The sides of many of the blockships and hulks were completely battered in, with huge gaps in their planking. Many were out of position, driven inshore onto the flats off Amager. Some still flew the Danish flag. Looking at the respective appearance of the two protagonists, the shattered Danish line to the west, the British battleships licking their wounds to the north east, Drinkwater concluded there seemed little to choose between them. Possession of the field seemed to be in the hands of the Danes, since no landing of the troops had taken place; no storming of the Trekroner from the flat-boats had occurred.

And then his tired mind remembered his own words of the previous night. Here they were, the line of little bomb vessels, the tubby Cinderellas of the fleet, holding the field for the honour of Great Britain and turning a drawn battle into victory.

'Sir, boat approaching, and I believe his lordship's in it!'

'What's that?' Drinkwater woke abruptly as Quilhampton's bandaged head appeared round the door. He stretched. His head, his legs and above all his mangled arm ached intolerably. He could not have slept above half an hour.

'What did you say? Lord Nelson?'

'Yes sir . . .'

Drinkwater dragged himself on deck to see the admiral's barge approaching *Explosion*. It passed down the line of bomb vessels. The little admiral wore his incongruous check overcoat and sat next to the taller Hardy. The Viragos lined the rail and gave the admiral a spontaneous cheer. Nelson raised his hat as he came abeam.

'Morning Drinkwater.'

'Good mornin', my lord.'

'I have been in over a hundred actions, Mr Drinkwater, but yesterday's was the hottest. I was well pleased with your conduct and will not forget you in my report to their Lordships.'

'Obliged to you, my lord.' Drinkwater watched the boat move on. Beside him Lettsom emerged reeking of blood.

'His lordship has paid a heavy price in blood for his honours,' the surgeon said sadly.

'How was *Monarch*?'

'A bloody shambles. Fifty-six killed, including Mosse, her captain, and one hundred and sixty-four wounded seriously. They say her first lieutenant, Yelland, worked miracles to bring her out. Doubtless he will be promoted . . .' Lettsom broke off, the implied bitterness clear. How many surgeons and their mates had laboured with equal skill would never be known.

'Flat-boats approaching, sir.'

'Mr Q, will you kindly desist with your interminable bloody reports . . .'

'Aye, aye, sir.'

Drinkwater was immediately ashamed of his temper. Quilhampton's crestfallen expression was eloquent of hurt.

'Mr Q! I beg your pardon.'

Quilhampton brightened immediately. 'That's all right, sir.'

Drinkwater looked at the flat-boats. 'Let me know what they are up to, Mr Q.' He went below and immediately fell asleep.

He woke to the smell of smoke rolling over the sea. Going on deck he found an indignant knot of officers on the poop. 'What the devil's this damned Dover court, eh?' He was thoroughly bad-tempered now, having slept enough to recover his spirits but not to overcome his exhaustion.

'Old Vinegar's ordered the prizes burned,' said Rogers indignantly. 'We won't have the benefit of any prize money, God rot him.' In a fleet that had subsisted for weeks upon rumour and gossip no item had so speedily offended the seamen. It was true that there was little of real value among the Danish ships but one or two were fine vessels wanting only masts and spars. Only the *Holstein* was to be spared and fitted as a hospital ship for the wounded. Nelson was reported to be furious with Parker and had remonstrated with his commander-in-chief on behalf of the common seamen in the fleet, arguing that their only reward was some expectation of prize and head money.

The vice-admiral seemed indefatigable. He was known to have arranged the truce and that evening went ashore to dine with his former enemies. Although peace had not been formally concluded the fleet had persuaded itself that the Danes were beaten.

Drinkwater shut the prayer book and put on his hat. The gospel of the resurrection had a hollow ring this Easter Sunday.

'On hats!' bellowed Rogers. Drinkwater stepped forward to address the men.

'My lads, I do not propose to read the Articles of War today, simply to thank you for acquitting yourselves so well on Thursday.' A cheer went up from the men and Drinkwater mistily realised it was for him. The shouting died away. 'But . . . but we may not yet have finished work . . .' The hands fell silent again, staring apprehensively at him. 'I received orders this morning that the truce ends at noon. If no satisfactory explanation is heard as to why our terms have not been accepted we will bombard the city.'

He went below and Rogers dismissed the hands.

'Sir! Mr Rogers says to tell you there's boats coming and going between the shore and the Trekroner . . .'

Drinkwater went on deck and stared through his glass. There was no doubt about it – the Danes were reinforcing the defences.

'So much for his lordship's toasts of everlasting fraternity with the Danes,' remarked Rogers sourly.

'Man a boat, Mr Rogers, and take command of the ship in my absence.'

The boat could not go fast enough for Drinkwater and it wanted a few minutes before noon when he clambered up *London*'s side and reported to the commander-in-chief. Parker astonished him by remembering his name. 'Ah, Drinkwater, the officer of the watch informs me you have intelligence regarding the Trekroner Forts.' Drinkwater nodded. 'By the way, my wife writes and asks to be remembered to you, it seems I was not appreciative of your services to her last year when we met before.'

Drinkwater bowed. 'That is most kind of her ladyship, sir.' He was desperately anxious to communicate the news about the Danish reinforcements.

'The Danes are pouring men into the Trekroners, sir, reinforcements . . .'

'I think you may compose your mind on that score, Mr Drinkwater. The Danish envoys have just left me. The truce is extended.' It was only much later that Drinkwater wondered if Lady Parker implied anything in her kindness.

For two days the British fleet repaired the damage to itself, took out of the remaining prizes all the stores that were left and burnt the hulls. A south westerly wind swept a chill rain down over them and once again all was uncertainty. The seamen laboured at the sweeps of the flat-boats as they pulled between the plundered prizes and the British anchorage.

The cutter *Fox* left to survey the shallows over The Grounds to the south, past Dragør, in an attempt to find a channel suitable for the deep hulls of the first-rates and enable them to get through to the Baltic. Eager to assist, Drinkwater was ordered to remain on his bomb and keep his mortars trained on the city of Copenhagen.

Nelson and Colonel Stewart again dined ashore and the truce was further extended. News came that letters might be written and transported to England. Drinkwater sat at his reinstated table, snapped open the inkwell and paused before drawing a sheet of paper towards him. There was one duty he was conscious of having put off since the battle. Instead of the writing paper he pulled the muster book from its place and opened it.

He ran his finger down the list of names, halting at Easton. He paused for a second, recalling the man's face, then his mouth set in a firm line and he carefully wrote the legend '*D.D.*' for 'discharged dead'. He repeated the process against the name Jex, suppressing the unchristian relief that clamped his lips even more tightly, then hurried down the list, and inserted the cryptic initials against four other names.

At the bottom of the column he paused again. Then, dipping his pen in the inkwell with sudden resolution he wrote '*D.D.*' against the entry '*Ed'd. Waters, Landsman Volunteer*', sanded the page and pushed the book aside.

He found his hand shaking slightly as he began his letter to Elizabeth.

> *H.M. Bomb* Virago
> *Copenhagen Road*
> *Wednesday 8th April 1801*

My Darling Elizabeth,

Cruizer is about to leave with despatches and I have time to tell you that on Thursday last the fleet was engaged before this city. The action was furious but I escaped unscathed, so your prayers were answered. Many brave fellows have fallen but you may tell Louise that James got only a scratch. He has done well and exceeded my expectations of him. Peace is still not confirmed, but I think it likely. You will read in the papers of great exertions by Lord Nelson and I flatter myself that his lordship took notice of me. Some good may yet come of it, although I must not be too sanguine, his lordship not having the chief command.

Tell Susan that Tregembo is fit and in good health.

I hope you continue in health and your condition is not irksome. Kiss Charlotte Amelia for me and remember me as your devoted husband . . .

He signed the letter, disappointed that it was not more personal. Somehow Elizabeth's remoteness made her existence unreal. Reality was this penetrating chill and the endless ache in his right arm.

The cutter *Fox* returned to the fleet anchorage on the following evening. She had found a passage over the shoals into the Baltic. The next day came news of a fourteen week armistice. The Danes would supply the fleet with water and other necessaries and in return the bomb vessels would haul off. Other news came aboard too, news that had little impact on anyone except Lieutenant Nathaniel Drinkwater.

Danish and Prussian troops had entered Hamburg and the port had been closed to all communication with Britain.

Kioge Bay

'General signal from Flag, sir: "All ships to send boat".'

'That ought to be for mails, see to it Mr Rogers.'

Every glass in the fleet had trained on *Lynx* when she arrived at Kioge Bay. Captain Otway was on board with news of the outside world. After the efforts and tribulations of the last few weeks almost any news that was not pure gossip about the fleet was welcome.

Strenuous efforts had been made to work the big ships, particularly *London* and *St George*, over the shallows. Their guns and stores had been hoisted out into merchant ships while the lightened battleships, riding high in the water, were hauled into the Baltic. Following the *London, St George* had grounded. Parker heard that the Swedish fleet was at sea and sent for Nelson to leave *St George* and rejoin *Elephant* anchored with the rest of the British warships at Kioge Bay. Nelson had his barge pull the twenty-four miles in the teeth of a rising and bitter wind to rejoin his former flagship.

While the big ships sailed to seek out the squadron from Carlscrona, the bombs and small fry waited in Kioge Bay and wondered if they were to sail against the Russians. Despite the recent carnage of the battle, relations with the Danes were good and the anchorage was usually enlivened by the sight of several Danish galliots among the anchored ship, selling cream for the officers' coffee and cheese and chickens to those who could afford them.

Then Parker had returned with the news that Tsar Paul had been assassinated and that his son Alexander had succeeded to the throne and declared his friendship with Britain. It was news already three weeks old.

So were the letters brought by *Lynx*, but nobody minded. The distribution of the mail had its usual effect. Men with letters ran off to sit in obscure corners or in the tops, painfully to spell out the ill-written scrawl of loved ones. Those without went off to sulk or affected indifference, according to their temperament. Saddest were the letters that arrived for the dead. There was one such for Easton, scented with lavender and superscribed in a delicate, feminine hand. It lay upon Drinkwater's table waiting to be returned unopened with his condolences.

There were three letters for Drinkwater. One was in Elizabeth's hand and one in Richard White's, but it was the third that he opened first.

> *Dear Drinkwater,*
>> *Your letters reached me safely and I desire that you wait upon me directly you return to London.*
>>> *Dungarth.*

It was frigidly brief and reawakened all Drinkwater's doubts about his conduct over Edward. Jex's death, though it had freed him from accusation from one quarter, had not released him entirely. It came as small consolation to learn that the Danish and Prussian troops had abandoned Hamburg.

He had gone on deck and paced the poop for over an hour before remembering the other letters. When he had sufficiently calmed himself he returned below and picked up the next. It was from his old friend Richard White, now a post-captain and blockading Brest in a frigate.

> *My Dear Nathaniel,*
>> *We are still here, up and down the Goulet and in sight of the batteries at St Matthew. I am sick of the duty and the incessant wearing of men and ships, but I suppose you would say there was no help for it. So thinks the First Lord, and no-one is disposed to argue with him. I heard you had command of a tender and if you can make nothing of it I would welcome a head I can rely on here. Write and let me know if you wish to serve as my first lieutenant . . .*

Drinkwater laid the letter down. If he could contrive to get transferred to White's ship directly, without the need to call upon Dungarth, he could serve for years on the Brest blockade. The affair of Edward Drinkwater would blow over. He picked up the third letter and opened it. Elizabeth had been right all along; he was no dissembler, he knew that he would have to face the music. Sighing, he began to read.

> *My Dearest Nathaniel,*
>> *Charlotte and I are well, although we miss you. I grow exceedingly rotund. Louise is a great solace and constantly asks if I have heard of James.*
>> *We are starved of news from the Baltic and I wait daily to hear from you. Unrest in the country grows and there is uncertainty everywhere. We long for peace and I pray daily for your safe return, my dearest . . .*

Drinkwater waited in *London*'s ante-room, nervous and tense, the subject of Edward uppermost in his mind. There had been ample time for the authorities to make arrangements for his arrest, perhaps Otway himself had brought a warrant . . . Sweat prickled between his shoulder blades. The dapper little midshipman who had brought Parker's summons had 'requested' he wore full uniform. Wondering if that insistence might not be sinister, he looked down at his coat and breeches.

The uniform was mildewed from languishing in his closet and the lace had become green. Tregembo's efforts prior to the battle had not been very successful and the smell of powder smoke was still detectable from the heavy cloth. Drinkwater felt exceedingly uncomfortable as he waited.

Parker's secretary appeared at last and called him into the great cabin. It was richly appointed; the furniture gleamed darkly, crystal decanters and silver candelabra glittered from the points of light that were reflected upwards from the sea through the stern windows and danced on the white-painted deckhead.

'Ah, Drinkwater . . .' the old man paused, apparently weighed down by responsibilities. 'I am to be superseded you know . . .' Drinkwater remained silent. 'Do you think I did wrong?'

'*I* sir??' That Parker should consult him was ludicrous. He felt out of his depth, aware only of the need to be tactful. 'Er, no, sir. Surely we have achieved the object of our enterprise.'

Parker looked at him intently, then seemed to brighten a little. 'It was not an easy task . . .' he muttered, more to himself than to Drinkwater. It was clear from his next remark that Drinkwater's acquaintance with his wife had allowed the friendless old man to speak freely.

'My wife reminds me constantly of my duty towards you in her letters . . .'

'Her ladyship is too kind, sir,' Drinkwater flushed; this solicitude on the part of Lady Parker was becoming a trifle embarrassing. Nelson had jumped to the wrong conclusion; was Parker about to do the same? Were not elderly husbands supposed to suspect young wives of all manner of infidelities?

'. . . And Lord Nelson is constantly complaining that I have failed to recognise your services both before and during the recent action. I believe you commanded *Virago* in the bombardment?'

'That is so, sir,' Drinkwater's heart was thumping painfully. Parker's nepotistic promotions after the battle of Copenhagen had aroused a storm of fury and it had taken all Nelson's persuasive powers to have a small number of highly deserving officers given a step in rank.

Parker picked up a paper and handed it to Drinkwater. 'Perhaps they will leave an old man in peace now.'

Drinkwater picked up the commission that made him Master and Commander.

The celebratory dinner in *Virago*'s cabin was a noisy affair. Out of courtesy Drinkwater had invited Lord Nelson, but the new Commander-in-Chief had taken his battleships off to demonstrate British seapower before the guns of Carlscrona and Revel.

The senior officer present was Captain Martin who did his best to hide his mortification at not being made post. He consoled himself by getting drunk. From some macabre source available in the aftermath of a bloody battle Rogers had acquired an old epaulette which they now presented to their commander.

"Tis a trifle tarnished, Drinkwater, but in keeping with the rest of your attire,' said Martin as he banged a spoon against a glass and called for silence. 'Gentlemen, I ask you to charge your glasses. To your swab, Drinkwater!'

'Drinkwater's swab!' The glasses banged down on the table and Tregembo and the messman moved rapidly to fill them again. Drinkwater looked round the grinning faces. Rogers flushed and half-drunk; Quilhampton, smiling seraphically, slipping slowly down in his chair banging on the table the fine, new wooden hand that Willerton had fashioned for him. Lettsom dry and birdlike; Tumilty red-faced and busy getting roaring drunk.

'An' I suppose I'll be having to call you "sir", Nat'aniel,' he shouted thickly, slapping Drinkwater's back in an insubordinate way.

'Sit down you damned Hibernian!' shouted Rogers.

'Take your damned fingers off me! An' I'm standing to make a pretty speech, so I am . . .' There were boos and shouts of 'Sit down!'

'I'll sit down upon a single condition . . . that Mr Lettsom makes a bit o' his versifying to mark the occasion.'

'Aye! Make us an ode, Lettsom!'

'Come, a verse!'

Lettsom held up his hand for silence. He was forced to wait before he could make himself heard.

At last he drew a paper from his pocket and struck a pose:

'The town of Copenhagen lies
Upon the Baltic shore
And here were deeds of daring done
'Twere never seen before.

'Bold Nelson led 'em, glass in hand
Upon the Danes to spy,
When Parker said "that's quite enough"
He quoth, "No, by my eye!"

'The dead and dying lay in heaps
The Danes they would not yield
Until the bold *Virago* came
Onto the bloody field.'

Lettsom paused, drank off his glass while holding his hand up to still the embryonic cheer. Then he resumed:

'Lord Nelson got the credit,
And Parker got the blame,
But 'twas the bold *Virago*
That clinched old England's fame.'

177

He sat down amid a storm of cheering and stamping. Mr Quilhampton's enthusiasm threatened to split his new hand until someone restrained him, at which point he gave up the struggle to retain consciousness and slid beneath the grubby tablecloth.

Drinkwater sat clapping Lettsom's dreadful muse.

'Your verse is like Polonius's advice, Mr Lettsom, the sweeter for its brevity,' Drinkwater grinned at the surgeon as Tregembo put another bottle before each officer. 'Mr Tumilty's contribution, sir,' he whispered in Drinkwater's ear.

'Ah, Tom, I salute you . . .'

Tumilty stood up. 'Captain Drinkwater . . .' he began, enunciating the words carefully, then he slowly bent over and buried his head in the remains of the figgy duff.

'What a very elegant bow,' said Martin rising unsteadily to take his leave. Drinkwater saw him to his boat.

'Good night Drinkwater.'

Returning to the cabin Drinkwater found Rogers dragging Tumilty to Easton's empty cot while Tregembo was carrying Quilhampton to bed. Martin had left and only Lettsom and Rogers sat down to finish a last bottle with Drinkwater.

Tregembo cleared the table. 'Take a couple of bottles, Tregembo, share 'em with the cook and the messman.'

'Thank 'ee, zur. I told 'ee you'd be made this commission, zur.' He grinned and left the cabin.

Lettsom blew through his flute. 'You, er, don't seem too pleased about it all, if I might say so,' said Lettsom.

'Is it that man Waters that's bothering you, sir?' asked Rogers.

Drinkwater looked from one to the other. There was a faint ringing in his ears and he was aware of a need to be careful of what he said.

'And why should Waters bother me, gentlemen?'

He saw Rogers shrug. 'It seemed an odd business to be mixed up in,' he said. Drinkwater fixed Rogers with a cold eye. Reluctantly he told the last lie.

'What d'you think I got my swab for, Samuel, eh?'

Lettsom drowned any reaction from Rogers in a shower of notes from his flute and launched into a lively air. He played for several minutes, until Rogers rose to go.

When the first lieutenant had left them Lettsom lowered his flute, blew the spittle out of it and dismantled it, slipping it into his pocket.

'I see you believe in providence, Mr Drinkwater . . .'

'What makes you say that?'

'Only a man with some kind of faith would have done what you did . . .'

'You speak in riddles, Mr Lettsom . . .'

'Mr Jex confided in me, I've known all along about your brother.'

'God's bones,' Drinkwater muttered as he felt a cold sensation sweep over him. He went deathly pale.

'I'm an atheist, Mr Drinkwater. But you are protected by my Hippocratic oath.' Lettsom smiled reassuringly.

A week later Admiral Pole took command of the fleet. The Baltic States were quiescent and, like Lord Nelson, the bomb vessels were ordered to England.

Chapter Twenty-One

A Child of Fortune

Commander Nathaniel Drinkwater knocked on the door of the elegant house in Lord North Street. Under his new full-dress coat with its single gleaming epaulette he was perspiring heavily. It was not the heat of the July evening that caused his discomfort but apprehension over the outcome of the forthcoming interview with Lord Dungarth.

The door opened and a footman showed him into an anteroom off the hall. Turning his new cocked hat nervously in his hands he felt awkward and a little frightened as he stood in the centre of the waiting room. After a few minutes he heard voices in the hall following which the same footman led him through to a book-lined study and he was again left alone. He looked around him, reminded poignantly of the portrait of Hortense Santhonax for, above the Adam fireplace, the arresting likeness of an elegant blonde beauty gazed down at him. He stared at the painting for some time. He had never met Dungarth's countess but the Romney portrait was said not to have done justice to her loveliness.

'You never met my wife, Nathaniel?' Drinkwater had not heard the door open and spun to face the earl. Dungarth was in court dress, his pumps noiseless upon the rich Indian carpet. Dungarth crossed the room and stood beside Drinkwater, looking up at the painting.

'Do you know why I detest the French, Nathaniel?'

'No my lord?' Drinkwater recollected Dungarth had conceived a passionate hatred for Jacobinism which was at variance with his former Whiggish sympathies with the American rebels.

'My wife died in Florence. I was bringing her body back through France in the summer of '92. At Lyons the mob learnt I was an aristocrat and broke open the coffin . . .' he turned to a side table. 'A glass of oporto?'

Drinkwater took the wine and sat down at Dungarth's invitation. 'We sometimes do uncharacteristic things for those close to us, and the consequences can last a lifetime.'

Drinkwater's mouth was very dry and he longed to swallow the wine at a gulp but he could not trust his hand to convey the glass to his lips without slopping it. He sat rigid, his coat stiff as a board and the silence that followed Dungarth's speech seemed interminable. Drinkwater was no longer on his own quarterdeck. After the heady excitement of battle and promotion the remorseless process of English law was about to engulf him. The colour was draining from his face and he was feeling light-headed. An image of Elizabeth swam before his eyes, together with that of Charlotte Amelia and the yet unseen baby, little Richard Madoc.

'Do you remember Etienne Montholon, Nathaniel?' Dungarth suddenly said in a conversational tone. 'The apparently wastrel brother of that bitch Hortense Santhonax?'

Drinkwater swallowed and recovered himself. 'Yes, my lord.' His voice was a croak and he managed to swallow some of the port, grateful for its uncoiling warmth in the pit of his stomach.

'Well, it seems that he became so short of funds that he threw in his lot with his sister and that fox of a husband of hers. The emergence of the consulate in France is attracting the notice of many of the younger émigrés who thirst for a share in *la gloire* of the new France.' Dungarth's expression was cynical. 'The rising star of Napoleon Bonaparte will recruit support from men like Montholon who seek a paymaster, and couples like the Santhonaxes who seek a vehicle for their ambition.'

'So Etienne Montholon returned to France, my lord?'

'Not at all. He remained in this country, leading his old life of gambling and squabbling, like all the émigré population. He served Bonaparte by acting as a clearing agent for information of fleet movements, mainly at Yarmouth in connection with the blockage of the Texel, but latterly watching Parker's squadron. The intransigence of the Danish Government was largely due to knowledge of Parker's dilatory prevarications and delays . . .' Dungarth rose and refilled their glasses. 'Etienne Montholon is dead now, he called himself *Le Marquis De La Roche-Jagu* and was killed by a jealous lover when in bed with his mistress at Newmarket . . .'

The point of his lordship's narrative struck Drinkwater like a blow. He felt his body a prey to the disorder of his mind which presented him with a bewildering succession of images: of Edward shivering on the bank of the River Yare, of Jex confronting him with the truth, of Edward walking ashore without looking back, of Jex's drunken death. Faintly he heard Dungarth say, 'By an odd coincidence the man suspected of the double murder had the same surname as yourself . . .'

Drinkwater turned to look the earl in the face. An ironic smile twisted Dungarth's mouth. ''Tis curious, is it not,' he said, 'how a man may flinch in perfect safety who would not deign to quail under a hail of shot?'

'I, er, I . . .'

'You need a little more wine, Nathaniel . . .' The glasses were again refilled and Dungarth resumed his tale.

'The suspect's cloak was found on the bank of the River Yare and it was supposed he drowned himself in a fit of remorse. Odd, though, that he should do his country such a service, eh?' Dungarth smiled. 'As for the girl, a certain Pascale Vrignaud, she suffered the fate of many whores. Odd little story, ain't it?'

'Yes.' Drinkwater swallowed the third glass of port at a gulp.

'I thought it would interest you,' added Dungarth smiling. 'You need give no further thought to the matter. Now, as to this fellow you feel may be of interest to me, whoever he is, I sent him from Hamburg with letters to Prince Vorontzoff in St Petersburg. The prince is a former ambassador to the Court of St James and has agreed to find him employment. Not unlike yourself, Nathaniel, this fellow Waters seems to be a child of fortune. Has a gambler's luck, wouldn't you say?'

Drinkwater returned Dungarth's grin. He felt no remorse for the death of Etienne Montholon, regretting that the man's rescue from the Jacobins had cost the lives of two British seamen. He wondered if Hortense would ever learn the name of her brother's executioner. It was a strange, small world. He saw the wheels of fate turning within each other and recalled Lettsom's observations on providence. As for Pascale, Edward would have her upon his own conscience. But Edward had a gambler's amorality as well as a gambler's luck. Drinkwater smiled at the aptness of Dungarth's last remark. The earl rose and refilled their glasses for the fourth time.

'I must thank you for your efforts . . . on my behalf, my lord,' said Drinkwater carefully, not wishing to break the delicate ice of ambiguity around the subject.

'It only remains,' replied Dungarth smiling, 'to see whether this man Waters is to be of any real use to us.'

Drinkwater nodded.

'And, of course, to drink to your swab . . .'